THE
HANGING WOODS

A NOVEL BY SCOTT LORING SANDERS

THE
HANGING WOODS

A NOVEL BY SCOTT LORING SANDERS

HOUGHTON MIFFLIN COMPANY
BOSTON 2008

This book is dedicated to my wife, Jocelyn,
who never stopped believing in me.
And also to my son, Mason, the light of my life,
who keeps me alive and strong.

www.houghtonmifflinbooks.com

The text of this book is set in Sabon.

Library of Congress Cataloging-in-Publication Data

Sanders, Scott Loring.
The Hanging Woods : a novel / by Scott Loring Sanders.
p. cm.

Summary: In rural Alabama during the summer of 1975, three teenaged boys
build a treehouse, try to keep a headless turkey alive, and become involved in
a murder mystery.

ISBN-13: 978-0-618-88125-3

[1. Friendship—Fiction. 2. Murder—Fiction. 3. Country life—Alabama—Fiction.
4. Alabama—History—1951—Fiction.] I. Title.
PZ7.S19792Han 2008
[Fic]—dc22
2007025773

Manufactured in the United States of America

VB 10 9 8 7 6 5 4 3 2 1

I wish I could
recollect that novel or short
story (by some contemporary writer,
I believe) in which, unknown to its author,
the first letters of the words of its last paragraph
formed, as deciphered by Cynthia, a message
from his dead mother.
—Vladimir Nabokov, *The Vane Sisters*

What's in a name? That which we call a rose
by any other name would smell as sweet.
—William Shakespeare

CHAPTER 1

IN 1975, WHEN I WAS THIRTEEN, I killed a fox. It happened a few weeks after I'd snuck into my mother's room and read her diary. That diary told me a lot of things that I didn't want to know. Or maybe I did want to know them. I can't say for sure. But what I can say for sure is that killing the fox wasn't pretty. And it wasn't an accident. I beat it over the head with a piece of stiff hickory about as long but not quite as thick as a baseball bat. I'm sure if my grandfather's .22 had been available, I'd have had an easier go of it.

Beating the fox was my first experience with death. I mean real death. Death by my own hands. I'm not talking about catching a catfish out of the Tallapoosa, throwing it on the bank, and watching as its pulsing mouth gasped for air. It wasn't the same as that. Killing the fox was brutal. I didn't enjoy it, exactly, though in a strange way it did fascinate me.

My grandfather, Papa, had taught me the basics of trapping the winter before. The first thing I ever saw caught was a big female raccoon. I actually heard it before I saw it. When we approached the set, near a small creek in a dense wood of live oaks and sycamores, the chain of the trap rattled through the morning air as the coon scooted from side to side. The steel jaws clamped her front right paw, and she hissed when she saw us. In the silt, on the edge of the creek, her little handprints overlapped one another as she stomped around, trying to free herself. The black band on her face couldn't hide the fear and hatred in her eyes. Papa walked up to the coon as casually as if he were lighting his pipe. He stuck the barrel about an inch from her head and fired. One shot and the coon was dead.

"You gotta be humane, Walter," he said as he picked her up, squeezing the release prongs, freeing her leg. "They should suffer as little as possible. You got it?"

"Yes, sir," I said, "but without a gun it's going to be hard."

He dropped the coon into the oversize wicker rucksack resting on his back, then reset the double-spring trap. "Your mama don't want you out here with a gun yet. You know how she worries. In a few years, maybe, but not yet."

"But how am I gonna do it?"

"You're gonna use a stick and hit it over the head," he said in his usual matter-of-fact way. "That's the way I learned when I was a boy, and you'll do the same. It ain't an easy thing to do, but it's important. With a stick you feel the life escape the animal's body, run up through the wood, and then into your hands and arms. It's a might troubling, but necessary."

"But why?" I asked. "Seems like it'd be easier with a gun."

"Because you'll respect the animals in these woods, that's why. Get an idea of how flimsy life is. There ain't no feeling with a gun. You pull the trigger and it's over. That's the easy way, and you gotta learn the hard way, really feel it with your hands, so you can appreciate the easy way. Got me?"

"Yes, sir," I said, "but I'd still rather use a gun."

After that first season of instruction, Papa told me I'd be ready to go out on my own the following year. I waited impatiently through the spring, summer, and fall, excited about the prospects of trapping solo. When the time finally came, Papa set me up with a half dozen Victor Oneida double-spring leg holds and let me loose.

Papa lived in a rundown house in the country, not much more than a shack really, on the other side of the Tallapoosa River, several miles from Woodley. During the trapping season, Mom dropped me off after school on Fridays and picked me up on Sundays. I liked spending time with Papa on weekends because he never bothered me or made fun of me. I felt at ease around him; it was definitely better than having to stay at home with my parents. Especially my father.

Every weekend, as soon as Mom dropped me off, I would grab the traps that hung on sixteen-penny nails in his toolshed and take off running through the woods. I placed sets near the creek for coon, and a couple in the field for fox. Since it was winter and the sun set early, I had to hustle. Alabama winters weren't all that frigid compared to most of the country's, but I still didn't want to get caught in the woods after dark. Things sometimes got eerie out there.

After several weekends went by and I hadn't caught a thing, I found that trapping wasn't as easy as Papa had made it look. But I stayed optimistic. On that third Saturday morning, I sprang out of bed feeling confident, but by the end of my round of checking traps, I had been shut out once again.

"Usually when you think it ain't never gonna happen is when it does," said Papa as I walked into the kitchen, miserable and dejected after my latest effort. He sat on a wobbly chair, his long legs stretched out in front of him, rubbing little circles into his glasses with a bandanna.

"Then I guess it's gonna happen real soon," I said, "because right now I don't think I'll ever catch a thing."

"It'll happen," he said with a smile. "Just keep at it. A weasel don't always catch a chicken the first time it enters a henhouse."

When I awoke the following morning, rain bounced off the tin roof, tapping beats like a child on a snare drum. I pulled on my flannel jacket, laced up my boots, and grabbed the heavy walking stick Papa had fashioned for me. He'd whittled off all the bark and carved my initials at the top. Smooth and sleek, the stick felt comfortable in my hands, as if it belonged there, as if it had grown in the woods all those years just for me. As nice a fit as it was, all I wanted to do was crawl back into bed, sleep, and wait for the smell of frying eggs and sausage. But Papa would never allow it. Checking the traps first thing, no matter how I felt or how nasty the weather, was his strictest rule. So I headed out, still eager despite the rain and cold.

I had trouble seeing more than a few feet in front of me as I made my way through the fog. My eyes still hung heavy with sleep. The morning light barely seeped through the loblolly pines that stood tall and thin all around. A cold, wet grayness surrounded me, and I started shivering within five minutes of being exposed to the chilly air.

I jogged to the first set in order to stay warm. It held nothing, but I wasn't surprised; I had gotten used to it by then. I walked beside the creek, which now rushed along, white and foamy from the heavy rainfall. Leaves and branches rolled and tumbled through the water as they journeyed to meet up with the larger body of the Tallapoosa. The rest of the coon sets were also empty, so I headed to the edge of the field where I had a fox set. The trap lay on the far side of an old rock wall that had once been used as a field divider. I climbed up and over the fallen stones to get to it, nearly slipping on a slick patch of moss growing on the rocks.

The wet leaves softened my steps, so as I approached the trap, I saw the animal before it saw me. A large gray fox, about the size of a small German shepherd, lay on its stomach, its whitish gray coat matted and soaked from the pelting rain. It had little pup tents for ears, and its black snout rested on the moist, rotting leaves. I took a step forward. As I did so, the fox immediately sprang to its feet and yipped with such vigor that chills shot through my body. I'd never heard anything like it in my life; it was worse than a fork raking across a chalkboard.

I didn't know what to do, so I did the only thing that seemed natural. I panicked. I gripped my walking stick tightly, which turned my red hands white. The fox hobbled around as best it could, pacing back and forth, though the few feet of chain didn't allow for much mobility. The hackle of its orange neck stood stiff and upright.

The fox's eyes locked on me and never strayed. The yipping continued, and I felt an overwhelming urge to let it go, but I saw no way of doing it. In order to open the jaws of the trap, I'd have to step on the release prongs, and there was no way to do that without being attacked. I thought maybe I should run back to the house and get

Papa to come with his .22, but I didn't want him to think I was a coward.

The moment I'd been dreaming of had come, and I realized it had turned into a nightmare. One part of me kept saying to let it go. The fox hadn't done anything to anyone; the only thing it had done wrong was to have the bad luck of stepping into my trap. But the other part of me, the stronger part, said that I had to kill it. And I always seemed to listen to my stronger part.

I grabbed my stick tighter still, as though preparing to swing for the fence. I took a couple of steps forward, which sent the fox into a fury. The fox kept attempting to walk backwards, trying to break free, but its captured leg prevented it from going more than a foot or two. I'd secured the trap by twisting thin baling wire around the steel trap chain and then wrapping the other end of the wire around the trunk of a pine sapling. The young tree bent and shook as the fox tugged; tiny drops of water flew from its needles, but the trap held fast.

When I got within a few feet of the fox, it pulled as far away from me as it could. I raised the hickory over my head and swung with all my might. The stick struck the ground, jolting my frozen hands. While I had been in midswing, the fox had leaped to the side. Just after it jumped, however, part of the chain somehow wrapped around the exposed root of a large loblolly, now making the fox immobile. I raised the stick again and swung. I heard the thud of the heavy wood connect with the fox's skull the same instant that I felt it. Its life seemed to flow through the hickory and into my body, just as Papa had said it would.

A heavy gasp exhaled from deep within the fox's chest. The fox instantly dropped to the ground, landing on its stomach, its legs splayed out spread-eagle style. Its tail stood straight up in the air, so I pulled back and smashed its skull again, and then again, thinking it was probably still alive. After the third blow, the tail gradually dropped to the ground, almost in slow motion, like the black-and-white barrier at a railroad crossing.

It looked beautiful. Hardly any blood leaked from the head, and only a trickle seeped from its mouth. Its tongue stuck out over the side of the ridged black jowls, and if not for that, the fox would have looked asleep instead of dead.

I poked its ribs with my stick a couple of times. I still wasn't completely convinced that it wouldn't wake up and attack. After a few moments of prodding, when it didn't stir, I finally opened the trap, picked the fox up—the soft fur and warm body comforting my numb hands—and placed it in Papa's rucksack. I then slung the pack over my shoulder.

The rain had stopped and the sun had peeked out from a window in the clouds by the time I made my way out of the woods. The warmth of the rays thawed my frozen skin. My clothes felt five pounds heavier from the rain, and the fox in the rucksack must have weighed at least twenty more. I panted and felt exhausted as I neared the skinning table that Papa kept set up in the backyard during the season. He stood on the deck filling his bird feeder, which was screwed into the trunk of a magnolia. The tree's glossy leaves hung over the deck, giving shade in the summer and fat white blossoms in the late spring.

"How'd you make out?"

"I got a fox," I said through a forced grin. "A gray."

"Get out of town, boy. Did you really?"

"Yes, sir, I really did."

"Well, hot damn, son, pull her out and let's take a look," he said, climbing down the steps to meet me.

"She" actually turned out to be a "he," which was easy enough to figure out when Papa helped me skin it. He pulled the pelt over a wire stretcher when we finished, but I didn't really pay attention to the process. He talked and rattled on and seemed so excited about the whole thing that he never looked at me. I automatically nodded when he asked me something, but my mind and thoughts had flown far away from that pelt on the skinning table. I couldn't think about anything except the feeling that had shot up through my arms and into my brain, settling there with a dull buzz. The new knowledge—that I possessed the power to kill—overwhelmed me.

The following weekend, instead of setting traps on Papa's property, I chose to stay close to home. It was an unusually warm day for December, so I decided to find my two best friends, Jimmy and Mothball. They lived down the road, and since I had given up trapping, I figured I'd see what they were getting into.

I set out walking down Douglass Street. Every house in the neighborhood was an exact replica of the one next to it. They were small two-story, two-bedroom houses that had been constructed by the Simmons pulp mill after World War II, when Woodley became a booming pulp town. Practically every man in Woodley worked there, including my father, as well as Jimmy's and Mothball's. Now, thirty years since that war, and with Vietnam only ending during the last year, the pulp mill still ran, but not the way it had in the past. Layoffs had hit families left and right, though so far my family had been spared.

The slowing down of the mill took its toll not only on the neighborhood but on the town of Woodley as well. Most of the houses were in various stages of ruin, and many of the stores had closed shop in the past few years. The five-and-dime, the grocery store, the only restaurant, they were all abandoned. The Phillips 66 sign, pocked with rust, still stood atop a white pole in front of the only gas station, though the pumps now sat useless under a thin, dusty layer of Alabama red clay. To purchase fuel, or just about anything else, we had to travel twenty miles to Lafayette—pronounced "La-fette" by everyone I knew. Lafayette barely fared better than Woodley, and I'd heard Dad say many times over that he didn't know what we'd do if the mill ever shut down. He'd even threatened that I might have to get a job.

The only house that looked different from any of the others was Mothball's. He lived in an old farmhouse positioned at the far end of the street. Mothball's farmhouse made the rest of the houses in the neighborhood look pristine by comparison. The only shutter left attached to the facing boards hung cockeyed, ready to drop at any moment. Lying in the bushes or leaning against the house were the remnants of other shutters that had already fallen. The once white siding now showed gray exposed boards beneath the patches of peeling paint. The wooden fence around the yard looked similar, with most of the railings either busted or hanging at forty-fives, barely clinging to the vertical oak posts. Rusted bicycle frames, with rusted chains and rusted wheels, lay scattered around the yard with the dead weeds of last summer still poking through the spokes. Peahens and chickens roamed freely around the yard, pecking the ground.

When laughter arose from the back of the house, I figured Jimmy and Mothball were in the chicken shack, so I headed in that direction and walked in.

"Look, Mothball, it's Davy Crockett, back from the wild frontier," said Jimmy as I walked under the low doorway of the coop.

"Where's your coonskin cap?" asked Mothball. "I thought you'd have made something by now with all them furs you been catching. Maybe a coat for your mom out of that fox." They both laughed, and I felt my cheeks flush.

"Yeah, yeah, yeah," I said. "Y'all are funny. I did what I wanted to do, and now I'm moving on to bigger and better things." I'd told them about the fox earlier in the week. I didn't want to go over it again, so I said, "Looks like you're up to no good, Mothball."

Mothball stood in the middle of the coop in front of an oak log cut into a firewood-size section. The log stood on its end, knee high, serving as a chopping block. The square coop, made of rough-cut boards, leaned so much to one side that with only a little push, it seemed, I could have toppled it over. And chicken shit lay everywhere. White streams of it stained the walls like dripping paint. Crusty clumps—turned green and gray with age—mingled with the moldy straw on the dirt floor. The odor was enough to knock out a pig.

Mothball, who was short and round with a baby face, had an ax in his hand and brandished it like a prison guard holding a rifle. He'd been dubbed "Mothball" when we were younger, back in the third or fourth grade. His older brother, Carver, had asked him if he'd ever smelled mothballs. When he replied that he had, Carver asked him how he'd gotten the moth's little legs apart to sniff them. Jimmy and I had fallen out laughing while Mothball's cheeks burned red. His lips puckered up as though he'd been sucking on persimmons from the tree in the backyard. The name stuck.

Jimmy, on the other hand, had a strong jaw line and sharp features. He possessed a thin frame and stood the same height as I did. We were similarly built, nearly the same exact age—I was two months older—and had the same green eyes. We were sometimes mistaken for brothers, though I didn't have the good looks that he had. Most of the girls at school made a big fuss over him, which didn't seem to bother Mothball, but I have to admit I got jealous sometimes. At the moment, he had a tiny sliver of wood in his mouth and sucked on it like a toothpick as he walked over and leaned against the side of the doorway next to me.

"Seems like both my friends have turned into murderers," said Jimmy. "You won't even believe what Mothball's up to."

"I'm not a murderer, y'all," said Mothball. "I'm going to be famous."

"Yeah, I'm not a murderer either," I said, though I wasn't necessarily convinced of that.

"Okay, Mr. Mothball the Famous," said Jimmy as he swept the sliver of wood across his lips, "why don't you tell Walter what you're planning to do and then we'll let him decide."

"Check this out, Walter," said Mothball. He smiled as he talked, his big brown eyes flickering with excitement. "I'm gonna be in *The Guinness Book of World Records*."

"For what?" I asked. "Having the dumbest nickname?"

"No, dickfor—I'm gonna cut off a chicken's head and keep it alive."

"What are you talking about?" I asked. "That's impossible."

"Is not. I'll prove it." Mothball forcefully slammed the ax into the oak log and reached for a worn, wrinkled softcover copy of the *Guinness Book*. It lay face-down and splayed open on a roll of chicken wire. The cover had a few splatters of chicken shit on it, and when he picked up the book his fingers landed in the stuff, smearing it across the word *Guinness*. But he didn't even flinch. Apparently the book had been opened right to the page he wanted, because he said excitedly, "Listen to this," and started reading aloud. "'Longest surviving headless chicken. On September tenth, 1945, a Wyandotte chicken named Mike was decapitated but went on to survive for eighteen months. The cut had missed the jugular vein, and much of the brain stem had been left intact. His owner, Lloyd Olsen (USA), fed and watered the chicken directly into his gullet with the aid of an eyedropper. Mike eventually choked to death in an Arizona motel.' So what do you think?" asked Mothball.

"Is there a picture?" I asked.

"No, there ain't no picture."

"Without a picture, I don't know if I buy it."

"Yeah, and what was he doing in a motel?" asked Jimmy. "That's what I want to know. Meeting up with a hen or something?"

"Shut up, y'all. I'm gonna do it. I'll take care of it, and feed it, and everything."

"And you'll love him, and squeeze him, and call him George," said Jimmy.

"Whoa, Jimmy," I said. "Since when did you start reading Steinbeck? I didn't even know you knew how to read."

"Steinbeck? What the hell is that?"

"You know, John Steinbeck? You just quoted him."

"I did not, dipshit. That's from *Bugs Bunny*."

I started to reply, but Mothball interjected.

"I'm serious, y'all," he said. "I bet I can make it live for four or five years. I'll crush the record. I'll be famous."

Jimmy almost choked on his toothpick as he started laughing. I couldn't help but join him.

"If you don't wanna watch, then don't," said Mothball, "but I'm gonna try it right now."

"Won't your ma get pissed if you kill all the chickens?"

"I ain't gonna kill all the chickens, Walter. I'm gonna try it on one, and if it dies, then we'll just eat it. Next time

Ma wants me to get one for supper, I'll try it again, and keep trying until I get it right."

"You're crazy," I said.

"And a murderer," added Jimmy.

"I'm not a murderer," Mothball shot back. "If we eat it then it ain't murder. Walter killing a fox for no reason but to sell its skin, now that's murder."

"Well, let's see it then, if you're gonna do it," I said, ignoring Mothball's dig.

In the back corner of the shadowed shack sat a small cage about the size of a couple of stuck-together milk crates, crudely fashioned out of pine slats and chicken wire. A hen the color of a rusty beer can bobbed its head within its confines and nervously paced around, though she didn't have a lot of room to do either. Mothball grabbed the cage and set it on the flat surface of the log next to the lodged ax. He unfastened the door, which was bound with a leather thong tied in a bowknot. The hen scuttled to the back corner, rattling the wire with her flapping wings, sending pieces of straw and shit into the air. She clucked angrily at Mothball, but he paid her no mind. With a strike quicker than a cottonmouth, his hand darted in and snatched the legs of the hen in one fluid motion. Her wings beat faster still, and she cackled with fear as he pulled her out. He held her as if she were a bouquet of flowers and stroked her back, which hunched with every caress. She calmed down immediately.

"Move the cage out of the way, will ya?" he asked Jimmy.

Jimmy worked the homemade toothpick back and forth across his lips as he moved the cage and set it on the dirt floor.

Mothball continued stroking the back of the bird, talking in a gentle whisper, saying, "It's okay, little hen. I won't hurt you."

"Yeah, right," said Jimmy.

"You gotta be quiet," said Mothball. "I gotta soothe her before I do it."

He went on petting the bird and talking to it for a couple of minutes. The hen kept cocking her head back and forth, blinking her eyes repeatedly, but she remained calm.

"All right, this is where I could use y'all's help," he said.

"*Our* help?" said Jimmy. "I thought this was *your* record. You gonna give us credit in the book if we provide our most valuable assistance?"

"Yeah, I'll give you some credit, but dammit, Jimmy, this is serious. If you don't want to help then you can go on home, but stop making fun of me. I'm trying to work."

Jimmy looked at me and raised his eyebrows. I shrugged my shoulders in response.

"Walter, pull the ax out, will ya?"

"Yeah, sure," I said. I reached over and dislodged it. The wooden handle felt smooth and comfortable in my hands, just like the hickory stick had, though the steel blade made it top-heavy.

"Now I'm gonna set her head down nice and gentle on the stump," said Mothball. "And when I do, I want you to chop her at the back of the neck, but at an angle toward the head. Kind of take off the back of it. I think that's how the guy did it."

"You want *me* to do it?" I asked. "No way. I'm not doing it."

"Oh, come on, Walter. I need your help."

I immediately thought of the fox and almost felt the death flowing through the ax handle. The idea sort of fascinated me, but I said, "I'm not doing it, Mothball. I'll hold the bird or something, but I'm not chopping its head off."

"Jimmy?" implored Mothball.

"Nope. No way. I'm with Walter. It's your record, you gotta do it."

Mothball looked at us with disbelief. "Well, shit, then. Some friends you are," he said. "And y'all want credit? Give me the ax."

He reached for it with his right hand, still holding the hen in the other. I slipped him the handle. He grabbed it near the curved neck, just below the blade.

"I'll hold her and do it, but at least pet her back while I get ready," he said. "Usually I can do it by myself, but I gotta be real careful so I don't mess up."

I complied with his request, reaching over and stroking her soft feathers. She twitched every time I touched her. Mothball slowly lowered her toward the face of the log, and I dropped my hand with him, still stroking the bird. When her neck stretched across the wood, Mothball's grip on the handle tightened. He shifted his weight from foot to foot and licked a light bead of sweat from his upper lip.

"Here it goes," he whispered.

He pulled up, but a little too quickly, and the hen, either startled by the movement or just sensing her demise, shifted at the last second. Mothball caught her square across the back of the neck. I heard the brittle snap as the steel sliced through her vertebrae and sank firmly into the wood. Rolling over the surface of the log, the head flopped onto the ground and settled in the dust.

"Son of a bitch," yelled Mothball, letting go of the legs as soon as he had decapitated her. The hen actually landed on her feet and took a few steps before toppling over, resting next to her head. The one eye that I could see remained open, and I could have sworn it blinked. Blood emptied from her body, pooling around the head in the dirt.

"You scared her, Walter," yelled Mothball. "She jumped just before I hit her."

"Me? I didn't do a thing except pet her like you told me to."

"That wasn't bad for your first try," said Jimmy. "She stayed alive for nearly five, no, maybe even ten seconds."

"Shut the hell up, Jimmy. Just shut the hell up."

"At least you got supper," he said.

"Would y'all just go on home and leave me alone?" said Mothball. "I gotta think of a new way of doing this."

"All right," I said, "but all I did was pet her. I swear."

Jimmy and I turned around and left the chicken shack. I thought about saying something further but decided it really wasn't worth it. On the way home, we discussed Mothball's antics.

"You have to give him credit," said Jimmy as he spat his makeshift toothpick into the street. "If nothing else, he's determined."

"That's for sure," I said. "I've never seen him this serious about anything in his life."

"Did you see the way that thing jumped around without a head?" asked Jimmy. "That was pretty cool."

"It was weird, is what it was," I replied.

When we reached Jimmy's house, about halfway between mine and Mothball's, we parted.

"I'm gonna get something to eat," said Jimmy. "All that chicken killing has got me hungry."

"All right," I said. "I'll catch up with you later."

I walked the rest of the way home, not feeling at all hungry like Jimmy. The only thing I thought about was that chicken's head covered in dust and how it winked at me.

CHAPTER 2

JIMMY'S DAD GOT LAID OFF IN THE SPRING, and it affected their family in strange ways. I first noticed it in Jimmy's mother. On Easter weekend, a few weeks after Mr. Haddsby lost his job, Jimmy invited me over to have Sunday supper with his family. Mothball had to go to his grandparents' house, so it was just the two of us, along with Jimmy's parents and his uncle, whom everyone called Ox. Ox was short, bald, and built like a whiskey barrel. He possessed an amazing talent that had made him famous in Woodley; he remembered birthdays. Not just birthdays of relatives and friends—he remembered everybody's. And what was even more amazing was that he never wrote them down.

He and Mr. Haddsby sat on the back deck, drinking Schlitz Tall Boys with salt sprinkled around the edges. Jimmy and I tossed a football and listened to the two men talk as we all waited for supper. They were discussing work prospects, since Ox had also been laid off.

"I heard the quarry might be hiring some people next week," said Ox.

"Shit, that's all the way over on the other side of

Lafayette. And besides, there ain't nothing but a bunch of niggers working over there."

"I don't reckon we can be too choosy right now," said Ox. "I'm putting in an application."

"Well, I ain't," said Mr. Haddsby. "I ain't about to lower myself and do no nigger's work." He took a pull from his can and set it back on the little table next to his rocking chair. He had a pronounced Adam's apple, and it pulsed with every swallow of beer. He always reminded me of the scarecrow from *The Wizard of Oz*.

"Nigger's work or not," said Ox, "it still pays more than what we're making now."

The evening sun started to drop behind the trees at the back of the property. The football became harder to see. Though it was still early spring, the air was warm. I loved that time of year because the mosquitoes weren't out in droves like they would be in a few more weeks. Peepers began singing a nighttime song along the creek near the tree line.

"Goddamn, I'm about to die of hunger," said Mr. Haddsby. As he salted the rim of his can with a salt shaker, he said to Jimmy, "Boy, get your sorry ass inside and ask your mama when supper's gonna be ready. Me and Ox is about starved."

"Yes, sir," said Jimmy. And then to me he said, "Come on."

I dropped the ball in the grass and followed Jimmy up

the steps of the deck, through the back door, and down the hall. The aroma of roasting turkey filled the house. Mrs. Haddsby, a pretty woman with high cheekbones, auburn hair, and a perpetual suntan, stood in front of the stove, stirring a pot of boiling potatoes. She wore a checkered apron over her dress, tied in a bow at her back. She didn't hear us enter and jumped like a spooked cat when Jimmy spoke.

"Dad says he's about starved and wants to know when supper's gonna be ready."

"Is that right?" she said. "You tell him that . . . No, I'll tell that no-good . . ."

She grabbed the handle of the pot with both hands, lifted it from the stove, and stormed off down the hall. The potatoes bounced around, forcing drops of hot water to spill over the sides. Jimmy and I followed. She pushed open the screen door with her shoulder, walked onto the deck, and tossed the whole pot, boiling water and all, at Mr. Haddsby. The pot bounced off the sun-bleached boards and barely missed him. Some of the scalding water hit Ox's jeans as both men popped out of their chairs. Mr. Haddsby's chair rocked violently back and forth as if caught in a windstorm.

"I'm cooking as fast as I can," she screamed. Her pretty face turned ugly, and the tendons in her neck tightened. "If you can do better, then come cook it your own self."

"Goddamn, woman, what in the hell're you doing?"

Mr. Haddsby had his arms outstretched, and foam over-flowed from his tall can of beer, trickling down his hand.

Mrs. Haddsby turned around and flew past us down the hall without answering. Jimmy and I just stood in the doorway, not knowing what to do.

"She's out of her goddamned mind," ranted Mr. Haddsby. "You all right?"

Ox grabbed at his thick legs, hopping from one foot to the other. "She got my legs some," he said.

Mr. Haddsby set his beer down on the table next to the salt shaker and reached into the cooler, grabbing a handful of ice. "Here. Sit back down and put this on them." Ox grabbed the ice, took his seat, and struggled with his pants. Mr. Haddsby kicked the steel pot with the toe of his boot; it caromed off a railing post and onto the lawn.

"Maybe we should help," I whispered. "Looks like Ox's having trouble."

We walked outside and not a moment later the door swung open again. Mrs. Haddsby, her hands covered with two red oven mitts, grasped a roasting pan, the browned turkey sitting atop it. She didn't hesitate for a second as she shot-putted the whole pan at Mr. Haddsby. It didn't make it far. Grease splattered all over the deck boards as the pan clanked against them. The turkey rolled over a couple of times, collecting dirt and other debris, before it settled on its breast. Steam rolled out of the opening that had held the stuffing, which now lay scattered across the deck. The golden arms pointed upward toward the darkening sky.

"Enjoy your stinking dinner," said Mrs. Haddsby. She looked to be on the verge of tears, and I saw fear in her eyes—a fear that said she couldn't believe what she'd just done. She busted out crying as soon as she made it past us and back into the house.

"What's got her all et up?" asked Ox. "She's acting about as crazy as a coot."

"Damned if I know," said Mr. Haddsby, who took a long swallow from his beer, then kicked the pan off the deck to rest next to the potato pot and the football.

"Maybe you should go," whispered Jimmy. "And don't ever say nothing about this to anyone, okay?"

"Yeah, okay," I said. "I'll catch up with you tomorrow at school."

❦

I never brought up the incident with Jimmy, and since he never said another word about it, I left it at that. However, a couple of weeks later something else took place at his house that was so crazy, not only did I talk about it, but it made the local newspaper.

I got up early that day, a Saturday, ate a bowl of cereal, and headed out the door.

"Where you off to in such a hurry this morning, mister?" asked my mother.

She stood in front of the stove, frying eggs and bacon. Her chubby little hand held a fork over the cast-iron skillet, and she jerked it back when grease popped and sprayed her apron. My father, who sat at the table dressed in his bathrobe, always read the paper before he did anything. Without fail, every morning he got up, poured a cup of coffee, went out to the paper box, and then sat at the kitchen table and read while my mother, also without fail, cooked him breakfast. This morning was no different.

"I gotta meet Mothball and Jimmy," I said. "We're building a tree house in Jimmy's backyard, out by the creek."

"Did you straighten up the carport like I told you?" said my father, looking up from his paper. His green eyes—the same ones I'd inherited—peered at me from over the tops of his reading glasses. When he looked at me that way, with the paper in his hands and the dark-rimmed glasses hanging on the bridge of his thin nose, he looked more like a college professor than a mill worker struggling to support his family.

"Yes, sir," I said. "Didn't you see it when you got home from work yesterday?"

"I was too tired to notice, but I got some other chores I need you to help me with."

"Can't I help you later?" I asked, hopeful, but also scared of his reaction. I never could tell if he'd relent or fly into a rage. "I'm supposed to meet them right now."

"No, goddammit. I need your help setting posts for that clothesline of your mother's. The old ones have rotted out."

"Oh," said Mom, "couldn't he go as long as he's back by noon?"

"I thought you needed that done today, Louise. He doesn't do a damn thing around here. For once I could use his help, and you want him to run off with his derelict friends?"

"I don't need to set out any laundry until later," said Mom. "How about noon?"

"Fine, goddammit, and not a second later or you'll be sorry."

"Okay. Back by noon," I said. "No problem."

"Walter," said Mom, "please be careful. I don't like you climbing up in trees. You could fall and break your neck. And put on your jacket before you catch cold."

I bolted out the door quickly, fearing my father might change his mind, and raced toward Jimmy's house. Other than Dad's mood swings and the way he constantly belittled me, I couldn't help but think how plain and boring both he and my mom were. Mom stayed at home and did the laundry, cooking, and cleaning. Every day she did the same thing. And as erratic as Dad acted when dealing with me, every other part of his life was just like his breakfast ritual. He woke up, went to work, came home, went to bed. Day in and day out, except weekends. Then, instead of working at the mill, he worked around the house. I knew I didn't want to end up like him, doing a job anyone could do. Actually, after I'd read Mom's diary, I didn't want to end up like him for a lot of reasons.

The morning was already warm—certainly no need for the jacket I stashed in the bushes as soon as I left. Honeybees darted around in the clover and fully bloomed lilacs. The lilacs were my favorite, mostly because they provided the only smell that could overpower the constant stench of sulfur from the mill that hung above our town. Simmons sulfur, we called it.

Spring had now busted out in full force, and I ached to get the tree house completed. Not because I yearned for a tree house especially, but because we had ulterior motives that I wanted to hurry up and implement. It had been Jimmy's idea. Sheila Brackwater, the best-looking senior in all of Woodley High, lived in the house next to his. He swore to us that when the weather turned warm, Sheila always sunbathed in her backyard in a pink bikini, sometimes even topless. We were willing to do anything if it meant catching a glimpse of that.

"We need more boards, is all I'm saying," Mothball said when I arrived at the base of the sycamore. He and Jimmy were already up in the tree, arguing about something. I climbed the pieces of two-by-four nailed into the mottled skin of the tree until I reached the floor, about fifteen feet off the ground. I popped up through the hole where the trapdoor would eventually be.

"Hey y'all," I said. "Fighting already?"

"King Chicken Killer thinks we need more wood," said Jimmy, his back turned to me. "I say we've got enough."

"We gotta get some plywood for the walls," said Mothball. "We hardly got anything for them yet."

As they bickered, I surveyed the small heap of scrap wood that lay scattered in the leaves below me. "Looks to me like Mothball's right," I said. "We've only got that one piece of plywood left, and a few two-by-fours. That's hardly enough for one wall."

"See," said Mothball. "We could rip down that old deer stand up in the field behind my house. Or even one of them duck blinds down by the river."

"Yeah, and if those duck hunters find out we did it," said Jimmy, "they'll shoot us just as quick as they'd shoot a bunch of ducks. Even quicker."

The majority of the wood we'd collected had been obtained in just that manner. We pilfered wood from our fathers' sheds, busted a couple of deer stands, and gathered it from just about anywhere else we could find it.

"Well, we gotta get it from somewhere," I said. "If not the deer stand or the duck blind, then where?"

"How 'bout if we steal it from the Troll?" said Jimmy. "We could sneak down to his shack and grab a bundle.

He's got crap sitting around all over the place down there."

"Yeah, right, that would work real well," I said. "If you think those duck hunters wouldn't think twice before shooting us, just imagine what the Troll would do."

"He'd slit our throats and eat us, that's what he'd do," said Mothball. He wasn't kidding—he meant it, and I didn't really doubt him. I felt the Troll capable of anything that had to do with the strangling and murder of young boys.

The Troll was probably in his early thirties, but he looked much older to me. His hair was long and straggly, and it crept from underneath a blue wool cap that he wore constantly, even in the thick of summer. He always dressed the same, wearing a pair of pants that looked as though they'd been fashioned from a burlap sack, a pair of worn brown boots held together with duct tape, and a ripped flannel shirt over which hung his olive drab army-issue jacket. He was thickly bearded, and his eyes—which I tried to make out when Mom and I drove by him on the road—were almost impossible to see because of all the unwieldy hair. It felt like he was staring through me when we passed, and I'd always turn away from the window when we got close to him. My mother tended to get nervous, too. She usually just gazed straight ahead, avoiding his eyes.

Dad had told me he was a Vietnam vet and mixed up in

the head. He warned me to stay away from him at all costs. He said he'd wear out my backside if he ever caught me near the man. I'd told Dad that that would never be a problem, as I was more scared of the Troll than of the devil himself.

The Troll lived underneath a dilapidated railroad trestle on the outskirts of town, right along the banks of the Tallapoosa. He'd constructed a shack out of tin and scrap metal, and oftentimes I saw a thin column of smoke rising from a rusted stovepipe when Mom and I would pass by on our way to get groceries in Lafayette. The trestle stood about fifty yards from the road, and I always looked down across the field of scrub pine and canebrake to see if I might catch a glimpse of him. Sometimes I saw his hunched figure when we'd cross over the Tallapoosa Bridge; he'd be sitting on the bank of the lazy chocolate river, fishing for channel cats. Usually, on the opposite side, were several colored boys, also fishing from in front of their shanties. Mom called the area where they lived Niggertown, and as much as I'd been warned about staying away from the Troll, that went double when it came to Niggertown.

"Well, you figure it out then, if you're so smart," snapped Jimmy, still frustrated about the wood situation. He turned around to make his way down the tree. A dark purple ring, the color of ripe eggplant, encircled his right eye.

"What happened to you?" I asked. "Looks like the Troll already got a hold of your face."

Jimmy stared me down. "I got up to take a piss last night and smacked into the edge of my door. What the hell do you care?"

"I don't," I said. "I just hope the door's okay."

"Go fuck yourself, Walter."

Jimmy slipped through the square hole of the floor, ducked out of sight, and climbed down. He started picking up two-by-fours and tossing them into a pile. Soggy leaves, clumps of mud, and white stringy residue stuck to the bottoms of the boards.

"What's his problem?" I whispered to Mothball as we watched him through the trapdoor hole. Jimmy slammed board after board into a haphazard stack.

"His dad left the house last night and never came home," he whispered back. "Second time this week."

"Where'd he go?" I asked.

"I don't know. But Mama said he's been going out with Ox, getting drunk, and causing all kinds of trouble around town. Mama said the sheriff had to bring him home the other night. Got in a fight or something and was too drunk to drive."

"What about Jimmy's face?" I asked. "You know anything?"

"You figure it out, Walter."

"What are y'all talking about up there?" yelled Jimmy. He glared at us.

"I was telling Walter about Mike the Second," said Mothball.

"Bullshit," said Jimmy, who went back to picking up half-buried boards.

"What do you mean?" I asked, turning my attention to Mothball. "Did you finally manage to keep a chicken alive?"

"No, but I'm getting better. I killed one last night for supper, and she stayed alive for almost two minutes. I swear to God."

"How'd you do it?"

"I cut her at the back of the neck. Her head flopped over but stayed attached, just barely hanging on. I saw the brain and everything. She finally just fell over and died. I think I gotta try a rooster next time. Mike was a rooster, so maybe they're tougher."

"You're not right," I said, tapping my head. "Something's wrong up there."

"You'll see. Go on and keep making fun of me, but you'll see."

A loud commotion from the side of Jimmy's house cut our conversation short. Mothball and I shifted our attention as Jimmy took off running from underneath us. The leaves of the sycamore were young and small enough that we still had a pretty clear view through the branches. Mr. Haddsby yelled to Ox, and Ox yelled back as they made their way from Ox's pickup truck to the backyard. They both stumbled and weaved, and I didn't see how either one of them kept from falling over. Mr. Haddsby held some kind of dark cable in his hands, which he seemed to be twisting.

"They're drunker than a couple of skunks," said Mothball.

"It's not even nine in the morning," I said.

"What's that in his hand? Looks like a pipe or something."

"It's not a pipe," I said. "See, it's limber in the middle. Like a piece of rope."

Jimmy approached his father as the two men made their way farther into the yard, closer to Mothball and me.

"Where've you been?" said Jimmy. As I looked down on them from above, I realized that Jimmy was nearly as tall as Mr. Haddsby. I'd never noticed it before, but being in the tree offered a new perspective. In fact, as they stood face-to-face, they didn't even look related. Jimmy was clearly going to be tall, and his sharp features already made the girls swoon. Mr. Haddsby, on the other hand, was short; his face was weak and splotchy. Jimmy was lucky to have inherited his mother's good looks.

Jimmy's voice now cracked as he tried to stand up to Mr. Haddsby. "Mama's been worried sick about you. She thought you were in jail, or dead, or something."

Mr. Haddsby stepped backwards, then forward, to keep his balance. The tails of an unbuttoned flannel fluttered from his thin frame, exposing his scrawny chest. Scrunched low on his head was a blue baseball cap. The bill hid his eyes. Though the men were closer to us now, I still couldn't figure out what Jimmy's father held, my view slightly obscured by a tree branch.

"You want a kiss, boy?" said Mr. Haddsby, thrusting the object at Jimmy. Jimmy reared back to avoid it. The thing suddenly made a noise like seeds inside a dried gourd.

"Holy shit," said Mothball. "It's a canebrake."

We both stared in horror as Mr. Haddsby continued thrusting the snake at Jimmy, faking as though he might actually throw it at him.

"Cut it out," shrieked Jimmy. "I'm getting Mom."

"Don't you dare, you sorry ass, or I'll make your eyes a matching set."

Jimmy paid him no mind and took off for the back door. Ox, who was only about six feet from Mr. Haddsby, hadn't said a word the whole time. He just stood in the grass with a can of beer in his hand while the top half of his body swayed in little circles.

"Listen to her sing, Ox." Mr. Haddsby held the cane-brake by the back of the head with one hand and grasped the end of its body—about a foot above the rattle—with the other. Goose bumps popped up on my arms, standing the fine little hairs on end.

Mrs. Haddsby and Jimmy appeared on the deck together. She raised her hand across her forehead, shielding her eyes from the morning light. "Macon," she yelled, "get over here this instant, you damn jackass. I ain't putting up with none of your foolishness this morning. You gonna get yourself killed."

"Don't you tell me what to do, woman," slurred Mr. Haddsby. "I'm the man of this house, and I'll do what I please."

"I'm calling the law," she yelled.

"You better not, Lydia, or you'll end up looking like that boy."

"Don't you dare threaten me. Kill that snake or I'm calling the sheriff right now."

Ox chuckled. Mrs. Haddsby turned to go inside, while Jimmy stayed leaning against the deck railing. Mothball and I hadn't moved from the floor of the tree house.

"Shit," said Mr. Haddsby, "I gotta stop her. Here, hold this, Ox."

Instead of handing the snake to Ox, he threw it at him. The snake rainbowed through the air, and Ox instinctively put out his hands, dropping his beer in the process. The snake, maybe three feet long and as fat as a fire hose, landed on Ox's outstretched arms. It instantly sunk its fangs into the thick of Ox's biceps. Ox screamed, unlatched the snake, and whipped it back at Mr. Haddsby. Ox fell over backwards after he threw it. The head of the snake locked on to Mr. Haddsby's calf, biting right through his jeans.

"Oh, shit," he yelled, swatting at his pants as if trying to ward off a swarm of angry yellow jackets. He kicked his leg furiously. The snake's body curled into a ball and it held on tenaciously, like a dog on the neck of a rabbit. Mr. Haddsby finally got the snake by the tail, ripped it away, and slung it toward the trees. Twirling through the air, boomerang style, the canebrake hit the trunk of the sycamore we were perched in.

Looking through the trapdoor opening, I saw that the snake had gotten tangled in the gray beard of some dead kudzu vines. Colored in bands of brown and pinkish gray, the snake looked beautiful to me. Its head bobbed from side to side, but it was unable to slink off. Toward the middle of its body was a strange protrusion, like a camel's hump.

"Jimmy, get back here," said Mrs. Haddsby as she reappeared on the deck. He had already started running toward his dad.

"We gotta get out of here," I said. "Come on."

Mothball looked at me. His face was the color of the dead kudzu.

"What about the snake? It's right there."

"We'll climb down to the bottom step and then jump. His back's broke. He can't get us."

"Of all the trees in the woods," said Mothball, "he had to smash against this one."

"Come on, you big baby, let's go. I'll even jump first."

I climbed down the steps, keeping my eye on the writhing snake. When I got to the bottom step, I turned around and leaped out as far as I could. After landing, I looked back at the snake and then up at Mothball; he still hadn't made a move to descend. Jimmy screamed at his father in the yard, but I didn't pay any attention to what he said.

"Come on, Mothball," I said. "He can't get you. He's practically dead already."

"He don't look practically dead, Walter. I hate snakes. I hate 'em."

"Just do what I did. I missed him by five feet easy."

Mothball slowly made his way down the steps. His shirt balled up under his armpits as his belly scraped against the trunk of the sycamore. Folds of pale skin rolled over the waistline of his jeans. The snake, unable to shake its rattle, still jerked underneath him, its mouth wide open and hissing.

"Look at it, Walter," he said. "It wants to kill me and eat me. Just like the Troll."

"Jump, Mothball."

"I wanna move to Ireland," he said.

"What? What the hell are you talking about?"

"I heard there ain't no snakes in Ireland."

"Jesus Christ, Mothball. Just jump already," I yelled. "Or I'm leaving."

Mothball pushed off the step. The snake tried to lunge at his shoes but couldn't. Mothball landed and rolled at my feet, tears streaming down his chubby cheeks.

"Let's get out of here," I said.

"Oh, shit, Walter. Holy shit."

I sprinted away from the wood line, Mothball blubbering behind me. We ran toward Jimmy, who now stood above his father with his fists clenched. Mr. Haddsby rolled around in the grass, screaming and grabbing at his calf.

Ox lay on his back a few feet from Mr. Haddsby, mumbling inaudibly, a giant lump of man in the greening Bermuda grass. His massive chest heaved up and down, up and down. Two little streams of crimson trickled down his arm, collecting in a puddle at his elbow. White foam oozed from his ear, and it took me a moment to realize that it was only beer spilling from the can that his head had just crushed.

"Jimmy," I said, "you okay?"

He didn't turn around; neither did he respond. He just stood there, glaring at Mr. Haddsby, his angry fists opening and closing as if he were flicking water from his fingers. I swear it looked as though Jimmy was about ready to kick Mr. Haddsby right in the face. And I wouldn't have blamed him if he had.

Chapter 3

Ox DIED. I don't know how else to say it. He just died. Everyone always said he was tougher than a pine knot, but the canebrake proved tougher. An ambulance rushed the two of them to Atlanta, but Ox died before they got there. Mr. Haddsby fared better. The doctors said that because the snake had bitten through his jeans and because it had already injected Ox with the majority of its venom, he survived.

The only good that came out of the whole mess was that we missed school on Friday for the funeral. It seemed like the whole town of Woodley showed up at the little Methodist church to pay their respects. There was a lot of talk about what a good man Ox had been, about how he remembered birthdays, and the preacher actually made a joke about how the casket maker had to use the wood from three full-grown pines to make Ox's coffin. That drew snickers from some of the people, but I didn't find it all that funny. He preached about how God worked in mysterious ways, or some such crap, but the whole thing seemed like a waste of time to me. As I sat on the pew next to my mother—my father had to work—I wondered about God. If there really was a God, why didn't He get rid of Mr. Haddsby instead of Ox? It just didn't make sense, as far as I could tell.

The other thing I thought about was how I had felt as I watched Ox gasping and dying. A feeling had come over me that was similar to when I'd killed the fox. It was a feeling of fascination and curiosity. It was as if I knew I should do something to help but that stronger part of me just wanted to observe, as if I'd been transfixed by a hypnotist's pocket watch. The first time I remember ever having that feeling was when I was a little boy, maybe six years old. I'd been playing down the street at the O'Kanes' house. They were away on vacation, and I liked going there because they had a jungle gym in the backyard. The house was tucked away in a stand of pines and isolated from the other houses in the neighborhood, so nobody knew I was there. My parents certainly didn't know. They'd been in one of their many fights, and Dad had screamed at me to get lost and go outside.

I played on the monkey bars and trapeze, but after a while, I got bored. Since I knew nobody was home, I started snooping around the house, trying to see if I could find anything of interest. On the back porch was a charcoal grill. Underneath it I found a box of matches and lighter fluid.

At first I just poured lighter fluid into the grill and lit it. But before too long I'd stacked a little pyramid of charcoal on the deck, doused it with fuel, and lit it. The flames rose as high as my bellybutton for an instant before settling down. Shortly after the charcoal started to take, the briquettes began glowing orange. And then the decking boards started to smolder. Before I knew what was happening, the cedar shakes on the side of the house caught fire. I pushed the grill over to try to smother the flames, but it was too late.

Within a few minutes, the entire house was engulfed. Because of the heat, I had to leave the deck, but I never took my eyes off the flames. I watched as the glass in the kitchen window melted and folded over on itself, as the flames came rolling out of the opening like waves in the ocean, as the yellows and blues started to spring to life when the heat intensified, as thick gray smoke began billowing off the roof. I watched it all, mesmerized. I knew I should have run to my house to get help, to get my parents to call for fire trucks, to tell them I was sorry. But that stronger part of me said to hide in the pine trees and watch. And that's what I did. Fire trucks arrived, as well as all the people in the neighborhood, including my parents, who watched the house burn as if it were an exciting sporting event. When I saw my mother, I ran to her and tugged on her pant leg. She seemed relieved to see me as she scooped me into her arms and squeezed me tight.

A few days later, the fire marshal stated that he believed the O'Kanes must have left some hot coals in their grill and that a strong gust of wind had probably blown it over, igniting the blaze.

I never got caught, and I never told anyone about it. Not even Jimmy or Mothball. I learned early on that children are never suspected of such things, and that silence is the key to keeping out of trouble.

🍃

The morning after Ox's funeral, I was sitting on my bed reading *The Catcher in the Rye* when I heard a knock on the front door. My mother's muffled voice filtered up the stairs.

"Well, hey, Raymond," she said, "come on in. You want something to eat?"

"Sure," said Mothball. "Yes, ma'am."

I knew that Jimmy probably stood right next to Mothball while my mother talked, but she usually pretended he didn't exist. She loved Mothball for some reason—I think since she'd always been overweight herself, she empathized with him—but she refused to call him by his nickname. Every time he came over to the house, she fed him something or other, but Jimmy was a different story. It always made me mad, because it wasn't Jimmy's fault that Mom had a grudge against the Haddsbys. "Haddsby blood's been tainted for as long as I can remember," she said. "Nothing good has ever come from a Haddsby except the choir music at their funeral." She'd used that line on me just the evening before, after Ox's burial.

I got dressed and went downstairs to find Jimmy and Mothball sitting at the kitchen table, a plate of pecan pie in front of Mothball, nothing in front of Jimmy. But Jimmy was so used to it by now that it didn't even seem to bother him.

"Hey," I said. "What're y'all up to?"

"You want to go to town with us?" said Jimmy. "Bum around or something?"

I noticed that the bruising around his eye had all but disappeared. "Yeah, all right," I said. "Let me get my shoes."

"Grab some quarters," said Mothball through a mouthful of Mom's pie.

"What for?"

"Oreo's got his pot up and running. First batch of the year."

"So why do I have to buy? Don't y'all got any money?"

"Because you're rich," he said, rubbing his fingers against the last traces of sticky goo that clung to the plate, then sucking them clean. "You already told us your granddaddy fetched twenty dollars for that fox pelt."

"I should've never opened my big mouth."

"Too late now," said Jimmy. "Hurry up, Walter. Watching Mothball stuff his fat pie hole has got me hungry."

Mothball stuck his tongue out at Jimmy, then used his moist finger to mop up the crumbs. He said, "Umm, this sure is good."

I went upstairs and grabbed a dollar and two quarters from a Mason jar on the desk next to my typewriter. The typewriter had been an inheritance from my grandmother, who prided herself on writing letters. "There ain't no better way than a powerful note to get your point across," she used to tell me. She'd promised that when she died that old typer would go to me, and she'd been true to her word.

I stuffed the money into the front pocket of my jeans, then put my tennis shoes on. When I came back down, Mom stood at the sink, washing off Mothball's plate with a sponge.

"You sure you don't want anything else to eat, Raymond?" she asked. "I got some peanut brittle."

"No, ma'am, but it was mighty good. We're fixing to go see Oreo anyway. I want to save some room," he said, grabbing his round belly with both hands and smiling.

"Walter, you watch that Oreo fella," said Mom, turning her attention to me. "Make sure he uses a ladle. His hands are filthy."

"*Hand,* Mom, not *hands,*" I said. "He's only got one."

"Well, whatever—you know what I mean," she said. Her lips pursed as she dried Mothball's plate with a dishtowel and stuck it on the slatted wooden rack next to the sink. I'd already had enough of Mom for the day, so I hastily pushed my friends out the door.

We walked to town in search of Oreo. As we passed in front of the Big House—Dr. Schuessler's house—Jimmy stopped. The Big House stood on the corner, just before you entered Woodley proper. Adorned with a two-level porch and huge bay windows, the grand white house was the pride of Woodley, hence its name. Concrete steps led from the street to a sidewalk in the yard. "Schuessler" was etched into the bottom step in fancy letters. Yellow daffodils flanked the edges of the sidewalk in a perfect row, all the way to the front porch. Live oaks, bigger around than the Doric columns that stretched to the roof, shaded the lawn.

"Mothball, let me see your knife, will ya?" asked Jimmy.

Mothball pulled his jackknife from his jeans pocket and flipped it to him. Jimmy opened it, sliced a splinter of wood from the white picket fence, and popped it into his mouth. He snapped the knife closed and tossed it back to Mothball. Little patches of bare wood dotted the fence where Jimmy had procured many of his toothpicks.

"Doc Schuessler's fence makes the best toothpicks in Woodley," he said as he sucked the flavor out of the wood, paint included.

We ventured away from the Big House, my mouth salivating as I thought of the goodness awaiting us at Oreo's stand. The town, as usual, was desolate. The hardware store appeared open, but the rest of the red brick buildings, with metal awnings hanging above the storefronts, were abandoned. From inside the five-and-dime, flashes of silver gleamed off the defunct soda fountain. In front of the counter were the red-topped swivel stools that I used to spin around on as a little boy when Mom would take me there for fountain-made Coca-Colas or root beer floats.

The candy stripe still hung on the brick façade of the old barbershop, and "Audey's" was painted across the window in faded cursive lettering. The little green and white striped awning above the entrance now sloped down precariously, ready to collapse with the next storm. The big cushy chairs with the steel footrests sat idle, not having held a customer in years. Papa used to sit in there for hours, shooting the breeze with the other elderly men in town. For a man who hardly had a hair on his head, Papa'd surely spent an awful lot of time at that barbershop.

Once we reached the far end of the hardware store, I caught sight of the steam stretching upward from Oreo's five-gallon steel pot. We hurried to his stand, racing to see who'd be first in line. The odor of boiling peanuts didn't smell like much more than warm dirt, but it was the taste, not the smell, we were after. I called it a stand, but really it was just a folding card table with a propane hot plate on top. A large burlap sack lay at Oreo's feet, filled with raw peanuts, and a huge box of Morton's salt sat next to it. Every spring, Oreo was out there, between the hardware store and the edge of a black-eyed pea field, selling boiled peanuts.

Oreo was an old man, a mulatto with skin not much darker than mine was in the summertime. His white hair gleamed in the sunshine, sitting on his head like a puffball mushroom. He always smiled, showing a few yellow teeth that were spaced out in his purple gums like kernels on a bad ear of corn. The most interesting thing about Oreo, though, was that he had only one arm.

"Hey, Oreo," I said, beating Jimmy to the table by a step.

"How y'all young'ns doing this morning?" asked Oreo in a slow, smoky voice.

"We're good. How the peanuts looking this year? Are they ready?"

"Pert nigh. Nice and green, just like they ought to be. Can't make boiled peanuts with them mature ones. They gots to be green."

Mothball started giggling, and I knew why. When Oreo said "boiled peanuts," it always sounded like "boilt penis." I smiled, trying not to laugh.

"We'd like three bags then," I said. "One for each of us."

"You treatin' today? Now that's a good man," he said, pointing at me with his ladle as he looked at Jimmy and Mothball.

"Yes, sir, I guess so," I said.

Oreo had a stack of skinny brown-paper sacks on the table, the kind that general stores put tall bottles of beer in, and he fingered one as though pulling a card off a deck. He snapped it open with a pop, then stuffed it under the armpit of his right arm—or what used to be his right arm. It was a light brown sausage of an arm now, rounded and puckered just above the spot where his elbow used to be. The tightened skin at the end of his stump looked like a balloon knot. Or the asshole of a tomcat.

I had to give it to Oreo though; he had his method down pat. He stuck that open sack under his arm and, with his left hand, ladled the hot peanuts, never spilling one. He set the ladle on the table, grabbed the sack, and handed it to me. As he doled them out, I handed one to Jimmy, then Mothball, and finally kept one for myself. I pulled the dollar bill out of my pocket and dropped it into the steel coffee can on the table. I pulled a quarter from the bottom of the can and held it up.

"It's still a quarter a bag, right, Oreo?"

"That's right, young'n. Quarter a bag. Y'all enjoy 'em, now."

I was about to tell him we would when Jimmy said

something so stupid and rude that I swear I wanted to strangle him around his skinny neck.

"How'd you lose your arm, Oreo?" He said it as matter-of-fact as all get-out. We'd talked about it plenty of times, speculating on what happened, but no one had ever actually asked Oreo about it. However, much to my surprise, it didn't seem to bother him in the least.

"When I was a puppy dog, younger than y'all," he said, "I had to help Mama and Daddy pick cotton. We got paid by the basketful, you know, so the more baskets we filled, the more money Mama had for groceries. One day, while I was dumping a basketful onto the wagon, I noticed some stray cotton that had fallen underneath. I reached down to grab it, figuring I'd sneak it into my basket and get myself a little extra without the work. Well, I must've spooked them horses because they lurched forward and that wagon wheel went right over my elbow. Snapped it backwards as easy as you'd break a stick for the campfire."

The three of us stood there, hot bags of peanuts in our hands, too entranced by his story to eat them.

"Arm weren't no good then, so Daddy took it off with a hacksaw when we got home. He give me a couple of shots of whiskey, stuck the blade in Mama's cookin' fire, then commenced to cutting. That's why it looks all ugly down there at the end," he said, pointing the stub at us so we could see. "Because that blade weren't all that sharp, he ripped up the skin something awful. It was bleeding worse than a stuck hog. Daddy said I deserved what I got, seeing's how I had my mind set on stealing and all."

I felt numb. I thanked Oreo for the peanuts and then we walked across the street to sit on the steps of the five-and-dime. I took the remaining quarters I had and bought three RC Colas from the machine on the sidewalk.

"Holy shit," said Mothball, tossing a shell into the street. "Now that was a story."

"I'd say," I said. "I can't believe you asked him that, Jimmy."

I placed a hot, wet peanut to my lips, splitting the shell with my teeth. The brown-skinned nuts sat in a neat little row. I sucked them into my mouth and chewed, the soft bullets forming a paste as they mixed with the salty water. Every person I knew had his own method for eating them. Jimmy, for instance, put the whole peanut, shell and all, in his mouth, chewed it into mishmash, then spat the bolus into the street. Sometimes, with the peanuts that had been overboiled, he'd simply eat the whole thing. "Those," he said, "give you the best juice."

"What were you thinking, Jimmy?" asked Mothball. "Oreo's a cool dude. There wasn't no reason for that."

"He didn't care," said Jimmy. "And besides, now we know what happened."

"I can't believe his daddy sawed his arm off," I said.

"He got what he deserved," said Jimmy. "No nigger

got any right to steal from a white man. That's all there is to it."

"He was a little kid," I said.

"Yeah, and besides," said Mothball, "Oreo ain't a nigger. He's half white."

"Bullshit," said Jimmy, spitting a wad of chewed shell on the sidewalk. "Daddy says once a man's got even a trace of nigger blood in his body, he's full nigger. He said whoever gave Oreo his name had it backwards, though. Don't matter how white he is on the outside, he'll always be black on the inside. Once a nigger, always a nigger."

"You're about dumb," I mumbled. I looked over at Mothball, who had his eyes locked on something across the street.

"Look, y'all," he whispered, "it's the Troll."

I couldn't figure out where he'd come from. But sure enough, there he stood, getting a bag of peanuts from Oreo. Just as soon as I got a bead on him, though, a logging truck slowly passed by, filling the air with the sweet smell of diesel. The butts of long pine logs bounced over the edge of the truck bed, rattling against the steel standards that shot upright on either side of the load like pitchforks. One log had a red flag tied to its end, flapping as it passed us by. Bits of bark bounced off the asphalt like raindrops as the truck headed toward Simmons, which operated just past town, right before the bridge that spanned the Tallapoosa.

"Watch this," said Jimmy, jumping up from the step.

"No, Jimmy," said Mothball. "Don't do nothing stupid. That's the Troll."

"I know it's the Troll, dipshit."

"Walter, make him stop."

"I don't even know what he's gonna do."

"Just watch," said Jimmy. He set his sack of peanuts on the step, then cupped his hands over his mouth and yelled, "Hey, you. Troll."

No one called him the Troll, as far as I knew, except us. I'd made the name up after telling Jimmy and Mothball about the story of Billy Goat Gruff.

"He doesn't know that name, you dumb-ass," I said.

"Jimmy, don't," said Mothball. "He'll come over here and kill us."

"You're such a pussy sometimes. I'm just having a little fun." He cupped his hands again and yelled, louder this time. "Hey, you. Troll." This time the Troll turned his head around, showing his hairy face. "You shot any gooks lately?"

Up until recently, the Vietnam War had been the only thing on the news. In fact, for as far back as any of us could ever remember, it had always been the main story every night. So we were pretty familiar with a lot of the lingo, including racial slurs toward the Vietnamese.

"Oh, shit," said Mothball. "You're crazy, Jimmy."

The Troll just stood there with a bag of peanuts in his

hand, his head cocked to the side. Then he slowly started walking across the street toward us.

"Oh, God," said Mothball, "we're gonna die. You really done it this time. He probably thinks we're the VC. He thinks we're the gooks." He popped off the step, dropped his bag of peanuts on the sidewalk, and took off running toward home, his flabby arms pumping furiously in front of him.

"What are we gonna do?" I whispered to Jimmy as the Troll took slow, deliberate steps toward us. As it turned out, Jimmy didn't have to answer my question because a blue pickup truck pulled in front of us, blocking off the Troll.

"Hop in, boys," said Papa, oblivious to what was happening around us. "I just talked to your mama on the phone. She said y'all were down here. Hurry up and get in. I'm hungry and want to take y'all to Mudcat's."

We flew over the tailgate and into the back of Papa's truck. I looked over at the Troll, who stood only a few feet from us in the road. Much to my surprise, he stared directly at me and not at Jimmy. And then he said something. I stared at him for a second and then quickly turned to Jimmy to see if he'd heard what I'd heard. Jimmy looked back at me, but then the truck lurched forward. As Papa pulled away, he waved at the Troll. I was too scared to turn and see if the Troll waved back.

"Where's your other buddy?" asked Papa, sticking his

head out the window, yelling back at me. The few strands of hair he had left flopped around in the wind like loose tassels.

"Keep going straight," I said, feeling confused and disoriented over what the Troll had said, but I tried to remain calm and normal. "He should be running up the road. We'll be on him any second now." And as soon as I said it, I saw Mothball, just past the Big House. His oval figure chugged along faster than I'd ever seen it move. His jeans slipped down, and he pulled them up every few paces, but he never slowed.

"Get in," said Jimmy, as Papa pulled up alongside him. Mothball turned toward us, his cheeks red and splotchy. He stopped, looked behind him as if the Troll were right on his tail, and jumped in back. Papa had lawn chairs in the bed, and I unfolded one and sat down as he turned the truck around in someone's driveway. Jimmy and Mothball each grabbed a chair too.

"What . . . the heck . . . is going on?" asked Mothball between heavy breaths.

"Papa's taking us to Mudcat's," I said.

"Well . . . what happened?" asked Mothball. "Where's the Troll?"

"Shortly after you so boldly left us to die," said Jimmy, "the Troll started coming toward us. Then, out of nowhere, Walter's grandpa pulled up and saved us."

"You're kidding," said Mothball, suddenly revitalized.

"That's unbelievable. And now we're going to Mudcat's? Man, what a day. Pecan pie, boiled peanuts, a near death experience, and now catfish. And it ain't even noon yet."

Mudcat's was the best catfish shack around. It was way out in the country and every Saturday he—Mudcat—had a fish fry. A dinner cost three dollars, and it included as much catfish, French fries, and hushpuppies as you cared to eat. My favorite part was the tails; they were like crisp potato chips. We'd eat outside under a pavilion, sitting at picnic tables covered with newspaper. I didn't know how Papa figured on paying for all of us, but at the moment I didn't really care. I was just glad he'd come up with the idea; I didn't know what would have happened to Jimmy and me otherwise.

As we passed back through town, we kept our eyes peeled for the Troll, but he'd disappeared. Mothball eyed our bags of peanuts on the sidewalk that now lay abandoned, but Papa kept on going. Oreo waved to us with his good arm, and Mothball and I waved back. When we made it to the bridge, Papa punched the accelerator. We all looked toward the trestle, scanning the path that led through the canebrake to the Troll's shack, but we saw nothing. I wanted to ask Jimmy if he'd heard what the Troll said, but I didn't have the nerve.

"Where do you think he went?" I asked instead, having to yell now that Papa had picked up speed. The warm air felt good as it whipped through my hair. It smelled fresh, which always surprised me. Sometimes I'd get so used to Simmons sulfur that I'd forget what air was supposed to smell like.

"He's probably out searching for Mothball," Jimmy yelled back. "I bet the Troll can sniff out a yellow-belly a mile away."

"What was I supposed to do?" said Mothball. "Stay there and let him kill me?"

Jimmy and I laughed while Mothball turned his head away, mumbling something I couldn't hear. And then Jimmy mentioned what the Troll had said.

"What do you think he meant, Walter? What the heck was that supposed to mean?"

"I . . . I don't know."

"What?" asked Mothball, now turning back to us excitedly. "What are y'all talking about? You mean, the Troll talked to you? What'd he say?"

Before I could answer, Jimmy replied, "He said, 'How's blue fleas doing?'"

"'How's blue fleas doing?'" repeated Mothball. "What the hell's that supposed to mean?"

"I have no idea," said Jimmy. "He said it real fast. It sounded like 'blufleeze,' not 'blue fleas.' Ain't that what you heard, Walter?"

That wasn't what I'd heard at all, but I was too dumbstruck to tell the truth. "Y-yeah, I think so," I stammered.

"The engine was kind of loud, and I was scared shitless, but yeah, I think that's what he said."

"I know, it was hard to hear," said Jimmy, "but that's what I heard. Or maybe it was 'blue trees.' Shoot, I don't know, but I'm telling you, that Troll is one cracked nut."

"'Blue fleas'?" said Mothball again. "'Blue trees'? Fleas are black. Trees are green. That don't make no sense. He's crazy, y'all."

I considered telling them what I'd heard, but I had to think about things first. I wasn't ready to do that yet. Even in the breeze, I felt sweat pouring down my forehead. And it wasn't because I was hot.

Papa really opened up the truck once we crossed the bridge and passed Niggertown. It flew by in a flash, but I still made out some young children playing on a bare patch of red dirt, chasing after a rubber tire they rolled along. Streams of smoke filtered up from stovepipes that poked out from the rusty tin roofs of their shacks. Not one shack was painted. Some had tarpaper tacked to the sides, peeling like wallpaper, but most just showed faded pine boards, turned the gray of rotting mushrooms. Scraps of clothes hung from lines, drying in the sun, and rusted-out trucks and cars with busted or cracked windshields sat in a clump at the far end, tall weeds growing up all around them.

It was impossible to carry on a conversation now, as

the roar of the wind drowned everything out. I sat back in my lawn chair, trying not to think about the Troll anymore, and just watched the countryside roll along. The straight road undulated slightly as Papa sped toward Mudcat's. We passed the Shady Oak mobile home park, a name I always found ironic, because there was nothing but slash pine and cypress surrounding it. Not an oak in sight. Right next to the trailers was the Jubilee Worship Center, which was nothing more than a doublewide with a wooden cross out front.

Papa turned onto the road that led to Lafayette, and we all had to lean way over so we didn't tip out of our chairs. Shortly after that, we took another turn that put us on a hard-packed clay secondary that led through the swamplands. The swamplands were desolate and eerie. Spaced far apart from one another, spindly scrub pines grew on little bumps of land, while broken logs and snapped-off stumps sat half submerged in the dark, brackish water. I knew that the cottonmouths were thick in there, enjoying the spring sunshine. I couldn't help but think of Ox for a minute, and I looked over at Jimmy, wondering if he might be thinking the same thing.

A small hill led us up and out of the swamplands and back to dry ground where the conifers once again grew tall and straight. About a mile past the swamp, Papa pulled into the driveway of Mudcat's. A load of cars already sat in the grass, and people milled around under the pavilion and in the lawn, talking and laughing or eating at the picnic tables. A group of boys stood at the edge of the catfish pond behind Mudcat's house, skipping rocks. The smell of frying oil reminded me that I hadn't had any breakfast.

Mothball was so excited that he jumped out before Papa had come to a full stop.

"Hey, Jimmy," he said. "I was just wondering about something on the way over."

"Yeah? What were you just wondering?"

"I wanted to know if you enjoyed sucking on Oreo's boilt penis this morning?"

Mothball took off running through the parked cars, nearly busting his hip on a rearview mirror. Jimmy jumped off the truck bed to give chase. I hopped out and gave Papa a hug, thankful that he'd saved us. But the Troll's words still echoed in my head. He hadn't said "blue fleas" or "blue trees." He'd said my mother's name. I was positive of it. He had looked right at me and said, "How's Louise doing?"

CHAPTER 4

TOWARD THE END OF MAY, just after Jimmy's birthday, school finally let out for summer vacation. We'd seen nothing more of the Troll (though I swear it felt like he was always lurking around somewhere) and as time passed, I started to doubt what I'd heard. It didn't make any sense, so I just tried to forget about it.

We were released early on the last day of school, and as we exited the building, I met Jimmy and Mothball outside. We followed the throng of other kids toward the center of town. The last day of school not only meant the beginning of summer, but also marked the day the Simmons pulp mill had its annual celebration: Merchants' Day.

Merchants' Day was a tradition in Woodley. It used to be held just before Thanksgiving, but Old Man Simmons switched it several years back so that it always fell on the last day of school. All the stores in town got together and threw a party, a celebration to say thanks to all of their patrons. Main Street got blocked off, and each proprietor set up a booth and gave away free stuff. In years past, Audey had brought a chair outside on the sidewalk and gave complimentary haircuts. The five-and-dime gave away candy. Simmons, being the largest business by far, supplied all the food and drink: hot dogs, hamburgers, and Coke. This year, however, since there were virtually no businesses left, Mr. Simmons had to run the whole show on his own.

Usually there was music and dancing, and the elementary students showcased the plays they'd been working on all year. But the real highlight was the turkey toss. It was all Mothball had talked about for weeks. He had a plan, and he wanted Jimmy and me to help. He could hardly stand still when we arrived at the celebration.

"Okay, y'all are going to have to really hustle," he said. "I think the smartest way is for us to hang back from the crowd, near the five-and-dime. That way, we'll have a better view of the roof. Usually after they throw 'em, they don't just fall straight to the ground. They flutter out away from the building. That's the mistake everybody always makes. They all stand right at the edge of the awning."

"We know what to do," said Jimmy. "You've told us every day for a month."

"I want to make sure. I ain't never caught one. This is my year—I can feel it."

"I've never caught one either," I said, "but I've never really tried that hard."

"Well, you gotta try this year. I'm counting on y'all. Take no prisoners. Knock people out of the way if you have to—I don't care, just catch one."

"I think you've officially lost your mind," said Jimmy.

"Yeah," I said, "maybe the *Guinness Book* has a record for the craziest person to ever live. You'd have a good shot at that one."

"Listen, all I've heard from y'all for the last few months is how crazy I am. How stupid I am. But I'm gonna do this. I was hoping for some assistance. I thought we were best friends. Best friends are supposed to take care of each other."

Mothball walked off through the crowd, toward the hot dog stand.

"He's crazier than a two-peckered billy goat," said Jimmy.

"Yep," I said.

※

It seemed that the whole town was gathered in the street, though one person I definitely didn't see was the Troll. I saw my mother talking to a group of women, but I went the other way as soon as I caught sight of her. Oreo stood in his usual spot, smiling, with a line of people waiting to buy peanuts. All of the lunch ladies from school were behind the food booths, dressed in Pilgrim costumes. Our teachers were all there too, some dressed in the same Pilgrim attire, others made up to look like Indians. They all looked hot and grossly out of place.

"Look, Jimmy," I said, nodding across the street toward a couple standing in front of Audey's barbershop. "Look who it is."

Sheila Brackwater stood in front of the doorway, holding hands with Arch Davis, a big football player wearing his letter jacket. It felt about ninety degrees outside, and I thought him a fool to wear one of those heavy coats in the sweltering heat. Sheila wore a short skirt, exposing her tanned, shapely legs, and a tight button-down blouse with the top few buttons unfastened. Jimmy and I stared as she laughed with Arch. When she stood on her tiptoes to give Arch a peck on the cheek, her calves tightened into balls of muscle.

"We've gotta get that tree house finished," I said.

Jimmy didn't respond. He only stared.

Mothball walked up while we gawked at Sheila. In his hands, resting on a paper towel, were two hot dogs covered in runny chili, mustard, and ketchup.

"Man, look at that," he said.

"I know," I said. "I can't pull my eyes off her."

"Not her," said Mothball, "Arch. He's wearing his letter jacket. It must be a thousand degrees out here."

Jimmy turned his head to say something but apparently decided against it.

"What's wrong, Mothball," I said, "didn't you get anything at lunch today?"

"What? These?" he said, looking down at the hot dogs. "These are energy food. They'll help me when the time comes. Y'all should go get a few for yourselves."

I ignored him and instead scanned the crowd, trying to get another glimpse of Sheila. But, unfortunately, all I saw was my mother walking toward me. The last thing I wanted to do was talk to her with all of my school friends around.

"There you are, Walter." She wore a flowery spring dress that was too tight, and she waddled as she approached. She had a pink pillbox hat on her head, and it appeared she'd used a whole can of hairspray, judging by the way the hat seemed to float like a little pink raft on a brown sea. I was mortified. "I've been looking all over for you. Isn't this fun?" She had a Coke bottle in her hand with a lipstick-stained straw curving out of the top. She leaned over and kissed me on the cheek. "I love Merchants' Day. It's—"

"Mom, stop it already." Her eyes widened, a pained look in them, but I didn't care. I caught Jimmy's eye over the top of her shoulder; he was doing all that he could not to bust out laughing. I knew I was in for it. "Don't ever kiss me in public like that."

"But Walter, I'm your mother."

"I don't care. You can't do that. It's embarrassing."

All I can say is thank God for Mothball. After finishing his hot dogs, he said, "Hey, Mrs. Sithol."

"Well, hello, Raymond, you sweet thing, you." She ignored Jimmy as usual. "I'm glad to see you're not embarrassed to be around me."

"Why would I be embarrassed? You're the nicest lady in Woodley."

"Well, I'm glad *you* appreciate me. You come over tomorrow and I'll have some brownies waiting." She glanced over at me. "I guess I'll see you at home then, Walter."

She turned to leave, patting Mothball on the head as she left. As she scuttled away, I noticed her pass right by Mrs. Haddsby. It appeared that Mrs. Haddsby said hello to her, but my mother turned her head the other way, pretending not to see her. It wasn't only Jimmy that she ignored. I looked at my friends to see if they'd noticed, but clearly they hadn't, because Mothball said, "Your mom is so nice. My mother never bakes me nothing."

"She doesn't need to," said Jimmy, "with Walter's mom feeding you all the time."

"You're just upset because she thinks you come from bad stock."

"Yeah, I'm upset, all right. I wish my mother would come over and give me a big fat kiss on the mouth like she just did to Walter."

"It wasn't on the mouth, asshole."

"Didn't you see it, Mothball?" asked Jimmy. "I'm pretty sure I saw a little spit-swapping going on. Maybe even some tongue."

"Shut the hell up," I said. "You're sick."

Jimmy and Mothball started laughing. I loathed my mother as I never had. I wanted to get out of there, but about that time, from a small stage at the end of the street, a voice came over the PA system. An elderly man stood in front of a microphone, tapping it with his finger. As soon as the man spoke, feedback whistled through the crowd, causing everyone to groan and cover their ears.

It was Old Man Simmons himself, the founder and owner of the pulp mill. He was thin and frail, dressed in cowboy boots, jeans, a white shirt with metallic buttons that glimmered in the sunshine, and one of those thin bolo ties I'd imagined only people in Texas wore. On his head, instead of a five-gallon hat, was a black-brimmed fedora adorned with a silver buckle, making him look like a western-style Miles Standish.

"Is this thing working?" he said into the microphone, his voice scratchy and old.

The crowd replied that it was.

"Okay, well, good, then," he said. "Happy Merchants' Day, everybody. It's time for the turkey toss. Good luck and happy catching."

"Come on," said Mothball. "Y'all get in your positions."

Jimmy and I stood where Mothball told us to, as if he were the quarterback and we were his wide receivers. And in a way, I guess we were. Across the street, a group of men—maybe ten in all—were making their way up the black iron fire escape on the side of the three-storied hardware store. The men had large, lumpy burlap potato sacks slung over their shoulders, looking like a group of Santa Clauses on their way to deliver presents.

"All right, y'all, just hang back and wait. This is my year. Oh, man, I know it is."

Jimmy and I looked at each other and shook our heads. The crowd clustered together in the street, looking up at the men. Mostly it was boys and girls my age and younger, but there were some adults too, mostly colored men and cotton farmers. The ladies, including my mom, stayed on the sidewalk, laughing and, no doubt, gossiping.

"Well, people," said Old Man Simmons over the scratchy speakers, "you know what time it is now. Are y'all ready up there?" he said, looking up at the men on the roof. They all gave a thumbs-up. "Then let the fun begin."

The men bent over, reached into their sacks, and held up fat, angry turkeys that violently flapped their wings.

"One . . . two . . . three," said Old Man Simmons.

The men held the turkeys about as easily as they could hold greased watermelons. All at once, they pitched them over the edge of the building. Their wings flapped furiously, but they still started dropping from the sky like a stack of wet newspapers. However, they all managed some type of awkward flight, and Mothball had been right—most of them came in our direction. Stray dark feathers snowed down on the crowd.

One landed on the sidewalk not more than five feet from me; it was a tom. I grabbed at him, but he darted off to the side. I chased him, his dark body bouncing along as he ran down the street, his head bobbing. The crowd roared and scurried around in all directions. The men on the roof then dropped the second wave upon us. It was madness.

A colored boy and I charged after the same tom. Like I said, they can't fly well, but they can sure run when they have to. The tom darted and weaved through the crowd, then shot up the alleyway between Audey's and the five-and-dime. The boy and I ran side by side up the narrow corridor. I grew excited when I realized one of us would get him; the alley dead-ended. Sure enough, when the tom got to the brick wall, he was trapped. He jumped up onto a steel garbage can, turning to face us. He puffed up his body, getting bigger around than a basketball. The snood hanging over his beak turned bright red. His throat changed to turquoise and his wattle a deep crimson as he readied for the standoff.

"That turkey's mine," I said. "I was after him first."

"The hell he is," said the boy. "I seed him first and I aim to catch him."

"Well, get him, then," I said. "Go ahead, he's yours."

The boy smiled and nodded, then slowly made his way toward the tom, walking as though trying to step quietly over dead leaves. The turkey shuffled around, its hard leathery feet making a ringing sound on top of the steel lid. As soon as the boy got in front of me, I shoved him hard in the back, sending him hurtling into the trash can, headfirst. I expected the turkey to drop off the lid, but he had no intentions of getting caught so easily. He flew off the can, beating his wings, leapfrogging right over me. I jumped with outstretched arms, trying to seize him. My fingers grazed his feet, but he landed behind me and took off trotting down the alleyway. I shot after the bird, knowing that the boy, being quite a bit larger, would beat me senseless if he got a hold of me.

I caught up to the tom right where the alleyway met the sidewalk. I lunged for him, sensing victory, when I felt a powerful jolt to my right shoulder. I went sprawling over the concrete, shredding my hands in the process. I lay facedown, spread-eagled on the sidewalk. I lifted my head to see Arch Davis holding my tom by the legs.

"Hell, yeah, I got me Tom Turkey," he whooped, not bothering to help me up.

Just as I started to pick myself up from the ground, a foot pressed into the small of my back; the breath shot out of me.

"Looks like neither one of us got that turkey," said the colored boy. He took off running into the melee of people, pushing harder than necessary off my back.

I stood up and inspected my palms. Black dots of gravel had embedded under the skin. Both knees of my jeans were ripped. My shoulder ached where Arch had slammed me, and to add the final insult, Sheila came up and gave him a big kiss, right on the lips.

I looked around for Mothball and Jimmy but couldn't see anything through the mass of people on the street. "To hell with this," I muttered, deciding to make my way home. I didn't give a damn about Merchants' Day anymore.

I started hobbling down the sidewalk, trying to avoid the people still chasing loose birds, when I saw Jimmy standing next to Mothball. I thought for a moment that I must have hit my head in the scrum, because I couldn't believe what I saw. Mothball was hunched over from the weight of not one but two turkeys—a tom and a hen—in his hands.

"Can you believe this shit?" said Jimmy as I limped up to them.

"Looky here, Walter," said Mothball, trying to hoist up the turkeys he held by the legs. They were upside down, hanging from his hands like slabs of meat in a butcher's shop. "Here, grab one. Help me out—they're heavy."

"I can't," I said, showing him my bloody hands.

"Take one, Jimmy," said Mothball. "I can't hold 'em both for much longer."

Mothball handed the hen to Jimmy. The turkeys futilely flapped their wings.

"Come on, y'all. We gotta get them to the chicken shack. Fellas, one of these two birds is gonna be Mike the Second."

We started to make our way home. As people passed us, they congratulated Jimmy and Mothball, admiring the birds.

"I caught 'em both myself," said Mothball to every person who offered praise.

"I hope you appreciate what I did for you," I said, once we'd escaped the crowd.

"What do you mean? I don't see no turkey in your hand."

"What happened, anyway?" asked Jimmy. "You look like you got beat up."

"Nothing," I said.

"Well, let me tell you how I caught 'em," said Mothball.

I had to listen to his story all the way back as we walked along. When we got to the corner of Douglass and Pine, I peeled off and headed to my house instead of following them to the chicken shack. I hoped my mother had already made it home. All I wanted was for her to clean me up and bandage my hands and knees.

CHAPTER 5

LATER THAT EVENING, I had trouble turning the pages of *Of Mice and Men*—I'd decided to reread it—because my mother had wrapped both my hands in gauze. I was at the very end of the book—George has the gun and is thinking of killing Lenny because he's become too much of a burden—when someone started pounding on the front door. I raced down the steps, hoping it was Jimmy and Mothball. But Mom beat me to it. She'd been in the kitchen, finishing the dinner dishes. Before turning the knob, she wiped her damp hands on her apron and patted her stiff hairdo as she glanced at the hall mirror.

"Well, hello, Raymond," she said, just as I reached the bottom step. Then her voice jumped in pitch. "What in the world? Are you okay?"

I poked my head around her wide frame to see what she meant. Mothball stood on the porch, his shirt and hands splattered in blood. He had a wide grin on his face.

"I'm okay, Mrs. Sithol. I've never been better."

"But the blood," said Mom. "Did you cut yourself? Do you need a rag to clean up?"

"No, ma'am. I've just been working on one of the turkeys I caught today."

"Working on? What do you—"

"Never mind, Mom," I said. "I'll explain it all to you later."

Mothball bounced with excitement on the porch. "Come on, Walter," he said. "You gotta see this. I think I finally did it."

"What did you do, Raymond?"

"Mom," I said, as I ran out the door, "I'll tell you later."

"Walter Elra Sithol, you get back in here, mister," she said as I ran across the front lawn alongside Mothball. "You don't have any shoes on."

I almost stopped dead in my tracks when she said my middle name. I hated that name—some sort of crazy, mixed-up family name—and I'd never told Jimmy, Mothball, or anyone else for that matter what it was. In fact, I'd lied to them both and said I didn't have one.

I looked over at Mothball to see if he'd taken notice, but clearly he had more important things on his mind. I ignored my mother and took off into the twilight, eager to see what grotesque creation Mothball had concocted. Yellow flashes from lightning bugs dotted the warm evening, flicking like dim caution lights at a railroad crossing. Crickets and katydids began their nightly concert as the orange-pink sliver of sky dissolved behind the loblollies.

"You two be careful," said the distant voice of my mother. "Stay out of trouble."

I ran on my tiptoes, trying to avoid bits of gravel in the road. After stinging my feet several times, I jumped over the curb and ran in the soft, cool grass. When we got to Jimmy's driveway, Mothball stopped.

"I need to get back," he said, breathing heavily. "Hurry up and get Jimmy, then meet me at the chicken shack. You're not gonna believe it."

"All right. I'll catch up with you in a minute. Did you actually do it?"

"Just grab Jimmy and come on. Hurry."

Mothball's white shirt glowed violet under the light of a streetlamp before he disappeared into the early darkness. I went to Jimmy's front door and knocked, praying either he or Mrs. Haddsby would answer. But it was Mr. Haddsby who swung the door open. He eyed my wrapped hands briefly, then said, "What do you want?" He wore a pair of bleached jeans and a cutoff T-shirt that exposed his stomach. A fine line of black hair shot up from just above the button of his pants, surrounded his bellybutton, and disappeared under the jagged edge of his shirt, which had obviously been cut in haste with a pair of dull scissors. The television blared, the unmistakable theme song of M*A*S*H emanating from the living room. The house smelled like an ashtray.

"Is Jimmy here?"

Mr. Haddsby took a long drink from the can of beer in his hand, his prominent Adam's apple bullfrogging with every swallow. He turned and walked off, closing the door behind him. He gave a muffled yell, and a moment later Jimmy stepped out.

"What's up?" he asked.

"Dr. Frankenstein thinks he's finally done it."

"What do you mean? The turkey?"

"Yeah, I guess. All I know is he wants us to meet him in his laboratory right away."

"Well, let's go then," said Jimmy. "This I gotta see."

We ran toward Mothball's house. My gauzed hands radiated like Mothball's shirt as we passed under the fluorescent streetlamp. A moth circled above my head in a frenzied elliptical pattern, orbiting something that didn't exist. My bare feet slapped the pavement once more, trying to keep up with Jimmy.

"So did he say he'd actually done it?"

"He had blood on his hands and a big fat smile on his face, but he didn't say exactly."

"So maybe it's something else."

"No. He told Mom it had something to do with one of the turkeys he caught."

"This better be good," said Jimmy. "I'm missing my favorite show. I hate not seeing Hot Lips."

We walked around the back of Mothball's house and headed toward the chicken shack. The door was shut, but a tiny line of yellow light seeped from the crack at the bottom, trickling onto the grass. I heard nothing from inside.

"Should we knock?" I whispered.

"Hell, no," he said, pushing the door open, busting in. As he did so, chickens in their roosts started cackling and beating their wings. The smell of mildew, ammonia, and shit wafted into the air as they went into a panic.

The flood of light blinded me for an instant as I entered from the darkness of outside. A single exposed bulb hung from the ceiling, and Mothball bumped it with his head as he jumped up from the dirty floor. Attached to a cord, it swayed back and forth, sending bizarre shadows across the room. Mothball's face lit up for a second, then faded to black as the light swung back and forth like a pendulum. Clutched in his hands was the strangest thing I'd ever seen.

Judging by its size, Mothball held the tom, not the hen, but I couldn't say for sure because its head was gone. Completely gone. It tried to beat its wings, but Mothball had it in a tight bear hug. The turkey's neck looked like a giant golf tee holding a grossly deformed ball. Dried blood streaked its neck and feathers. The way it struggled—despite its appearance—told me it was very much alive.

"Close the door, will ya?" asked Mothball.

I pushed it closed with the back of my bandaged hands, the cloth on the left hand snagging on the splintered wood for an instant. Once I shut the door, and after the light stopped swaying, the chickens calmed down and order was slowly restored. Warm chicken shit squished through my toes as I surveyed the scene. Instead of disturbing me, it actually felt good, as though the shit were moist mud on the riverbank. The dust under my arches felt soft and comfortable. Mothball sat on the dirt floor next to the oak chopping block, his back to us, caressing the turkey's feathers the same way he'd done with the chicken a few months prior.

"What in the hell have you done?" asked Jimmy.

"Isn't he beautiful?" asked Mothball, looking over his shoulder at us.

"I'm not sure 'beautiful' is the word I'd use," I said.

"What do you mean? He's a miracle, and we're gonna be famous."

"How are we gonna be famous?" asked Jimmy. "We didn't do anything."

"Not you two," he said, continuing to stroke the bird. "Me and Mike the Second."

"You know, Mothball," I said, "since the original Mike was a chicken, and this is a turkey, you don't have to name him Mike the Second. You can name him anything you want."

Mothball looked up at me, perplexed. He had four stripes of blood on each side of his T-shirt where he'd obviously wiped his fingers after handling Mike. Pieces of straw stuck to his back, and a few scraps were in his hair. "I hadn't thought about that. What would I name him?"

"If it had been a girl," I said, "you could have named her Marie Antoinette."

Mothball still looked confused.

"You know—she got beheaded by her husband, Henry the Eighth."

"Hey, that's good, Walter," said Jimmy. "And you could get a little nametag and put it on a necklace for her. Get it. Put it on a neck-less." Jimmy and I started cracking up, but Mothball didn't find any of it funny.

"He's still got a neck, you dumb-ass," he said to Jimmy. "It's the head that's missing." He turned to me then. "And I ain't no scholar like you think you are, Walter. I ain't Mr. Know-It-All, but wasn't her name Anne something or other? The one that got her head chopped off?"

My cheeks filled with blood, and I immediately got warm. He was right. I'd just been corrected by Mothball on English history. "I was just saying," I said, attempting to cover my blunder. "Trying to make a joke."

"That's all both of y'all are ever doing. Making jokes," said Mothball. "Why don't y'all just get out and leave us alone?" A bowl sat next to him, filled with corn he'd ground to a powder and watered to a yellowy mush. He squeezed the black rubber end of an eyedropper, then sucked up some of the food.

"When did you have time to make that?" I asked, suddenly transfixed on what he was doing.

"I mixed it just before I ran over to get you. Stole the eyedropper from a bottle of iodine Mom had in the medicine cabinet. I figured he'd be hungry after the day he's had, so I pounded out a little chicken feed."

Mothball raised the eyedropper toward what appeared to be a hole in the turkey's neck; it must have been the spot where his mouth had once been. The hole, about the size of a dime, rhythmically expanded and contracted like a dilating pupil. Mothball poked the tip of the dropper in, then squeezed the rubber end. Mike's neck stiffened and pointed straight at the ceiling after Mothball fed him a dose. He'd shake and twitch as he choked down the mush. Mothball had to wiggle the dropper loose after each feeding because the turkey's aperture would clamp down on the end of it, not letting go.

Jimmy and I started laughing. It was interesting to watch, but also so strange that it was humorous.

Mothball shot me a look of contempt. "It's not funny," he said. "This is the way I gotta do it. He's gotta eat, you know?"

I tried to stifle my laughter, but it was hard, and things became even funnier once I saw how serious Mothball had become. Jimmy didn't seem to care.

"Mothball," he said, "you're squeezing and holding on to a turkey like it's a stuffed teddy bear you won at the fair. Oh, yeah, and by the way, did I mention the turkey doesn't have a head? And you want us to take you seriously? Come on, man, I think you've lost your mind."

"It is serious," said Mothball. "Maybe not to you, but to me it is. I thought y'all could understand that."

"You can't expect us not to have a little fun over this one," said Jimmy. "I mean, shit, this is pretty weird if you think about it." He laughed again, and I couldn't hold back anymore either.

Mothball chose to ignore us, continuing to feed Mike instead. Jimmy and I stood behind him, watching as he squeezed dropper-full after dropper-full down the turkey's gullet. When the bowl of mush had nearly disappeared, Mothball turned to us. He seemed to have already forgiven us for laughing at him. "You wanna see him walk?" he asked. "Watch this."

He stood up with the big bird in his hands, then hunched over and set him on the ground. Mike the Second stood motionless for a moment but then started walking around normally. If I kept my eyes trained at his leathery feet picking through the dust and then slowly lifted my gaze to his legs and body, I'd never have known he was headless. But when I looked at that distorted, shriveled lump, a shiver ran up my arms every time.

Mike the Second made his way toward me. I shuffled to the side when he approached my feet—my toes were stained a greenish brown from the grass, the dirt, and the chicken shit—not wanting him to bump into me. I pasted myself to the wall of the shack. It seemed strange that earlier in the day I'd worked so hard to try to catch a turkey and now I feared this headless one as though it carried a deadly virus.

"He won't hurt you, Walter," said Mothball, now getting a laugh of his own as he watched me squirm.

"What did you do with the head?" I asked, shuffling again to avoid Mike, keeping my eyes locked on top of the veiny, multicolored mass of tissue that bobbed near my lower thighs.

"I don't know," he said.

"What do you mean, you don't know?" asked Jimmy.

When Mike started toward him, Jimmy turned into an elephant around a mouse.

"The door was open when I did it," said Mothball. "When the head flopped on the ground I didn't pay no attention. I was in shock he hadn't fallen over dead like the rest of them had. Anyway, one of them damn cats snuck in here and grabbed it. I saw the head hanging out of its mouth just before it darted out. Who knows where that head is now? Cat probably ate it already."

"So what now?" I asked. "What happens from here?"

"First thing I need to do is figure out how to get a hold of *Guinness Book*," said Mothball. "I'll need to write a letter and explain everything. You think I can use your typewriter, Walter?"

"Sure."

"I mean, I've probably set a record already. I didn't see anything in there about a headless turkey. Anyway, I'll have to do that. I was thinking about something else, too. If I cut off the hen's head, and then the two of them screwed or something, do you think they'd have babies born without heads?" He appeared perfectly earnest.

"Mothball," I said, "I don't think it quite works that way."

He remained unperturbed.

"I'll need to build Mike a pen too, and make him a leash."

"A leash?" asked Jimmy. "What are you going to do? Walk it around like it's a dog or something?"

"Well, yeah, I kind of thought so. Why not? It's my pet."

"They're going to lock your fat ass up in the loony bin, Mothball," said Jimmy. "I swear to God they are. You're nuts."

"If they do," said Mothball, "then at least I'll have your mom for company."

"What's that supposed to mean?"

"If I ain't allowed to walk a turkey around on a leash, then she ain't allowed to throw one at people."

Jimmy shot me a scathing look, and I shot the same one toward Mothball, realizing I could never trust him with a secret again. Jimmy walked out of the shack without saying a word.

"Thanks a lot, numb nuts," I said. "I told you not to say anything about that."

"I don't care," said Mothball. "If he can give me hell, I don't see why I can't fight back."

"I'll talk to you tomorrow," I said. "I'm gonna catch up with him."

"See ya," said Mothball, his eyes locked on Mike. I felt as though he hadn't heard a word I'd said. Neither did he care.

I chased after Jimmy, whose silhouette walked ahead toward his house.

"Jimmy," I said when I sidled up next to him.

"Shut up," he said.

He didn't say another word, and I didn't bother to say anything either. I didn't really care if he was mad at me. Mothball was right; he should be allowed to defend himself. I listened to the crickets sing and enjoyed the dew in the grass as I walked along; it helped clean the shit from between my toes. The gauze around my hands stood out against the dark night, making me look like a boxer with white gloves. I headed home, excited to finish up my book.

CHAPTER 6

THREE DAYS INTO SUMMER VACATION, we were already bored. Maybe I should say, Jimmy and I were bored. Mothball had his hands full with Mike, and his enthusiasm for that bird grew more disturbing with every passing day. Behind the chicken shack, he had built Mike his own pen with some rotting two-by-fours and chicken wire. He'd placed a blanket in a wicker basket for Mike's bed and put it inside a small hut that looked like a miniature doghouse. A bale of straw was strewn all over, serving as a groundcover.

"These first few days are critical," said Mothball as he sat down to lure Mike out of his little house. He wanted to feed him. Jimmy and I watched from the other side of the chicken wire.

"Seems like you're always feeding him," I said. "Every time I turn around, it's time for him to eat again."

"Well, he ain't exactly able to feed himself, now is he, Walter?"

Mothball made a sharp cluck with his tongue, as if calling a horse, and instantly the bird darted out of his house. Mike didn't have ears anymore, so I've got no way to explain it, but as soon as Mothball made that noise,

Mike came running straight for him. He had a little black hood over his stump that Mothball's mother had sewn. It looked like a hood that a guillotine executioner would wear—which seemed hauntingly ironic—though there were no eyeholes.

Mothball had a bowl of corn slurry by his feet. He pulled the hood off Mike while holding him under his arm. The bulb that had been his head had changed from a bright red that first night to a dull grayish blue. Apparently, Mike had grown accustomed to the feeding routine because he accepted the stopper and sucked the food without hesitation.

After Mike had finished eating, he started roaming around in his pen. When he walked toward me, I stuck my fingers through the chicken wire to give him a little pet. I touched the feathers on his back for a moment, and as I pulled my hand away, the sharp end of a stray piece of chicken wire sliced the side of my finger. Blood started dripping immediately.

"Dammit," I said and popped my finger into my mouth to ease the pain.

"What did you do?" asked Jimmy.

I pulled my finger out of my mouth and said, "I sliced the shit out of my finger."

"You gonna live?"

"Yeah, I'm gonna live, asshole. I'm just bleeding a little bit."

An expression crept over Jimmy's face as though he were suddenly in deep thought. "Hey, Mothball, let me see your knife."

Mothball walked out of the pen and closed the gate. "What for?" he asked.

"Just let me see it. I wanna try something."

Mothball handed the knife over, and Jimmy unfolded it. He stuck out his left pointer finger and then, with the tip of the knife, made a quick slice through his skin. A tiny crimson stream started flowing.

"What the hell are you doing?" asked Mothball. "Are you nuts?"

I was wondering the same thing.

"You'll see," said Jimmy, a devilish grin now on his face. He handed the opened knife back to Mothball, and as he did so he said, "Now you do it."

Mothball folded the knife and stuffed it in his pocket. "Yeah, right. Sure, Jimmy. How about if I just slit my throat and kill myself. Would that make you happy?"

"Okay, fine, don't," said Jimmy. Then he turned to me, his bloody finger pointing in my direction. "Stick out your finger, Walter. We're gonna be blood brothers."

I looked at Jimmy, shocked. "What did you say?"

"Come on. Give me your finger. We'll mix our cuts together. Then I'll have some of your blood and you'll have some of mine. Blood brothers, get it?"

I stared at Jimmy's finger and then into his eyes. "I don't know," I said. "That's a little freaky."

"What's freaky about it? We'll be brothers forever."

His words chilled me. I didn't want to do it. Something about the whole idea didn't seem right, yet I found myself reaching out toward him. He grabbed my finger and rubbed it against his as if blending paint. As I watched the blood mix, my mother's words—*Haddsby blood is tainted*—sang through my head.

"Well, I guess it's official now," said Mothball.

I wiped my finger on the side of my jeans and then pressed it against them, trying to stem the bleeding.

"Come on, Mothball," said Jimmy. "There's still time. Prick your finger. Then we'll all be brothers."

"Gee, thanks for the offer, Jimmy, but I'll pass. You guys are a little too weird for me."

"*We're* weird?" said Jimmy. "You chopped off the head of a turkey and now you're keeping it as a pet. And you're calling us weird?"

"Yeah, I'm calling y'all weird. Why'd you come over here anyway? To lure me into your devil-worshiping cult?"

"Actually, we stopped by," said Jimmy, "to make sure you're still cool for tonight."

"Yeah, I'm cool. Midnight at the corner. I'll be there."

"Okay, just making sure," said Jimmy as he squeezed his finger in the folds of his shirt. "I'll tell you, though,

Mothball, I think Walter might be turning yellow-belly on us."

"I am not," I said.

"What do you mean?" asked Mothball. "Is he chickening out?"

"I don't know, but he doesn't seem too excited about it."

"I'll be there," I said. "But it's late, that's all. I don't see what we're going to do in the middle of the night. How much fun can we have?"

Jimmy winked at Mothball. "What'd I tell you?"

"Yep, he's gone chickenshit."

"I told y'all I'd be there. I bet I'll show and then you two won't even make it. Then we'll see who's yellow." I turned to leave. "I'll see you lily-livers tonight."

"Bock, bock," they called out as I walked off. I knew they had their fists tucked tightly into their armpits, flapping their elbows, but I didn't bother to turn around. Instead, I sucked on my finger, tasting the blood, and wondered about what I'd just done.

❧

My parents were always in bed by ten o'clock and up with the roosters. I stayed up reading until eleven, then turned out the light and lay in bed, wide-eyed, staring at the ceiling. I got up every ten minutes or so and peeked out my window, looking down at the street. The sky was clear, and the half-moon did a good job of illuminating everything. A light breeze trickled through the screen, caressing my bare stomach; it carried with it the sweet scent of honeysuckle.

Just before twelve, I put on a pair of shorts and the darkest T-shirt I could find, then grabbed my tennis shoes and carried them downstairs. Walking quieter than a cat stalking a bird, I tiptoed across the wooden planks of the kitchen floor. I eased through the screen door, cringing when it squeaked, knowing my father would be down at any minute to brain me with the nightstick he kept under his mattress. I slipped on my shoes, then bolted down the street to the corner of Douglass and Pine.

I leaned against the trunk of a crape myrtle, its red blooms closed for the night, and waited. The moon cast a faint shadow of my figure on the blacktop while the same pleasant odor of honeysuckle filled my head. A wall of it covered the fencerow across the street in front of a vacant lot. During the day, we'd often pull the delicate little hairs from the trumpets and slurp the balls of nectar. It never tasted as sweet as it smelled.

I only had to linger a couple of minutes before I saw the faint forms of Jimmy and Mothball running toward me. Jimmy loped effortlessly while Mothball labored with every step. When they got to the corner, I popped out from behind the crape myrtle, trying to startle them. Jimmy didn't flinch.

"Listen to those crickets sing," said Jimmy. "There must be a million of 'em."

"This is pretty cool," I said. "Other than those crickets, it's so quiet out here. I didn't know things were so peaceful this late at night. Y'all have any problems?"

"Everything went according to plan," said Jimmy. "I couldn't believe it. Mothball was actually out before me."

"So what do we do now?" I asked.

"We could peep in some windows," said Mothball.

"We could go spy on the Troll," said Jimmy. "Find out what he does at night."

"No way," I said. "I'm not going near the Troll."

"What are you worried about, Walter? If he comes after us, he won't catch you or me. He'll snag the Polish Pudgeball before he gets anywhere near us."

"Shut up, Jimmy," said Mothball. "Don't call me that."

"Let's save the Troll for another night," I said. I didn't want to show it, but the idea of being anywhere near the Troll terrified me. Especially after what he'd said. "I'm with Mothball. Let's go peek in some windows. Maybe we could go see Miss Walters in her nightie."

Miss Walters was the fifth grade teacher at the elementary school and was unquestionably the prettiest woman in all of Woodley. Sheila Brackwater was a girl; Miss Walters was a woman.

"Yeah," said Mothball, "or maybe even naked. Can you imagine that?"

"I imagine it every night before I go to bed," said Jimmy.

❧

We never did see Miss Walters naked, though we did end up making her dog bark loud enough for her to turn on the outside lights to see what was the matter. For the next few nights, we snuck out and terrorized the town by peeking in windows or ringing doorbells and running. I was having plenty of fun with our adventures, but apparently the luster had started to fade for Jimmy. As much as I was against it, Jimmy's fascination with the Troll increased until spying on him became the inevitable next step.

On one particular night, the night we decided to go to the Troll's, we walked toward town, none of us talking. Usually we'd joke a little as we went on our missions, but tonight we didn't say anything. All I could think about were the morbid things that the Troll would do if he got a hold of me. I speculated he'd kill me for sure, after a lot of gruesome torture. I had a feeling that Jimmy and Mothball were thinking the same thing.

We passed through town, stopping only once for Jimmy to use Mothball's knife to slice a toothpick from Dr. Schuessler's fence. The night was eerily quiet. For some reason, even the crickets weren't out like they usually were. The only sound was the dull hum of the mill in the background.

When we reached the guardrail, which started just before the bridge, we halted to go over the plan. Sweat beaded on my forehead, caused not only by my anxiety but also by the thick humidity smothering the night. Only a sliver of waning moon hung in the sky, so I could barely discern the silhouette of the railroad trestle against the backdrop of the distant tree line. The trestle seemed to hover above the ground, magically floating. A trail of moonlight wavered and slid across the surface of the Tallapoosa below, dancing and transforming with the flow of the water. Orange dots flickered from a couple of oil lanterns on the opposite bank, and an unintelligible murmur occasionally broke the stillness of the night; the colored men were fishing.

"What do you think we should do?" whispered Mothball.

"I was thinking while we were walking," said Jimmy, "and I reckon we might not wanna get too close to the Troll's place. At least not this first time."

"I think we're close enough as it is," I said. "I mean, this is the farthest we've ever gone before. All the way to the bridge and everything."

"Walter's sounding chickenshit again."

"Yep," said Mothball.

I didn't say anything as my face warmed.

Jimmy said, "Let's each get a couple of rocks and pelt his shack."

"Are you crazy?" I said. "He'll kill us for sure if we hit his house."

"He'll never catch us. It's like ding-dong ditching, except better. Since he doesn't have a doorbell—at least, I don't think he does—we'll just use the rocks. That way, when we take off running, we'll have an even bigger head start."

"I don't like it. What do you think, Mothball?" I was hoping for some backup, but I didn't get it.

"Jimmy's right. Usually we gotta get on the porches to ring and run. This way, we'll already be farther away. Besides, it'll take him a while to wake up and come outside, and by that time we'll practically be back to town."

"Exactly," said Jimmy. "Are you lily-livered, or what, Walter?"

"Okay, I guess you're right. But I still don't like it."

"Who's going first?" asked Mothball. "Not me."

"Rock, paper, scissors," said Jimmy. "Odd man out goes first."

Mothball and I agreed.

We slapped our right fists into our open palms, keeping time with Jimmy's chant of "Once, twice, three, shoot." I showed rock, while they both showed paper. I had a strong suspicion I'd been set up.

We all knelt and searched for suitable stones. I grabbed

two, holding one in each hand. The coarseness of the rocks felt comforting against my sweaty palms, and their weight, at least, made me feel like I had a way of defending myself.

We hopped the guardrail and slowly made our way down the vague path leading to the Troll's shack under the trestle, with me in the lead, Mothball in the middle, and Jimmy in the rear. Mothball walked so close behind me that I felt the soft pant of his breath on my neck.

The path meandered through the canebrake at a slight decline. Though I tried to keep quiet, the crunching underfoot sounded louder than the whirring of the machines and saws running at the pulp mill during the day. With every step I took, the pungent smell of creosote grew stronger because of the railroad ties looming overhead. I kept beating at my neck with my clenched fist, trying to deter mosquitoes. Their incessant whine filled my ears, as did the distant bark of a dog from across the river at Niggertown.

Coming around the last turn of the path, I realized that some of the lanterns I'd seen from the bridge—the ones I thought had all been on the far side of the river—were actually on our side instead. In between the glow of the orange light was the hunched, shadowy figure of the Troll, his back to us, looking out at the black water. He sat only forty or fifty feet away. Two cane poles rested on forked branches that he'd stuck in the soft riverbank. Steel coffee cans were on either side of the log he sat on, smoke rising slowly out of them, shrouding him in a creepy haze. They were smudge pots to keep the mosquitoes away, but the smoke—the way it hung around him, encircling his head—made him look even more sinister than usual.

As I stopped, Mothball ran into my back, knocking me a few steps forward. Something grabbed at my ankles. A loud clanging sent my heart jumping into my throat. The Troll swung his head around, looking straight in my direction.

"Who the hell is that?" he yelled. His voice was deep and husky, just as I'd remembered it. Mothball and Jimmy screeched.

They both took off, the canebrake snapping under their feet as they scrambled away. It sounded as if Mothball had fallen because I heard him wrestling around on the ground for a few seconds before he ran, but I was too scared to turn around and look. My eyes were locked on the muddled figure of the Troll.

I kicked at the thing around my ankles as the Troll rose from the log. I realized the clanging sound came from several steel bean cans tied together with fishing line. I dropped my stones, turned, and shot up the path, the cans clinging to my feet and clattering as if I were a freshly decorated "Just Married" car. I continued making a racket for several yards before the cans finally kicked free.

"Hey, come here," yelled the Troll. His voice bounced along the river, echoing off the opposite bank and the shanties of Niggertown. I thought for sure he would grab me from behind at any moment. But I made it back to the road without being apprehended, though I was certain he was right on my tail. And then he yelled again, but this time his words nearly froze me. "Walter, come back here." He'd said my name. How was that possible? First my mom, and now me. Adrenaline shot through my body like I'd never felt before. I leaped the guardrail and bolted down the road, just able to discern Mothball's frumpy body twenty feet ahead. As I passed him I shouted, "Keep running!" and heard a whimper in return.

I ran all the way home without stopping. I never passed Jimmy, nor did I ever see him in front of me. He must have hidden somewhere; he was fast, but not that fast. I didn't stop at the corner to meet up with them the way we usually did. I went straight to my house, not stopping until I'd made it to my screen door. I grabbed the handle, leaned my forehead into the crook of my elbow, and tried to catch my breath before I opened the door. Sweat streamed down my face and something—not mosquitoes—buzzed in my ears; it was just a dull ringing that wouldn't go away. And the ringing kept echoing, *Walter, come back here.*

I went straight to my room, closed the door, and locked it. Only after I was safely under the covers, my heart still pounding, my body engulfed in sweat, did I start to wonder if Mothball had escaped. And more important, I wondered if the Troll would come searching for me.

❦

"I lost my damn jackknife," said Mothball. We stood on his driveway the following morning, shooting baskets and talking about the previous night's events, though I didn't dare mention that the Troll had said my name. "My granddaddy gave that knife to me."

"At least you're alive," I said. "If the Troll had gotten a hold of you, you'd be missing a lot more than your jackknife."

"I guess so, but still, I loved that knife."

"We could go back and hunt for it tonight," said Jimmy as he swished the ball through the hoop. "You probably lost it on the trail when you ran me over. I've never seen anyone so scared in my whole life," he said, laughing.

"Shoot, you were looking pretty scared yourself," said Mothball. "Walter was the only one who kept his cool. And we were calling him chickenshit."

"I couldn't move, I was so damn scared," I said. "The only reason I seemed calm was because I was frozen solid." *If they only knew why,* I thought.

I grabbed Jimmy's rebound and tossed in a lay-up,

bouncing it off the homemade plywood backboard. The afternoon heat was stifling and the humidity made it almost impossible to breathe. "How did y'all make it home?" I asked. "I ran all the way to my house without stopping."

"I cut into the alley by the five-and-dime," said Jimmy. "I saw you fly past, but I waited on Mothball. You should've seen the scare I put into him."

"What do you mean?" I asked.

"I peeked around the corner after you went by and saw Mothball giving it all he had. The Troll wasn't behind him, but he didn't know that. I waited until he ran past me and then I took off after him. When I got right up on his ass, I yelled in my deepest voice, 'I'm gonna kill you, boy!' You never heard a scream like the one that come up out of Mothball. He sounded like a stray cat getting pounced by a tom."

"It wasn't funny," said Mothball. "I thought I was dead for sure."

"I grabbed the neck of his shirt," continued Jimmy, "and he flopped down in the middle of the street, begging for mercy."

Jimmy and I laughed until Mothball hit me in the stomach with the basketball. The ball bounced away and landed in the front yard near a rusted wheelbarrow.

"Hey," I said, "I didn't do it. It was Jimmy."

"It's not funny," yelled Mothball. "I got the hell scared out of me. You wouldn't be laughing if it had been you."

"So you wanna go back tonight and find that knife?" said Jimmy.

"No way," said Mothball. "I'm never going near the Troll again. He can have my knife for all I care."

I agreed completely. I thought about telling them what I'd heard, but for some reason, once again, that stronger part of me said to stay quiet. I had never revealed anything about the Troll saying my mother's name, and now I couldn't bring myself to tell them that he knew my name too. I wondered if the Troll knew Jimmy's and Mothball's names. And where we all lived. I had an eerie feeling that he probably did, and that sent a chill through me.

"Well, what're we gonna do tonight then?" asked Jimmy. "How are we gonna top that one?"

"It's so hot," I said. "Let's go swimming and talk about it down at the river."

"I can't," said Jimmy. "I've gotta get my chores finished. My dad'll beat me if I don't mow the lawn."

"Yeah, me too," said Mothball. "Plus, I gotta give Mike a bath. I haven't figured out how I'm gonna do that yet." He picked up the basketball from the yard and dribbled it on the hard-pack of the driveway. Tiny puffs of red dust exploded underneath the ball.

"I say we go swimming tonight, then," I said.

"Yeah, we could go down to the rope swing," said Jimmy. "Let's go camping. I got that tent Ox gave me. And then we could play capture the flag in the morning or something."

"I didn't say anything about camping," I said. "I was just talking about swimming."

"Uh-oh," said Jimmy, "sounds like Walter's turning chickenshit on us yet again."

"Yeah, whatever. I'll see you tonight," I said, though the thought of sleeping outdoors so close to the Troll scared the hell out of me. But I had to at least pretend to be brave. "Be ready for some midnight skinny-dipping."

"What about Mike?" asked Mothball. "I can't leave him here by himself."

"Get Carver to watch him," I said. "All he needs is some food, right?"

"There's more to it than that," said Mothball. "I gotta bring him."

"You can't take a turkey camping with us," I said. "I don't care if he is missing his head—he can't go."

"Oh, hell, why not?" said Jimmy. "If we get hungry, we'll just throw him on the fire and have a feast."

Mothball shot Jimmy a vicious look. "Yeah, and your mom can give us the recipe, since she's so good at cooking turkeys. What is it with your family wanting to throw turkeys around?"

"Don't start that shit with me again, Mothball," said

Jimmy, flaring his chest. "I'll make you wish the Troll had gotten a hold of you instead of me."

I turned around and started to walk toward home. "I'll see you this evening," I said over my shoulder. "Make sure y'all kiss and make up before then. I don't want any fighting."

The basketball whizzed past my shoulder, barely missing the back of my head. It rolled to a stop in the road, resting against the curb. I picked it up and punted it back in their direction. I could still hear them arguing as I headed home.

CHAPTER 7

"HOW MUCH LONGER YOU GONNA BE?" asked Jimmy. "The sun'll be setting soon."

We stood outside Mike's cage, watching Mothball feed him once again. We were both eager to get to the river, set up camp, and go swimming.

"Let me finish up, would ya?" said Mothball. "Then all I gotta do is get some food for Mike. I'll be ready in just a couple."

"What do you mean, 'get some food for Mike'?" I asked. "I thought we went over this already. You're not taking him with us, are you?"

"No. Carve said he'd feed him, but I gotta have all the food prepared. Just give me a few more minutes."

Shortly, he got up, put the hood over Mike, brushed the straw off the rear of his pants, and walked out of the pen. "Let me go get my pack."

"Get some matches," I said. "We both forgot."

Mothball came back out with a stuffed knapsack over his shoulder. Things were tied haphazardly to it, and everything—pots, pans, a metal canteen, a long red bandanna—swung to and fro as he walked.

We then headed out for the Tallapoosa. The low sun

burned an orange swath in the sky, but we still had more than an hour of daylight left. My pillowcase, which had all of my things in it, bounced against my back as I walked toward town. As Mothball's knapsack flopped around, the pots beat together, keeping almost perfect time.

When we got to the far side of the hardware store, we cut into the black-eyed pea field. I walked in between the rows of the plants, their soft, heart-shaped leaves brushing against my bare knees as I headed toward the tree line looming ahead. Grasshoppers popped away in scattered directions, and heat rose off the exposed field in snaky waves. The Simmons sulfur hung in the air, rank and thick. I broke a sweat as we worked our way through the field. The tree line stood about a quarter of a mile away, covered in the green draperies of thick kudzu. Just on the other side was the Tallapoosa.

A clearing between a clump of sycamores was where we planned to make camp. It was a flat spot near the edge of the river embankment, the water running maybe six feet below. One dappled sycamore in particular was our favorite because it held the rope swing. The tree was unique because it grew horizontally from the side of the embankment for about ten feet, hovering over the river before it then elbowed skyward. The roots were a knotty mess, barely clinging to the soil, making it appear as if the tree would topple into the water at any moment.

The only problem with the rope swing was that it was

a little too short. It hung above the water, just out of reach of whoever tried to grab it. So one of us would have to get into the river and use a stick to swat the rope to the guy standing on the base of the tree, waiting for his turn to jump.

"Oh, man, that water looks good," I said to Jimmy. "Let's go."

"We gotta put the tent up first, Walter. Let's get camp set up, collect some firewood, and then we'll go. Think how much better it'll feel once we work up a sweat."

"Wow, okay, Dad—yes sir. Shoot, I think it'd feel pretty good right now."

We worked on the tent while Mothball took firewood duty. The tent wasn't very big, and I could tell right away that when it came time for bed we were going to be sardined in there. That worried me for a couple of reasons, but I tried to put it out of my mind.

Mothball had collected a healthy pile of dead twigs and branches and left them next to a circle of rocks we'd set up for the fire ring. I busted pine branches that snapped easily underfoot and built a small teepee out of the kindling. The quicker we got a fire going, the less we'd have to worry about the mosquitoes.

"You got those matches, Mothball?" I asked.

He fished a book from his pocket, then headed back into the woods for another run. I struck a match and held it to a pinecone. Once the resin took fire, I stuffed it under the teepee of sticks. When the wood started crackling, I placed larger branches on the pile in increments, careful not to snuff it. Even after what had happened at the O'Kanes' house years before, I still loved fire, loved how it ate up everything in its path. I was lost in thought as I stared at the flickering. Jimmy brought me out of my stupor.

"Let's go swimming. What do you say?"

"Yeah, okay," I said, coming back to reality.

I placed a piece of rotten sycamore, normally horrible firewood, on the fire. It smoldered nicely, creating a thick white smoke that hung under the pine branches like a heavy fog. My goal was not to get hit by one mosquito if I could help it.

I heard two splashes and turned to see my friends' heads bobbing in the water. Soft shafts of sunlight splintered through the trees onto the river's surface, creating puzzle-shaped patterns that danced over their faces. Jimmy's tanned shoulders were almost camouflaged against the murky water, while Mothball's white T-shirt contrasted sharply. He said it kept him warm, but I knew he didn't want us seeing his fat pale belly.

"Throw me a stick, Walter," said Jimmy. He stood just below the end of the dangling rope. I pulled a long stick from the firewood pile and tossed it into the water, where it submarined for a second before popping up right in front of him.

I took off my shirt and tennis shoes and crept out onto the thick balance beam of the sycamore trunk, waiting for the rope. Jimmy swatted it with the branch, sailing it directly into my outstretched hand. The rope was dry, and as I pulled, testing its strength, the coarse, hairy fibers dug into my hands, stinging them. The branch bounced slightly with my pulls, but it was very much alive and in no danger of breaking under my weight.

I pushed off the trunk, arcing out slightly, and then rushed through the air at tremendous speed. When I reached the maximum height, almost stopping dead still in midair, I let go and dropped into the river. The water washed away the sweat and grime in an instant. I popped to the surface, opened my eyes, and couldn't help but smile.

I swam around and watched as Jimmy climbed onto the tree. His wet footprints dripped down the slick sides and into the water as he waited for Mothball's toss. When he had the rope, he tugged on it, the same as I had. His muscles tightened as he did so, sending little ripples up his arms to his neck and chest. "Watch this," he said. "Penny drop." Jimmy swung out over our heads. At the rope's peak, he tossed his head back and did a flip into the water.

We swam and took turns on the rope for a while longer until the sun dropped out of sight behind the trees, leaving only a residual glow over the river. Back at camp, the heat of the flames dried the droplets that trickled down my chest and legs. My feet were caked in orange mud, and pine needles and leafy debris clung to the muck like sprinkles on a scoop of ice cream. I scraped my feet, one against the other, trying to remove the thick mud. Jimmy and Mothball did the same as we squatted around the fire, drying out.

Jimmy grabbed a steak knife and started sharpening the end of a green branch of slash pine. He whittled it into a spear point. "I'd say it's about dinnertime."

"I'm starved," I said. "I'll get the food."

I walked over and unzipped the door of the tent. I reached into my pillowcase and grabbed the hot dogs, the bag of buns, and the pecan pie Mom had packed. A pile of red ants had already sniffed out the sweetness of the pie, and I had to swat them away with the buns as I walked back to the fire. We immediately started cooking.

"Bring any ketchup?" asked Mothball.

"Nope," I said.

"Mustard?"

"Forgot."

"This'll do then," he said, closing a bun over his blackened dog and sliding it off the end of his stick.

The fire threw a yellow light around the campsite, flickering off the trunks of the trees. Crickets began singing and a bullfrog belched from downriver. Lightning bugs pulsed through the woods like blinking eyes, dancing over the pea field in the distance. None of us talked as we stood around, staring at the fire. We must have gazed at the flames, eating silently, for nearly fifteen minutes, until Jimmy finally got up.

"I gotta take a piss," he said. He walked off, nearly stumbling over a tent spike as he disappeared into the darkness.

I grabbed a slice of pie and angled it toward the firelight, checking for ants. Satisfied, I stared up through the trees as I ate, looking for stars in the twilight, the sky a deep blue slowly fading to black. The crickets hummed and the wood smoke filled my head as I gazed upward. I heard Jimmy walking back, but I paid him no mind.

"What's that?" asked Mothball as Jimmy reentered the circle. Suddenly a loud crack ripped from the fire, echoing off the rock wall across the river. Ashes and embers shot up from the pit. Jimmy started laughing.

"What the hell was that?" I yelled. "What'd you throw in the fire?"

Jimmy continued to laugh, now pointing at me. "Oh, shit," he said. "You should see your face, Walter."

"What did you do?" I was angry. My heart raced. Tiny pieces of white ash floated in front of my face and fell in my hair.

"It was a firecracker. I tossed it in. Brought 'em for capture the flag tomorrow. You know, figured we could use them as a signal or something."

"That wasn't funny. You about scared the shit out of me."

"Oh, come on, Walter. Lighten up, man—it was just a joke."

Mothball poked his hot dog stick into the embers but said nothing.

"Y'all are no fun," said Jimmy.

I eventually calmed down, grabbed another slice of pie, then passed around the aluminum tin. Jimmy and I, working together, had pulled a large sycamore branch from the woods behind the tent and set it near the fire. It made a perfect bench for two. Mothball sat in the pine needles across from us, Indian-style. Jimmy had a canteen filled with grape Kool-Aid, and he passed it around, each of us taking sips as if it were a bottle of whiskey. The distant sound of a train's horn sounded, breaking the silence of the evening. The steady rumble of the engine and the high-pitched squeal of steel on steel comforted me.

"That train," I said, "used to go over the trestle where the Troll lives now."

"Really?" said Jimmy. "No shit, Walter? Is that what that big thing with the train tracks on it used to be for?"

"Screw you, dickfor. I was just saying."

"Well, thanks for bringing him up, Walter," said Mothball. "That's just what I needed. It's not like I didn't get my fill of him last night."

"You know, we're less than a half mile from him right now," said Jimmy in a low voice. "Think about it. If we followed the river downstream, we'd only have to walk a little ways until we got to the bridge. If we crossed the road, we'd find him down in the canebrake on the other side."

"Shut up, Jimmy," said Mothball. "You're just trying to scare me."

"He could even be walking around right now," I said. "If he heard that firecracker, he might want to come investigate. See what the noise was all about. See if he can find out who messed with him last night and get some revenge." Though I was screwing with Mothball, the idea seemed highly plausible, and suddenly I realized I was scaring myself as much as I was him. Probably even more so. And the Troll definitely knew the identity of at least one of the people who'd messed with him.

"Yeah," said Jimmy. "I'd be scared if I was you. I bet he knows you yelled at him that day when he was at Oreo's stand."

"Me? You're the one that yelled at him."

"Yeah, but since you ran off like a bat out of hell, he thinks it was you."

"No he don't. I was—"

We all turned our heads as something sounded near the edge of the wood.

"What was that?" asked Mothball.

"Sounded like a mourning dove," I said, though I felt my heart suddenly pounding much harder than any bird had ever made it beat.

"Mourning doves don't sing at night," said Jimmy. "Maybe it was the Troll."

The night was quiet once more, except for the drone of the crickets and the occasional bullfrog. The train had moved on and the mourning dove—or whatever it was—hadn't cooed again. Tingles prickled my neck. Being out in the woods at night, that close to the Troll, gave me the heebie-jeebies.

"I know what you're doing, Jimmy," said Mothball. "And it's working, okay? Carver once told me a story about the Troll. I didn't want to tell it, but maybe this'll shut you up."

"Uh-oh, Walter—Mothball's got a ghost story," said Jimmy, elbowing me.

"It's not a ghost story. It's real. Last summer, Carve and some of his buddies came down here to do some catfishing. Mostly they came to drink beer, but they had to have an excuse."

"Who was with him?" I asked, trying to catch him if he was lying.

"It was Carve, Jerry Collins, Runway, and I think Richie Stackson. They'd set up some poles, tossed out some beef livers to chum with, and were sitting around drinking. They forgot a lantern, so all they had was one little flashlight between them. After a while, the little bell started jingling on one of Runway's poles."

"Yeah, yeah," said Jimmy. "So what's this got to do with the Troll?"

"I'm getting to that, dumb-ass. Let me finish."

"Go ahead, Mothball," I said, resting my elbows on my knees. "I'm listening."

"Well, anyway, Runway needs to borrow the light to unhook the fish because the thing has done swallowed it deep. So that leaves the rest of them up on the bank with no light while Runway is down at the water, using a pair of needlenoses to rip out the hook. Carve told me that he was watching the flashlight dance around over the water, starting to get a buzz on, when he heard something."

"What'd he hear?" asked Jimmy, now apparently immersed in the story too. I watched Mothball as the firelight glimmered over him, creating eerie shadows on the tree trunks. Outside the ring of light, it had become pitch black.

"Carve said he heard something that sounded like an owl, just like what we heard, and then branches snapping, as if something was racing right at them. It was the Troll, and he started screaming, said he was gonna kill them all."

"Get out of town," said Jimmy. "Why haven't I ever heard this story before?"

"I'm telling you. Carve told—"

Suddenly I heard a deep growl, like from a dog or something, and then a large flash caught my peripheral vision as a figure leaped out of the woods, then popped back into the cover of darkness. I jumped up and grabbed a thick stick from the dwindling pile, ready to smash whatever it was. When Jimmy got up, he tripped over the sycamore bench and fell over backwards, screaming like a girl as he struggled to right himself. He acted as if a rat or something had just run over his foot. Confusion followed as the thing ran behind the tent, growls and yells filling the air. I glanced back at Mothball as I readied myself with the stick, blood racing through my veins, my heart pumping violently. He still sat on the ground; he hadn't moved. All he did was laugh. It took me a second to register everything. Then I knew we'd been had.

The thing stood behind the tent, shaking the top of it, making wild noises. Jimmy yelled in its direction, screaming as loud as he could. "What the fuck! What the hell is it?" I grabbed Jimmy's elbow, shook my head, and pointed back at Mothball.

"What the fuck is it?" he yelled again.

Mothball grabbed at his ribs as he laughed. He couldn't stop. I turned around to see the hulking figure of Carver come out from behind the tent, pulling his shirt down from where he'd had it covering his head. He held a can of Budweiser, laughing just as hard as Mothball. He set the beer down, clasped his hands together, raised them to his lips, and blew on his thumbs, recreating the coo of a mourning dove perfectly.

"Oh, shit, Mothball—we got 'em good," he said as he picked up his beer. "Did you see their faces? Oh, damn, man. I wouldn't be surprised if y'all both got a steaming pile hanging in your shorts." He pulled a pack of Marlboros from the front pocket of his jeans, tapped one out, and lipped it. He flipped the top of his lighter open, let the flint roller glide against the thigh of his jeans, and lit the cigarette in one fluid motion. A billow of smoke washed over his face as he talked, the cigarette bouncing in his lips. "Mothball, you were right. We got 'em."

We both turned toward Mothball and glared.

"What?" said Mothball. "You two are always trying to freak me out. Always trying to scare me. I knew tonight wouldn't be no different, so I prepared myself. Had Carve hang in the woods and wait for the right time."

I eventually calmed down, though I still felt a little shaky. I could tell by Jimmy's expression that he didn't feel the same way. A fury hid behind his eyes that I'd never seen before, not even when he'd stood over Mr. Haddsby after the snake incident.

Carver finished his beer and tossed it into the fire, then grabbed another one from the edge of the woods. "Hell, you should've seen Haddsby's face. I thought he was about to damn near keel over and die. Mr. Tough Guy didn't look so tough just then."

I glanced at Jimmy. He had his head lowered and was staring at the fire.

"Y'all got us good," I said. "I hate to admit it, but y'all got us. That's two nights in a row the Troll's about made me shit myself."

Carver took a final draw off his cigarette, then flicked it into the flames. "What do you mean, two nights in a row?"

Mothball looked over at me, then immediately jumped in before I could answer. "Walter saw the Troll on the road yesterday. He got all scared and ran home. Thought the Troll was gonna kill him."

Mothball obviously didn't want Carver knowing about us sneaking out last night, and for a moment I figured I'd spill the beans just to get him back, but then I decided he must have his reasons. I opted to play along.

Carver laughed again. "Y'all are gonna run yourselves ragged worrying about that guy. He ain't gonna bother you none. He's harmless."

"I don't know about that," I said. "I've heard stories."

"Shoot. They's only stories, is all. He ain't never hurt no one that I heard of. He's like a snake. Stay away and he won't bother you."

Jimmy still hadn't said a word.

Carver finished his beer fast and tossed it into the fire; it landed right next to the first one. He smoked another cigarette and made fun of us some more before he decided to leave. "I'm out of beer," he said. "I gotta raid Dad's supply when I get back."

"Don't forget to feed Mike. You promised."

"Yeah, I know. I'll feed the stupid son of a bitch." He looked at me. "You ever seen anything so weird in all your life, Walter? That damn thing ain't got no head."

"I know it," I said, shaking mine in the negative.

Carver gave a half wave in our direction. "Y'all be good."

"See ya, Carver," I said. I'd always liked him. I kind of looked up to him, the way a boy who doesn't have a big brother often does.

"Hey, Haddsby," said Carver.

Jimmy looked up, his face tight with hatred.

Carver raised his hands above his head and said, "Boo." We snickered while Jimmy turned as red as a pin cherry. Carver walked off, disappearing into the woods.

"I gotta tell y'all something," I whispered, once I knew he was gone. "Last night, when the Troll was coming toward me, he said my name."

"What? What're you talking about?" asked Mothball.

"He said, 'Walter, come back here.' I swear to you he did. He knows my name."

"Bullshit, Walter," said Mothball. "Sorry, I already used all the good Troll stories for the night." Jimmy just sat on the log and poked at the fire with a stick.

"I'm telling y'all, it's true. And remember when Jimmy

yelled at the Troll? When the Troll came toward us, he actually said, 'Louise.' My mom's name."

"Yeah, right, Walter," said Mothball. "Give it up. The joke's already over."

"He didn't say your mom's name," said Jimmy, finally breaking his silence. "I was right there. Mothball's right— you need to work on your timing, Walter. You picked the wrong time to try and top Mothball's bullshit practical joke."

"Well, it's good to see you're back with us," said Mothball.

"You need to shut the hell up, you flabby fucker," blurted Jimmy. The anger in his voice startled me. "You'll pay for this."

"Oh, come on, Jimmy. Can't you take a joke? You mess with me all the time. For once I get you and now you're all mad. I'd say we're even."

"You'll pay."

"Fine. Whatever. I'm going to bed," said Mothball. He got up and walked to the door of the tent, unzipped it, and disappeared. He was noticeably flustered. I was too; neither one of them had believed me.

Thirty minutes passed and Jimmy said nothing; he just tossed tiny twigs into the fire, one after the other. I sat on the bench and stared as the flames died down, watching smoke twirl off the end of a scorched log. I played the whole incident over in my mind. Mothball had completely fooled me with his story. He'd suckered me in so deeply that I never saw it coming. I'd felt sure that the Troll was about to kill us all.

"This'll teach him," said Jimmy. I pulled my gaze from the fire to see him holding the handle of a stainless-steel pot. Water sloshed over the sides. He'd apparently filled it at the river while I'd been in my trance.

"What?" I said, confused.

"Gonna dip his hand in the water once he's asleep. So he pisses himself."

I jumped up from the log and knocked his arm, spilling the water into the brush. I got in his face and said, "No you're not."

"Fine, then," said Jimmy. "Jesus, I just thought we should get him back."

"Not that way."

I walked off to take a piss in the woods before I got ready to bed down. As I relieved myself, I stared at the arc of urine raining on the dead leaves in the fading firelight. I prayed that I'd make it through the night.

CHAPTER 8

A WHIPPOORWILL WOKE ME early the next morning. Faint light pierced the shell of the tent, telling me it couldn't be any later than six. It took only a second to realize what I'd feared most. My shorts were warm and wet, as was my sleeping bag. I peered at Mothball and Jimmy. Mothball snored lightly, curled in a tight package, while Jimmy seemed to be everywhere, arms outstretched, one foot poking me in the ribs.

I hated myself, hated that the problem still hadn't "solved itself" as my mother had promised. She'd been telling me for years that it took some boys longer than others but eventually I'd be fine. I'd believed her, desperately wanting her to be right, but the bed-wetting hadn't gotten any better. At least Mom hadn't told Dad about it. As far as he knew, I hadn't wet the bed since the day I stopped wearing diapers. If he found out, I knew he'd call me a sissy or a mama's boy. And that was if I was lucky. He'd called me far worse for things that were much less serious than wetting the bed as a teenager.

I unzipped the tent door as quietly as I could and tossed my sleeping bag out. To my horror, some of the pee had leaked downhill and onto Mothball's mummy bag; there was a dark moist stain on the side of it. I couldn't come up with any solution for drying it, so I left it there, hoping for the best.

The early-morning air caused goose bumps to bubble on my arms. Through the trees, a sliver of moon dropped on the horizon. I knelt on the ground, straightened out my sleeping bag, and began rolling it up. A wet spot had seeped through, but once I had it rolled tight, the spot didn't show. I thought of Mothball's sleeping bag and only hoped that it might dry before either of them awoke.

I walked down the embankment to the edge of the water and took a dip. A ghost of fog hung over the river, floating lazily. A hatch of sulfur flies hovered above the surface, coming off like yellow raindrops in reverse. The water was warm, just as it had been the night before. It immediately helped clear my mind of the disgrace I felt for peeing in the tent, but not of the anxiety of getting caught.

After exiting the river, I went back to camp and quickly built a warming fire with some of the previous night's coals. I slid off my wet shorts and underwear, reached into my pillowcase, grabbed my swimming trunks, and pulled them on. I went about it backwards, but my trunks were the only dry thing I had left.

"Morning, Walter," said Mothball, startling me as he walked up from behind.

"Hey," I said. "How'd you sleep?"

He yawned and stretched his arms above his head, his shirt rising up as he did so, exposing his gut. Pale lines of stretch marks, like bear claw scratches, wrapped around his body from either side of his bellybutton. "Pretty good. But Jimmy's pointy knees kept poking me all night."

I laughed nervously, nodding in agreement. It appeared that Mothball hadn't noticed anything. "I know. He kept kicking me in the ribs."

"So, what do we got to eat?"

"Pop-Tarts," I said. I threw him the box, relieved. He didn't say anything as he pulled out a package, tearing at the wrapper with his teeth.

Before we got started with capture the flag, Mothball and I sat around the campfire while Jimmy finished his breakfast. We discussed Carver's antics from the night before. Jimmy glanced at us occasionally but didn't say anything. I had a feeling that whatever he was thinking about had something to do with retaliation.

When we split in different directions to hide our flags, I feigned heading up toward the patch of peas before doubling back, setting off along the riverbank in the direction of the road, the bridge, and the Troll. The red bank sucked at my tennis shoes as I made my way over rocks and logs. Just past a downed sycamore, I found scattered pieces of crawdad shell near the river's edge. A pink and white claw stuck up out of the mud, surrounded by tiny imprints of raccoon tracks. They looked like children's handprints in a concrete sidewalk. A blue heron silently lifted from a paddy of swamp grass and parrot feather, its long, sharp beak leading it downriver, its broad wings flapping in slow motion.

After hiking for a little while, I found an oak sapling vying for establishment between a stand of loblollies. It looked like a perfect spot to tie my bandanna, so I fastened it to a branch and then headed out in search of Jimmy and Mothball. Sometimes I'd choose to stay near my home base and wait in ambush, but on this occasion I resolved to go on the prowl. After all, the thrill of the chase is the most exciting part; the actual kill isn't nearly as gratifying as knowing that you outsmarted your opponent.

I worked my way through the woods, following the faint skid of a deer trail, though it was heavily overgrown in places with nettles and other weeds. And the humidity was already thick. I thought it was probably similar to what the jungles in Vietnam that I'd seen so often on TV must have been like. The buzzing of grasshoppers sounded from the distant pea field, but in the thick of the woods it was hauntingly quiet. I had the creepy feeling that someone was watching me, but I often felt that way when I was alone in the woods.

When I smelled a faint trace of wood smoke, I knew I

wasn't too far from camp. My T-shirt stuck to my body like shrink-wrap, and my swimming trunks were moist with perspiration. I was considering sneaking down to the Tallapoosa, just to dunk my head, when I heard a scream. It wasn't a joking scream; it was a high-pitched, terrified scream. It came from Mothball, and he kept yelling my name.

After a few minutes of fighting the underbrush and thickets, I busted into the clearing where the fire lay smoldering, but Mothball wasn't there. Different scenarios flooded my mind: Was Jimmy messing with Mothball because of last night? Or was it someone else? The Troll? Or maybe they were just screwing around, trying to scare me. If that was the case, it was working.

I stopped for a moment, waiting for another scream, but nothing came. I followed another deer path cutting through the scrub, running quickly now but trying to stay quiet. The path wound through the woods for a short distance, then crept back toward the river. Briars scratched my bare shins, tearing my skin and drawing blood. I was about to yell Mothball's name when I heard a gunshot rip through the woods. My pulse thumped in my ears, blood rushed to my face, and my neck went cold with a sharp tingle. And then I heard the low murmur of a voice through the trees, just across the clearing.

I jogged the perimeter of the field, making my way toward the voice, which grew louder with every step. It was

Jimmy, and for a moment I felt a flood of relief, but his inflection quickly changed that feeling.

"Listen, you fat fucker. Walter might've forgiven you, but I sure ain't about to."

I crept out of the woods and into a sparse stand of young pine, still about twenty feet from where Mothball stood tied to a tree. Jimmy fiddled with a rope around Mothball's gut. Mothball groaned but didn't speak. I shook slightly, unable to control it.

"Why don't you shut up, you fat bastard? You're getting what you deserve."

I ran up to Jimmy. He wheeled around, not really surprised, it seemed.

"What in the hell are you doing?" I said.

"Hey, Walter," said Jimmy, calm and cool. "I'm teaching my prisoner a lesson."

Mothball couldn't speak because he'd been gagged with Jimmy's camouflage bandanna, tied tightly around his head. There was no mistaking the bandanna as Jimmy's; he'd once used it as his flag. It had blended in perfectly with the trees, making it impossible to find.

Mothball's arms were bound to the trunk of the pine with the piece of rope, and his shirt was hiked up and caught in it. The rope—actually a section of clothesline— cut a divide over Mothball's gut, disappearing where his fat rolls enveloped it. Fragments of bark peeled away from the tree as he frantically shook his head. Tears rolled down his cheeks, collecting with beads of sweat.

"What in the hell do you think you're doing?" I repeated.

"Mind your own business. This is my prisoner."

Jimmy had the pack of firecrackers in his hand. The crumpled red tissue paper that had held them lay at his feet on a bed of pine needles. He unwound the thin string holding the mat of explosives, letting them drop into his palm one by one. When he had three firecrackers loose from the pack, he stuffed them underneath the clothesline around Mothball's waist. They pinched between the rope and his skin.

"Jimmy, are you crazy?" I yelled.

"Hey, he's my prisoner. Besides, I wanted to stick his hand in water last night, but you wouldn't let me. Remember? I guess you didn't want him to wet the bed, did you, Walter?" He laughed and said, "Mothball told me everything."

Suddenly, nothing seemed real to me. *Mothball told me everything* reverberated in my ears. I saw Mothball. I saw Jimmy. I saw everything Jimmy did, but somehow nothing registered. Even when he pulled out the pack of matches, I still didn't believe it. It was like watching a movie in slow motion. I knew I had to do something, knew I had to do the right thing, but I couldn't. That other part of me, that stronger part, wouldn't let me. Sometimes I hated that other part, but it was as though I had no control over it. So I just stood there.

Jimmy struck a match, holding it down for a second to let the flame get a good hold. Mothball's neck flopped back and forth; he screamed through the cloth of the bandanna; he stomped his foot in the needles around the base of the tree. His wide, pleading eyes made him look like my fox. Or that first chicken he'd beheaded. Trapped. Vulnerable. Scared.

I stepped forward, maybe to intercede, maybe just to make it appear that I wanted to help—I don't know. I had a quick flash where I thought that maybe Mothball was getting what he deserved. After all, he had betrayed me.

Jimmy managed to light two of the three firecrackers before he pulled the match away. The snake hiss of the fuses sizzled rapidly. Two loud explosions, one right after the other, blasted through the woods.

Mothball uttered a gurgling scream while tears poured from his eyes.

"That should teach you to try and mess with us," said Jimmy.

"What the hell did you do?" I said. I didn't yell or scream; I barely mumbled.

"He deserved it," said Jimmy. There was no sign of remorse.

"You just blew up Mothball, for Christ's sake. And you don't even care."

"Don't get your wet little panties in a wad, Walter. He deserved it." He laughed and walked away, stuffing the remaining firecrackers into his shorts pocket.

"You're fucked up," I yelled at his backside. "Completely fucked up."

The smell of burnt powder hung heavy as I untied the bandanna from Mothball's head, dropping the spit-soaked thing to the ground. He swallowed gulps of air, nearly on the verge of hyperventilating. I untied the knot in the clothesline, which took me a few minutes because Jimmy had it bound solid. The bark dug into my fingers as I pulled and jerked on the line. When the rope fell from his waist, he slid down the trunk and collapsed on his side. Pine resin had stained the back of his shirt brown.

"Jesus, he went too far this time," I said. "Are you okay?"

Mothball didn't answer. He heaved for breath, sobbing.

"Let me see your stomach." I pulled up his shirt to get a look. Red welts swelled over his stretch marks like mosquito bites, powder burns branded in the center. Worse than the welts, however, was the rope burn that circumnavigated his midsection. It looked like someone had taken a red marker and drawn a line around his body.

Little trickles of blood oozed from the rope burn above his hips.

"Man, Mothball, are you okay?"

"Fuck you, Walter. Go fuck yourself."

"What? I didn't do this to you."

"You didn't *do* it," he yelled, spit flying from his mouth as he gasped, still crying, "but you didn't stop it either. You just stood there and watched."

Mothball massaged his jaws where the bandanna had been, then picked himself up from the ground. When I tried to assist, he smacked my hands away. He limped off, leaving me in the clearing, alone. My stomach churned as I watched him hobble off into the woods. I leaned my hands against the coarse bark of the tree and dropped my head. I began puking chunks of strawberry Pop-Tart all over the exposed roots as I tried to figure out what was wrong with me—what was happening to me.

CHAPTER 9

BY THE TIME I MADE IT BACK TO CAMP, there were only a few things left, mainly my clothes drying on the rocks by the smoldering fire and my sleeping bag, soaked in urine and steeping in the sun. Jimmy had apparently broken down camp, taken his tent, and rapidly departed. Mothball wasn't anywhere to be found. I grabbed a pot and walked down the embankment to the edge of the river.

Brass-colored minnows scurried away, darting in all directions, and a giant crawdad, nearly as long as my hand, rocketed backwards under a stone. I felt as if I were in a daze, not believing anything that had just happened. Something that sounded like a handful of pebbles smacking the water caught my attention. A school of mosquito fish jumped and sprinkled the surface, followed by a large wake chugging upstream. Something huge, a bass or a snapping turtle, maybe even a gar, was after its brunch.

One evening the year before, in the same spot where the baitfish now jumped, I had watched a family of water moccasins chasing frogs. There were two big ones, several feet long, and three babies. They essed across the surface effortlessly, their heads well above the water like a troop of periscopes. The parents nailed the frogs with ease, showing the babies how it was done. I'd been jealous of those baby snakes—jealous because they had two parents who were trying to show them the right way of doing things.

I dipped the pot in the river until it filled. Silt and golden motes flickered as the water jostled and spilled with each step back toward the fire. When I flipped the pot over, smoke rose with a hiss. Carver's steel beer cans still held their shape, though the labels were now illegible, encased in a thick gray crust. I stuffed my clothes, the sleeping bag, and the pot into the pillowcase, and then departed, homeward bound.

The heat hit me hard as I broke free of the woods. I moped along through the rows of black-eyed peas, the leaves tickling the fine dark hairs on my legs. My eyes focused on the path between the plants, staying wary of the holes of gopher tortoises. Plenty of people had broken a leg or wrenched a knee after they'd unwittingly stepped into the burrow openings. And I also watched for snakes. Papa had always vigorously warned me about the poisonous snakes in our area. Especially cottonmouths, or "trapjaws" as he called them. When he was a young man, a friend of his had died when he'd run into a nest of them while gigging for bullfrogs along the river.

As I focused on the ground in front of me, I played over in my mind what had happened with Jimmy and Mothball, then rewound the scene and played it again, over and over. Every time I got to the part just before Jimmy lit the firecrackers, I'd modify it. One time I tackled him; another time I punched him. But even after I went through all the different possibilities, I still felt worse than I had originally. My failure to help Mothball haunted me. I tried to convince myself that I didn't know why I'd done nothing, but in reality I knew. Mothball had found out about me peeing in the tent, and as bad as that was, I still could have lived with it. But then he had to tell Jimmy. That I couldn't live with. Or forgive.

When I got home, the smell of fried baloney filled the kitchen. My mother stood over the stove with the handle of a cast-iron skillet in her hand, browning the meat. Faint light gleamed from under the hood, and the vent fan squeaked as it scattered smoke around the tight room. My father sat at the table, sipping on a glass of tomato juice, waiting for his meal. As my luck would have it, this was a Saturday, and when Dad had to work them he always came home for lunch because he got an extended lunch hour. When he had to work on Saturdays, usually every other weekend, he was always in a foul mood. All I wanted to do was go to my room and be left alone. Talking to him was the last thing I needed.

"How was the camping?" asked Dad. From where I stood, I could smell the pine resin that stained his T-shirt and covered his blue jeans. Even the baloney smoke couldn't overpower it. His hair was moist and slicked back with sweat. His glasses looked in danger of sliding off the tip of his nose if he moved at all.

"It was okay."

"Did you sit around the campfire and tell ghost stories?" asked Mom, turning from the stove. She held a plate with a fried baloney sandwich on it; a pile of potato chips leaned against the Wonder Bread. She opened our old icebox, white with small splotches of rust on the fat belly of the door. If a refrigerator could look pregnant, ours did. She grabbed a jar of mustard, then carried it over to my father and set it and the sandwich in front of him. My father immediately grabbed a butter knife and dug into the jar, the steel of the knife clinking against the glass. He painted his bread yellow.

"No," I said. "We just sat around and talked mostly. It was okay."

"When I was a little girl, in Girl Scouts, we used to tell scary stories. It was so much fun. And we'd roast marshmallows too. I meant to pack y'all some, but you were out the door so fast yesterday, I plumb forgot."

"That's okay. They'd have probably gotten all stuck together anyway," I said. I wanted to escape to my room, but I knew I had to endure the interrogation first.

"Did Raymond get enough pie? I hope you shared. He just loves my pies."

"Yeah, we had plenty, Mom, but not much sleep. I'm gonna go up for a nap."

"A nap?" said my father between a bite of his sandwich. Moist white clumps of bread stuck to his top gum as he spoke. He made a sucking sound with his tongue as he cleaned his teeth. "Must be nice to be able to take a nap while I work all day. You better have the lawn mowed by the time I get home this evening. And it's about time you got a job. Or maybe you need more chores around here. Napping, for Christ's sake."

"Gene, he's only a child. There'll be plenty of time for work when he's older." Mom looked at me. "You hungry? You want a sandwich?"

"No, thanks. I'm gonna go up to my room."

"A child?" said Dad. "He's a goddamned teenager, Louise. Jesus—I started picking cotton when I was ten. Made a quarter a day if I was lucky. You're raising that boy soft, is what you're doing."

I slipped out of the kitchen and headed down the corridor to the stairs. I heard Mom arguing with him as I climbed. "Don't you remember how much you hated having to pick cotton when you were a boy? Remember when you said you wanted something more for Walter? Something more than him just becoming another common laborer?"

"Are you calling me a common laborer? I put food on this table, don't I? I work my ass off so you two have—"

I shut my door and drowned them out, deciding to let them do battle without me. It was the same fight they'd had a hundred times anyway. I knew my dad would get the last word, though my mother would win the argument, which meant that the whole notion of me getting a job would dissolve and be forgotten.

My parents' voices eventually softened until I could no longer hear them. I wanted to block out the whole firecracker incident, but that sizzle of fuse and Mothball's muffled screams wouldn't leave me alone. Neither would *Mothball told me everything.*

A beam of sunshine shot through my window, stinging my eyes, so I went over to pull the shade. I looked down the street toward Jimmy's house but saw no sign of him. I wondered what he was thinking about. I wondered if he had even given it another thought. I wondered if he felt guilty, but knowing him, he'd probably already forgotten the whole thing. I wasn't even sure that I felt guilty. *Mothball told me everything.*

Suddenly, my father's voice boomed from downstairs, breaking me out of my daydream. "Walter, get your ass down here."

I left my room and walked back into the kitchen, wondering what I'd done this time. He still sat at the table, rubbing his stained, flaking hands together, trying to remove the pine resin that seemed to grab at everything he touched. He looked at me over the rims of his glasses with a gaze that immediately made me feel stupid.

"Pick up that goddamned pillowcase and take it to

your room. You expect your mother to clean up after you the rest of your life?"

"No, sir."

"And I was thinking you needed to get a job? Shit, you can't even pick up your clothes off the floor. You'd probably get fired your first day."

Mom walked over and took away the dirty dishes in front of Dad. Her round face looked disturbed, causing her cheeks and nose to wrinkle like a rotting, caved-in jack-o'-lantern. "Why don't you stop it?" she said. "Enough is enough." She huffed back to the sink and dropped the dishes into the stainless-steel basin. I heard the faucet start running, but I just scowled at Dad as I picked up the pillowcase, not paying attention to her.

"Why don't you get me a job at the mill, then?" I yelled. I was angry and said it in a tone that I knew wouldn't sit well with him, but I didn't care. "Then we'll see how irresponsible I am. If you can do it, I know I can."

He rubbed his face with his dirty hands, anger and contempt showing in every weathered wrinkle. "There's nothing you could do there. It's man's work. The mill is a tough place. Tough work for tough men. You're nothing but a soft little boy."

"Maybe you should've just had a different son then. Maybe he'd do a better job," I yelled. Tears tried to force their way out, but I fought them back. I felt powerless against my father. "Get me a job, and I'll prove to you that I'm tough."

"You'd just end up embarrassing me. You don't got the brass, boy. Your mama's raised you soft, just like I said." He looked at me, steely-eyed, as he rose from the table. I thought for a second he might come after me. "I gotta get back to work. Make sure that yard's mowed before I get home. And if you ever raise your voice to me like that again, I'll make it so you can't speak for a week." He walked across the kitchen, his boots thumping against the wooden slats, and slammed the back door as he left. I turned around and ran upstairs, the loaded pillowcase thumping me in the back as I went, not wanting my mother to see me cry.

My pillow was already soaked with tears by the time she knocked. The door opened and then closed behind her, but I kept my face buried in the pillow. I didn't want her in my room, yet at the same time I did. The mattress sunk down as she sat on the edge. My body slumped toward her, my hip gently resting against her back. She lifted my shirt. Goose flesh prickled my skin as her smooth hands rubbed the small of my back. I continued to cry, though more quietly now.

When I'd nearly stopped, she began talking in a soft, placid voice. "Walter, your daddy didn't mean all of what he said. He gets frustrated, that's all. He wants more for you than what he's become. He's a hard-working man, and he likes working at the mill okay, I guess, but he doesn't want to see you end up there."

"Then why does he make me feel like crap for not having a job, and then when I say I'll work, he tells me I can't handle it? I could work at the mill. I could do something there."

"That'd kill him worse than anything. That's why he said the things he said."

But that was one of the main problems I had with my father. He was inconsistent. I couldn't ever trust him because I never knew how he might act. I remember one time coming home from Mothball's with a crude wreath on my head that we'd made out of honeysuckle. My mother commented on how nice it smelled, while my father didn't say anything. The following day, I came home with a similar wreath, but this time when he saw it, he went crazy. He ripped it from my head and started whipping my bare legs with it. Said I looked like a faggot. Said no son of his was going to wear a bunch of sissy flowers.

"Then why didn't he just say that?" I asked now. "Why'd he have to make me feel like I'm useless? And why didn't you say anything?"

Her back was to me, so when she spoke, she spoke to the typewriter on the desk. "I wanted to, but I knew that'd just make him more upset. You know how he gets."

"I don't care," I said. "That doesn't make it right. He's embarrassed by me."

"No, he's not."

"He said so himself. He's as bad as Mr. Haddsby."

As soon as I said it, I wished I hadn't. I immediately thought about what I'd read in her diary and knew bringing up the Haddsby name wasn't a good idea. I almost wanted to tell her that I'd read it, tell her I knew everything, tell her I knew why she was so mean to Jimmy and the Haddsbys.

She turned her head sharply. "Don't you dare say that. That's an insult to your father. The Haddsbys are trash and nothing more. Every one of them. Your father loves you and should never be mentioned in the same sentence with that sorry family. I've got strong suspicions about that man. If you think your father is tough on you, just put yourself in Jimmy's shoes for a day and then see how rough you've got it. It's no secret in this neighborhood how he treats that boy." She twisted her upper body to get a better look at me; her blouse bunched up, exposing a roll of mushy skin hanging over the waistband of her slacks. "Come up here and sit next to me." She patted the bedspread as her demeanor shifted and softened entirely. "You need your mama right now."

I eased up, swung my legs over the bed, and sat next to her, our legs touching. She put her arm around me and pulled my head to her shoulder. She smoothed my damp hair and stroked me as if I were a dog. She started humming a song that she used to sing to me as a child; the vibrations in her chest soothed me.

"You need your mama right now," she said, her voice gentle and consoling.

All of my earlier thoughts of Jimmy and Mothball, of my father's words, of everything, disappeared into a foggy, milky haze. Sometimes I loathed my mother, but at that moment, I needed her more than I'd ever needed anyone.

Chapter 10

A COUPLE OF DAYS WENT BY with no sign of either Jimmy or Mothball. Neither of them came around, nor did I venture to their houses. Mostly I stayed in my room, reading books in bed, my body covered in a sticky film of sweat. A small rotating fan, along with the cool of the evening thunderstorms, was my only salvation. The only air conditioner in the house was in Mom and Dad's room. At first I enjoyed the solitude, but a bout of cabin fever eventually took hold; Papa had always called it "getting woods queer." The shock of what had happened subsided to some degree, but I still couldn't get that instant—just before Jimmy lit the firecrackers—out of my mind.

A few evenings later, someone knocked on the front door. I sprang from the couch in the den to answer it. Mothball stood on the brick steps of the stoop.

"Hey," he said. "Whatcha doing?"

"Nothing. Just reading." I pulled the door closed and joined him outside. Dusk wasn't far off, yet the humidity still hung thick. The rotten-egg stench of Simmons sulfur was so prevalent that I could almost taste it. A tall mountain of gray clouds was stacking in the distance, the tops glowing pink as the sun dropped behind them. Katydids chirped in the woods, but the birds had gone silent. Robins and catbirds darted in different directions, heading for cover. The clouds looked so ominous that I was temporarily distracted from Mothball. And his companion.

"What in the hell are you doing with him?" I asked.

"What? Mike? I'm taking him for a walk. He gets hateful when he's been cooped up for too long."

Mothball held a leather leash, the other end tied in a loop around Mike's neck. The little black hood hung loosely over his "head." Mike kept trying to climb onto the first step where Mothball stood, but he couldn't seem to figure it out. The leash slacked, then tightened, as the bird tried to maneuver over the stair.

"You're walking your turkey around on a leash?"

"Yeah, sure—why not?"

"Seems like it would slip right off his neck if he pulled hard enough."

"Nope," said Mothball, smiling proudly. "That's what I thought too, at first. But the knob of his head is just big enough to catch it. Besides, he don't run off."

"Mothball, you've . . ."

"What? I've what?"

"Nothing," I said. "Forget it."

"Listen," he said, his voice now a whisper. He glanced at the front window, checking for my parents. "I wanted to let you know that we're back on for tonight. Jimmy said he's ready for another mission."

"You're talking to him again? After what he did?"

"Sure, I'm talking to him. We've been together all day. And yesterday too."

I immediately became jealous. "Jesus, Mothball, I can't believe you. He practically blew you up, and you don't care? Did he at least apologize?"

Mothball hesitated. He glanced down at Mike, who had given up with the porch step and now poked around in the lawn, just off the concrete walkway. As the sky grew darker, the wind increased in intensity. Random leaves whipped through the air in scattered directions. The power lines in front of the house swayed back and forth like a slack jump rope. The temperature had dropped significantly, and the cool wind sent goose flesh tingling up my arms.

"He didn't apologize exactly, but I know he's sorry. You gotta cut him a break, Walter. You know, with his dad and everything."

"Christ, don't you remember those Black Cats exploding against your gut? You gotta stop letting people walk all over you, Mothball. You're a damned jellyfish."

"The Bible says to forgive and forget. That's what I'm doing."

"The Bible? Since when did you start reading the Bible?"

"Let's just forget about it," he said. "The summer's too short to be holding grudges."

"Holding grudges? That sounds like something Jimmy told you to say."

He turned his head away, feigning a checkup of Mike.

"And if you two have been bumming around together," I said, "why didn't you come get me? I've been locked up with my mom while y'all've been goofing off. Thanks a lot."

"Jimmy said you probably needed to cool down for a little while."

"Me cool down? Y'all are both out of your minds. I swear to God y'all are. Jimmy needs to be paid back for what he did to you. I can't believe you're going to take that from him without even trying to fight back."

"There ain't nothing I can do to him. You know that."

"Bullshit," I said. "If you don't do something, he's gonna pull this crap on you for the rest of your life. There are a million things you could do."

"Yeah, like what?" he asked.

I rattled off several of the different sinister possibilities I'd been thinking about for the past couple of days. Mothball showed only a mild interest, but at least he listened and asked a few questions. I paced around on the concrete slab of the porch, mapping out the plan that I'd worked out. I felt determined to get Jimmy back, even if Mothball didn't want to.

Rumbles of thunder rolled toward us. A pair of swallows darted from a magnolia, seeking shelter under the eaves of my house. They found a rectangular hole where a soffit vent had fallen out. They scuttled inside, disappearing. A few sporadic drops of rain stained the walkway in front of the porch.

"There's a frog-choker coming," I said. "You better get home."

Mothball looked up at the piled wall of cauliflower clouds. Mike stamped his feet and pulled hard on the leash, either sensing the storm or just feeling the raindrops.

"So you gonna meet us or what?" he said, fighting Mike's thrusts.

"Yeah, I guess so. Where at?"

"Same bat time. Same bat channel." He dropped off the step to outrun the storm.

"So we're good? You're in, right?" I yelled to him as he reached the street. "Our plan?" Just as I said that, it started pounding down.

"I reckon," he yelled back, waddling along, Mike in the lead. Mike's breast feathers puffed out and his tail turned into a fan, looking ready to either fight or mate.

I stayed under the metal awning of the porch and watched them trudge toward home. A bolt of lightning, followed immediately by a tremendous smack of thunder, made me jump. The trees swayed violently now, exposing the pale underbellies of the leaves. The rain, mixed with pebble-size hail, clinked off the metal above my head, spraying a fine mist over my face as the wind sent the water horizontal. The hail bounced off the road like Ping-Pong balls. I picked up a piece from the porch and popped it into my mouth, where it dissolved like a chilly sugar cube.

Five minutes after the storm started, it was over. The fresh air was cool and the stink of the pulp mill erased. The hail on the street melted away, surrendering to the macadam's heat. A thin veil of steam rose from the burning road, traveling slowly downwind like fog over the Tallapoosa. Lightning bugs manifested from nowhere, hovering over the icy white lawn. My heart pounded with the anticipation of the night's mission and how to repay Jimmy. The boys were back in business, though I wasn't overly confident of how it would go.

The night sky was clouded over, starless. A light breeze made it feel like another storm might be on the way. I made it to the corner, thinking I was first as usual, but then I realized Mothball was already there, leaning against a crape myrtle.

"Where's Jimmy?" I was slightly suspicious, not yet ready to fully trust either of them. Since they'd been hanging out together for a couple of days, there was no telling what scheme they might have brewed up. I knew I needed to stay on my guard.

"I don't know," said Mothball. "I waited at the end of his driveway, but he never came out."

"Maybe he fell asleep," I said. I squatted and grabbed a handful of gravel that had collected in a crevice by the storm drain. Using the other drain across the street as my goal, I tossed rocks at the black mouth nestled in the face of the opposite curb.

"Maybe, but I doubt it." He still leaned against the crape myrtle, one leg pulled up against the trunk, making him look like a fat flamingo. "Earlier today he seemed pretty gung-ho about sneaking out."

"I'll give him a few more minutes," I said, "then I'm going to bed."

"He'll be here. He probably had to wait till his dad passed out or something."

I grabbed another load of rocks and took shots at the storm drain, the iron pinging as the stones pelted it. "It feels like it's gonna pour again. I'll tell you right now, I'm not gonna get caught up in a storm."

"Yeah, tell me about it," said Mothball. "You shoulda seen my arms when I got back from your place. I had little welts all over. That hail stung like fire."

I laughed. "How'd Mike make out?"

"Shoot, not so good. He freaked out. Probably thought

he was getting shot at. He was shaking something awful. The poor guy had little cuts under his feathers."

"So," I said, whispering now, "are we all set for tonight?"

"I guess so, Walter. But I've been thinking that—"

Mothball cut it short and stood wide-eyed as Jimmy suddenly appeared.

"Y'all ready?" he asked, his hands stuffed in his cutoff jeans pockets. He seemed a little distant, as if he had something on his mind. Though the light was poor, it almost looked as if he'd been crying.

"Let's go down to the river and go swimming," said Mothball.

"Yeah," I said. "A swim'll be good."

"I'll do that," said Jimmy, "but first let's get a few supplies for our mission."

"What do you mean, 'supplies'?" I asked. "What do we need to go swimming?"

"Come on. I'll show you." He started down the street, jerking his head for us to follow. He had a crooked, devious grin crawling up the side of his face. It worried me. I couldn't shake the feeling that maybe I was getting set up.

He stopped next to a Chevy pickup. "This is what I'm talking about."

"A truck?" I said. "You wanna steal Mr. Williams's truck? Are you insane?"

"Not the truck, dipshit. Just whatever's inside."

"I ain't stealing nothing," said Mothball. "My dad'll tan my hide if he finds out."

"To hell with your dad," said Jimmy. "To hell with all our dads. I wish I didn't even have one." Mothball and I glanced at each other, not knowing how to react to his sudden outburst. But Jimmy just continued on as if everything were normal. "Besides, we won't get caught. Haven't we been sneaking out for the past couple of weeks?"

"Yeah, I guess," said Mothball.

"And we haven't been caught, have we? So I say we make things a little more interesting. We should each have to take one thing, just to make it fair. I'll even go first."

Before we could argue, the truck handle gave a slight squeak as Jimmy pulled on it. The dome light popped on. A sinking feeling anchored in my gut as he poked his head in, the yellow light illuminating his profile. He surveyed the cab, stretched across the seat, grabbed something, and then pulled back, stuffing the contraband into the front pocket of his cutoffs. He silently closed the door. "Come on. Let's get out of here."

We ran about two blocks, our tennis shoes slapping against the pavement. Jimmy stopped under a streetlight, presumably to reveal his loot. Beetles swirled above our heads, clicking and bouncing off the frosted glass globe. Blue light rained down on us.

"What did you get?" I asked. My previous anxiety had changed to a curious fascination. My hostility toward Jimmy had also dissipated for the moment.

Jimmy showed that same devious grin, reached into his pocket, and pulled out a green box of Salem cigarettes. He also palmed Mr. Williams's butane lighter with the initials "JRW" embossed on it. He proudly displayed his wares for us.

"What are we gonna do with those?" I asked.

"Uh, we're gonna eat 'em, Walter," said Jimmy. "What the hell do you think?"

I glanced over at Mothball to see what he thought, but his smile told me everything I needed to know. His chubby face looked funny under the unnatural light. His teeth glowed, and I could nearly make out each individual freckle dappling his nose.

"Cool," said Mothball. "I ain't never smoked before."

"Me neither," said Jimmy. "But don't you reckon it's about time we learned?"

Jimmy shoved the box and lighter back into his pocket. "Now it's y'all's turn."

Quick bursts of sheet lightning lit up the clouds every so often, and the soft breeze continued to roll. The tops of the trees swayed slightly, just enough to sound a rustle in the leaves. My stomach tightened as we walked toward town. Shortly before the Big House, on opposite sides of the street, two vehicles sat like ducks in front of a blind.

Mothball veered toward a pickup truck while I approached the door of a paneled station wagon.

I opened it, wary of the dome light, but it didn't come on. The car had a musty, wet-dog smell. Because of the darkness, I had to feel around like a blind man. My hands surveyed the Naugahyde seat, but all I grabbed was the female part of a seatbelt buckle. I reached for the glove compartment, located the knob, and turned it. Searching around, my hand brushed over papers, a few coins, matchbooks. Then my fingers grasped something square and leathery; I had a wallet. I flipped it open and felt several bills inside. I balled them up, stuck them into my pocket, then returned the billfold. As I backed out of the car, my shoulder bumped the steering wheel, causing the horn to blare for a quick second. I slammed the door, creating even more noise, and took off running toward town. Jimmy and Mothball had already gotten a good head start on me. I followed their blurred figures into the alley next to the five-and-dime, the same alley where I'd momentarily trapped the turkey and pushed the colored boy, the same alley Jimmy had hidden in when the Troll chased me and Mothball.

"What the hell did you honk the horn for?" asked Jimmy, his voice a stifled yell.

"It was an accident," I whispered between heavy breaths. "My shoulder bumped the horn." I poked my head around the corner of the brick building, looking down the street in the direction we'd just come from. Everything remained calm. Not even a light came on. "Looks like the coast is clear."

"Well, what did y'all get?" asked Jimmy. "Show me your loot."

"I got some money," I said, reaching into my pocket. As I did so, the tips of my fingers touched the twine I had put in there before I left the house.

"How much?" they both said in unison.

"I'm not sure, but we'll split it three ways."

The cash was illegible in the dark of the alleyway, so I held it up to the sky, trying to see it with the aid of some residual light from a streetlamp. "Looks like it's just three ones. At least it'll be easy to split."

"Better than nothing," said Mothball.

I handed them each a bill, which they stuffed into their respective pockets. "What about you?" I asked, looking at Mothball. "What'd you get?"

"I found me a new jackknife. Can you believe it?" He pulled it out, opened it, and held it up for us to see. "I lost my old one, and then just like that"—he clumsily snapped his round fingers—"I find a new one."

Jimmy flicked his lighter so we could get a better look. Mothball smiled, ogling the blade as it reflected the flame.

"How're we gonna split that, dipshit?" asked Jimmy, closing the top of the lighter. "You were supposed to kipe something we could all use. I got cigarettes, Walter got some cash, but you stole a knife? What're we gonna do, alternate weeks?"

"You never said it had to be something we were gonna share. You just said take something, and that's exactly what I did."

"Fine, then," said Jimmy. "You won't get any of my cigarettes. And you need to give Walter the dollar back."

"Oh, come on, Jimmy. That ain't fair. You never said nothing about sharing. Did he, Walter?"

"I guess not," I said. "But you should've gotten something we could all use."

"Can I keep the dollar?"

"Yeah, I don't care," I said. "Let's go swimming, though. I'm dying after that run."

"Y'all can borrow it anytime," said Mothball. "I swear, anytime." He pressed the blunt edge of the knife against his jeans, closing it, then stashed it in his pocket.

A cool blast of wind met my face as soon as I stuck my head out from the harbor of the alleyway. The tops of the trees brushed against one another lazily. A low rumble of thunder sounded far in the distance. "If we're gonna swim, we better get a move on it," I said. "The storm's coming."

"I think we should go through the Hanging Woods," said Jimmy.

"The Hanging Woods?" I said with a tremor in my voice. "Why?"

"Because I don't wanna get caught. We did just steal, you know? That way we don't have to cut across the street right here in the center of town. And we'll be hidden better in the woods than in the black-eyed peas. Just to be on the safe side."

"Jimmy's right," said Mothball. "I don't wanna get caught."

"Yeah, but the Hanging Woods?" I said. "They're kind of creepy."

"What're you afraid of?" asked Jimmy.

"People go in there and don't ever come back. Bad things happen in there."

"Jesus, Walter, lift up your skirt and let me see your yellow belly."

I shot him the middle finger. He and Mothball started laughing.

"Let's go," said Jimmy.

We left the alleyway and snaked past Audey's, clinging to the wall as we crept away. On the other side of Audey's was another alleyway, but this one didn't dead-end; it opened up to an abandoned lot. Scattered in the lot were old dented hubcaps, the rusted shell of a stripped '57 Chevy, and steel barrels filled with debris. A combination of chicken wire and barbed wire sat in a huge ball in the middle of the lot like a stalled-out clump of tumbleweed. Sheet lightning flashed, lighting up the ball of wire for a moment before leaving it in the darkness once more.

The far side of the lot was bordered by the Hanging Woods, which was a thick, dark cluster of forest that acted as a buffer between town, the Troll's shack, and the river. We picked our way across the lot and slid into the cover of the trees. I felt a bit uneasy because we hardly ever ventured into the Hanging Woods, especially at night, and I wondered again if I was being set up for some big joke. Or worse.

The Hanging Woods were so named because in the late twenties a colored man got lynched there for stealing some chickens from a white man's coop. A couple of days later it was discovered that the chickens had actually gotten loose because of a hole in the fence. The man had been falsely accused and then put to death for a crime he didn't commit. A few years back, on Halloween night, Carver told us that he and his friends had made a scarecrow dummy of a colored man and strung it up over the branch of a live oak. He said it had been freaky. I didn't doubt him one bit. The Hanging Woods were freaky enough without a scarecrow.

Within the woods, the pines stood straight and tall. The live oaks were fewer in number but more massive in girth. Spanish moss hung from the limbs like tattered gray draperies, and I had to bob and weave like a boxer to avoid getting a face full. The dead needles on the floor made the walking smooth and quiet. Every time the lightning flashed, lighting up the forest as if it were blue daylight, I tensed, half expecting to see a body still hanging from a limb. Crickets and frogs sang near the river, but in the Hanging Woods, nothing stirred.

Jimmy led, Mothball walked in the middle, and I took up the rear, the three of us packed together and stumbling along like the tin man, the scarecrow, and the lion as they entered the witch's castle. The walking was difficult because it was so dark. I could hardly see my hand in front of my face, let alone Jimmy or Mothball, and we kept bumping into one another, scaring ourselves silly. Jimmy lit his new lighter to help shed some light, but it tricked our eyes and caused such eerie shadows that we opted to find our way without it. After a few minutes of nervous walking through the thick woods, Mothball spoke up.

"Don't you think we've gone far enough? If we walk too much more, we're gonna come out at the Troll's shack."

"Let's go a little farther," said Jimmy.

"I think we need to head toward the road," said Mothball. "We're past town now, so all we gotta do is run across and we'll be at the river in no time."

"All right, I guess so," said Jimmy. "Let's cut down to the road. Or we could head toward Simmons, bypass the Troll altogether, and swim downstream of his shack."

"No way," I said. "I want to jump off the rope swing. And if we go the other way, that's where the pulp ponds are. The mill dumps all their shit down there. I went there once with my dad. Smelled so bad you couldn't help but gag. Besides, going that way only leads us deeper into the Hanging Woods. If we go toward the rope swing, the forest isn't as thick, and we should at least be able to see a little better."

Jimmy had a three-needled cluster of slash pine in his mouth and was chewing on the end of it. "Fine, then. Like I said, let's head to the road."

We made it to the edge of the woods and emerged well past town but still a little ways from the bridge and the path to the Troll's. Though still dark, it might as well have been daytime compared to the deep of the Hanging Woods. The open road and pea field were at least discernible, and my eyes quickly adjusted. "Last one there's a rotten egg," I said.

I bolted across the street and dropped down into the black-eyed pea patch, running down the far edge between the tree line and the field. Jogging along, I had a brief altercation with my conscience. I couldn't help but think about my mother and the reaction she'd have if she found out I'd been stealing. I heard her sobbing voice in my head. *I taught you better. How could you do something like this?* But it had been so easy, and it certainly hadn't seemed to affect either Jimmy or Mothball.

A moment later, I busted into the clearing where we'd camped only days before, stripped off my shirt, and ran down the embankment. The click frogs and crickets instantly ceased their chatter. All went hauntingly quiet. The only sound was the mosquitoes attacking the hollows of my ears, so I waded into the water to escape. It was eerie being alone in the river. Despite the darkness, I could still discern the rope swing hanging from the sycamore.

"Hey, y'all, check this out," I said as they broached the edge of the embankment. "Somebody messed with the rope swing." I reached up and swatted at the clothesline someone had attached to the end of the rope. Whoever had done it had been pretty smart about it. The piece of clothesline—maybe four or five feet long—was tied to the rope above the knot, forming a loop at the end of it. So now, instead of fooling with a stick and having to smack the rope back to the next guy, all we had to do was snatch the loop, which hung just a couple of feet over the surface of the water, and snap it like a horse's reins, sending it to the next jumper. "It looks perfect. I wonder who did it."

"I don't know," said Jimmy. "Maybe it was the Troll."

That thought had already occurred to me, which only added to the eeriness of the night.

"We can test it out in a minute," said Jimmy. "Don't you wanna try one of these cigarettes first?"

"Oh, yeah," I said. I walked up the slick embankment and sat in between the two of them. I used my shirt to wipe my face and dry my hands. "The water feels good."

A bolt of lightning sparked, illuminating the understory of the forest. The piebald skin on the trunk of the sycamore seemed to glow for a second after the strike, leaving a lingering image, as if a camera had flashed.

Jimmy handed us each a cigarette and then popped one between his lips.

"How do you do it?" asked Mothball.

"I don't know," said Jimmy. "Just suck on them like our folks do."

I pictured Mr. Haddsby, the way his cheeks indented when he took heavy draws. The smoke would curl around his face and sometimes mysteriously slither up his nose.

Jimmy took out his lighter and lit my cigarette first. I puffed hard, the flame of the lighter pulsating as I drew in the smoke in quick spurts. My lungs filled with the coolness of the menthol, and as I exhaled, a stream of smoke flowed from my mouth in a column in front of me. I liked it immediately and didn't even cough. The mosquitoes dissipated as soon as I lit up.

Mothball coughed furiously when Jimmy lit his for him. Jimmy and I laughed. I took another draw, staring at the orange glow as it slowly burned down the paper. After the third puff, my head went light and my body relaxed. Any guilty feelings I'd had about stealing were now completely gone. I didn't even mind being with Jimmy. Neither was I worried about the Troll or the plan Mothball and I had worked out.

"This feels cool," I said, talking to no one in particular.

A bullfrog croaked on the opposite bank. I lay back

and looked up through the trees, waiting for another flash of lightning. Mothball coughed again.

"How you making out over there, Mothball?" I asked.

"These things taste like shit. They're disgusting."

"I'll take the rest of your share then," I said. "I love it."

"Yeah," said Jimmy, "and since you only swiped a knife, that's only fair."

"Fine. You can have 'em. I'm going swimming."

Mothball got up, walked to the edge of the water, and jumped in, fully clothed, shoes and all. His splash silenced the click frogs once again.

"How's it feel, Mothball?" asked Jimmy, smoke tumbling from his mouth as he spoke. I thought he looked pretty cool.

"It feels great."

"Watch out for moccasins," I said. "You know they come out at night."

"Shut up, Walter. You don't scare me." But he waded back toward the bank.

"Wait a sec," I said. "Don't get out yet. Stay there and toss me the rope. I wanna jump."

The tobacco pulled at my brain like waves in the ocean; I felt good. The orange trail of my cigarette arced through the air and into the water as I tossed the butt away. I walked onto the smooth bark of the sycamore that edged over the river as if I were walking the plank. Once I was over the river, I rested my hand against the vertical part of the trunk—the part that grew skyward—for balance.

"Toss it here," I said. Mothball grabbed the loop, pushing and pulling a few times to build up momentum. He snapped the rope into my waiting palm.

The coarse fibers bit into my skin as I grabbed the rope above the knot where the clothesline was now tied. I pushed off the trunk, scrunched my knees to my chest, and felt the wind rush across my face as I flew over the river. I let go and crashed into the warm water, my feet barely hitting the silty bottom.

Mothball had already made his way out, while Jimmy stood on the sycamore awaiting his turn. The rope swung above my head as I treaded water.

"Toss it to me, will ya?" asked Jimmy.

The current pulled me downstream slightly, the water a little higher than usual from the earlier storm. I swam toward the bank and shallower water, waiting for the rope to slow before I seized it. I grabbed the loop and tossed it to Jimmy. As I made my way to shore, I instinctively ducked as he sailed by overhead. He whooped as he dropped to the water, bouncing an echo off the rock face of the far bank.

Mothball now stood on the sycamore, awaiting Jimmy's toss. I climbed the bank and sat down. Jimmy grabbed the rope and sent a good toss to Mothball, but he missed it and nearly slipped off the tree while scrambling for the rope.

"Come on, Mothball. That was perfect," said Jimmy.

"Sorry. I missed it. It's dark, you know?"

Jimmy sent it toward Mothball again. This time he caught it. Jimmy waded toward shore and walked up the bank, sitting down next to me.

"How about another smoke?" he said. "You know Mothball. He'll probably be there for another hour before he jumps."

"I heard that," said Mothball, looking over his shoulder.

"Well, it's true," said Jimmy. "You act like a little girl when it comes to that rope swing." He dried his hands on his shirt, which lay next to him, then picked up the pack of cigarettes.

"Oh, yeah?" said Mothball. "Well, I've been thinking about doing a penny drop."

Jimmy lit my cigarette, then his own. The cool smoke filled my lungs.

"That'll be the day," said Jimmy. "If you flip over backwards, I'll personally come down there and kiss your fat ass."

"Okay, I'm gonna hold you to that. And maybe, if you're a gentleman, you could use a little tongue to clean my butt crack."

"Sure, I'm not too worried about it," said Jimmy. "Go ahead, we're watching."

Even during the day, Mothball rarely used the rope swing. His pear-shaped body was so weak that he had trouble holding himself up when he leaped.

"The sun's gonna be up soon," I said. "You gonna jump sometime tonight?"

"Shut up, Walter. I'm just picturing how Jimmy's gonna lick my ass. You know, I'm starting to grow some hair down there."

"And I'm picturing how you're gonna do another one of your famous belly flops, you sick bastard," said Jimmy. "That is, if you even jump."

"You'll see, butt licker. I just gotta get myself ready in my mind."

Jimmy reached over and grabbed at something underneath his shirt. "Maybe this would help him jump," he said. He chuckled as he held up a pack of firecrackers.

My heart plunged. Just when I thought things were getting better, he had to drop another bomb. "Jesus, Jimmy, don't you ever give up?" I whispered, not wanting Mothball to hear. Anger rose in my voice. "What you did the other day was messed up."

"Come on, Walter. You need to lighten up. It wasn't that big a deal." Though he still wouldn't admit any wrongdoing, he did drop the firecrackers back on his shirt. "I paid him back for that trick he pulled with Carver, that's all. We're friends again. He's forgiven me. And besides, just in case you forgot, you didn't exactly try and stop me."

Embarrassment, and the feeling that he was right, crept through me. "Yeah, but Mothball didn't deserve that."

"Even after he ratted you out about pissing yourself? You can't tell me you didn't want me to light him up."

Mothball yelled, "What are y'all talking about? I can hear you over there."

"Nothing," I yelled. To Jimmy I said, "Can we just drop this whole thing? I'll never mention it again if you'll swear to keep quiet about what happened in the tent."

"You mean just like you promised to never say anything about my mom throwing the turkey?"

I felt his gaze upon me. I understood now.

"I'm sorry about that," I said. "I guess I can't blame you if you tell the whole school."

"Hell, I wouldn't do that. I ain't cruel or nothing. We're blood brothers, man. Let's just forget it." He stuck his hand out. I shook it, though I wasn't entirely convinced of his sincerity.

"Goddamn," he said. "We're getting a little too mushy."

"Yeah, no kidding."

We both tried to detect Mothball in the darkness. He still hadn't jumped.

"Bet you a dollar he doesn't even go," whispered Jimmy.

I felt better about things, as if everything was finally resolved. I wasn't sure if I could trust him, but I had to believe that he'd keep quiet about it.

"You're on," I whispered back. "Come on, Mothball," I yelled, "just jump already. We don't have all night."

"Bock, bock, bock," cackled Jimmy. "Mothball's chickenshit."

"Shut up. I'm getting ready."

"Jump, chickenshit," I said. It felt good to say that to someone else for a change.

Mothball continued to fumble around. After a minute more, he wrapped the loop of the clothesline around the broken stub of a branch on the side of the sycamore, securing it, and walked away from the tree, back onto the embankment.

"What're you doing?" I yelled. I envisioned myself reaching into my pocket for the dollar I'd just stolen and having to hand it to Jimmy. "Where the hell are you going?"

"I gotta shit," said Mothball, scuttling away into the weeds. "I think that cigarette screwed up my stomach."

I pulled the wet dollar from my pocket and slapped it into Jimmy's open hand. My fingers had again touched the two pieces of twine I'd brought along, but now I wasn't sure if I wanted to go through with it. He chuckled and stuffed the dollar into his shorts.

"Well, I'll do a penny drop then," said Jimmy. He flicked his cigarette into the river. I heard a faint sizzle as it hit the water and disappeared.

"Damn that Mothball," I said. "All he had to do was jump in the water."

Jimmy laughed again as he stood up and walked onto the sycamore. A bright flash of lightning lit him up, followed soon after by a loud clap of thunder.

"Shit, where'd that come from?" he said. "That was close."

"We better get heading back soon," I said. "Storm's gonna be here any minute now." The leaves of the trees rustled together as the breeze picked up and light drops of rain started to fall.

"We still got a few minutes," he said. "Besides, who knows how long Mothball will take? You know him when he's gotta go. I'm gonna jump, Piss Boy."

I realized right then, in that instant, that I had to do what Mothball and I had planned on my porch. That stronger part of me suddenly erupted. Pages of my mother's diary flashed in my head. Things were never going to change with Jimmy. It was now or never. I stood up and walked toward the tree.

"What did you call me?"

"I was just joking," said Jimmy. "You know that."

"I thought we were gonna drop it."

"You're right. It's dropped."

"Well, come here, then, before you jump," I said. "I wanna show you this trick my dad showed me. It's the least you can do."

"To hell with that. I'm jumping."

"Just check this out real quick, then you can jump." I reached into my pocket and pulled out the pieces of twine.

"What's that?"

"They're pieces of rope. It's called Houdini's rope trick," I said, looking into the dark woods, trying to discern if Mothball was ready. I couldn't see anything.

"What do you mean?"

"Houdini was a famous—"

"I know who he was, dipshit. What's the trick?"

"Give me your wrists," I said. "I'm gonna tie them together with a special knot, and then your feet. You got one minute to escape."

Even though it was dark, I could tell he eyed me suspiciously. "I wasn't born yesterday, Walter. I'm not stupid."

I knew he wouldn't just fall into it, but I'd been planning this for days, and I was ready.

"Fine, you don't have to try it," I said. "But my dad did it to me, and I escaped in less than thirty seconds. It's easy . . . if you can figure out the secret."

"What do you mean? What's the secret?"

"I'm not gonna tell you," I said. "My dad didn't tell me. You gotta be smart enough to figure it out on your own. Shit, I bet Mothball can even do it."

"You aren't tying me up. To hell with that."

"Come on, we're blood brothers, just like you said. What, you don't trust me?"

"Hell, no, I don't trust you."

"Fine, then. I bet Mothball's not chicken." I needed him right then if I was going to pull it off. "Mothball, what the hell are you doing?"

I heard him slowly making his way toward us. As he emerged, he pulled at his shorts, hoisting them up. "Oh, man," he said. "There ain't nothing like taking a good shit in the woods."

"Come here," I said. "I wanna show you a trick."

He sidled up next to us, and I explained it to him.

"No way," he said. "If y'all think I'm gonna get tied up again, y'all're crazy. Not after what happened last time." He glanced hard at Jimmy. I was proud of him; he was following along just as I'd instructed.

"Come on, Mothball," I said. "You can show Jimmy you're not chickenshit. He's afraid to do it."

"I'm not afraid," said Jimmy. "I just don't trust you."

"See?" I said. "He's chicken."

"Yeah, looks that way," said Mothball. "Okay, go ahead. I can do it. How much time I got?"

"One minute," I said. "Give me your wrists."

Mothball extended his arms. I tied them loosely, and then his ankles.

"Who's got a watch?" asked Mothball.

"Me and Jimmy'll count."

"All right, but count slow."

"Yeah, okay," I said. "Ready . . . get set . . . go."

Jimmy and I counted aloud as Mothball began struggling with the cuffs. At thirty, he still hadn't gotten his wrists free. I started to wonder if I'd tied them too tightly.

"You're counting too fast," he said. "Slow down. I've almost got it."

At forty-three he freed his wrists, and then it only took him a few more seconds to undo his ankles. We stopped counting at fifty-two.

"Hell, yeah," he yelled. "Less than a minute. What do I win?"

I had to admit, I was pretty impressed with his acting job.

"You don't win shit," said Jimmy, laughing.

"Sure he does," I said. "He just proved he's not as chickenshit as you. Unless you can beat fifty-two seconds."

"Yeah," said Mothball. "What's wrong, Jimmy? You afraid you can't beat me?"

"If your fat ass can do it, then I know I can."

"Then prove it. Or else you can start calling me 'King Mothball' from now on."

Mothball laughed and I joined in. We had him. Jimmy was an apprehensive puppy on the edge of a dock, wanting to jump in but still not sure.

"To hell with it," he finally said. "How long did it take you, Walter?"

"Twenty-eight seconds."

"Bullshit."

"You can ask my dad. I did it in twenty-eight, and he was using his watch."

"I'll beat it," he said, offering me his wrists.

I picked up the twine from the ground, sneaking a peek at Mothball.

"Put your hands together," I said. "Like you're praying." I wrapped the piece of twine around Jimmy's wrists, cinching it down tight. I did the same with his ankles.

"Dammit, Walter, you're drawing blood. You didn't tie Mothball up this tight. How am I supposed to get out of this?"

Mothball stood next to me now, facing Jimmy, and said, "You're not supposed to get out of it . . . dipshit." He pushed Jimmy in the chest and Jimmy fell over backwards, landing hard on his butt. He rolled onto his side, scrambling to get up, but couldn't. The rain started to sprinkle down, hitting the leaves, with the occasional drop sneaking through and getting us wet. Jimmy struggled with his hands, trying to get them loose.

"You fat prick. You're gonna pay for this one."

"I've already paid for it, Jimmy," said Mothball. "And now you're my prisoner."

"I can't believe I fell for this shit. Okay, you got me. Ha-ha. Now let me go."

Mothball and I each grabbed under an armpit and pulled him up. We had him trapped, and I wasn't about to release him just yet. Adrenaline started pumping through me. And I liked it.

"Now, soldier," I said, "it's time to march."

"March? How am I gonna march with my feet tied together?"

"I said march. Toward the tree. Or else you're gonna end up in the mud again."

We guided Jimmy, his feet shuffling along in little baby steps, toward the base of the sycamore that held the rope swing.

"Hey, Mothball," I said. "Guess what he brought along?"

"I don't know," he said. We stopped Jimmy at the base of the tree. "What?"

"Firecrackers."

"Oh, really? Very interesting, Jimmy. Were you planning to blow me up again?"

"No," he said. He sounded as if he was starting to get scared. "I just brought them for the fun of it."

A feeling of dominance started to grow inside me. It

felt pretty good, having the power for once. I had just planned on messing with Jimmy a little bit, but his bringing the firecrackers was a bonus. I wondered if Mothball would go through with it or if he'd chicken out. If he wouldn't do it, I realized that I would. I wanted Jimmy to pay. I wanted him to pay for everything. I said, "Maybe it's your time to return the favor, Mothball."

"Yeah, maybe so."

"Get your hands off me, you fucking pervert," said Jimmy as Mothball dug into his pockets, looking for the firecrackers. Jimmy twisted and turned his body.

"They're over there under his shirt," I said.

When Mothball turned toward me, Jimmy socked him over the head with his tied hands, Captain Kirk–style. I laughed.

"Our prisoner is getting ornery, Walter," said Mothball.

"Yeah, well, I've got an idea," I said. "This should calm him down." I grabbed the sides of Jimmy's shorts and pulled them to his ankles, leaving him stark naked. "Help me get him out on the tree, Mothball."

"Walter," he said, "I . . . I don't know."

"Don't wimp out on me now," I yelled. I couldn't believe the way I felt. Anger, almost a rage, started to build in my head. But it wasn't unpleasant. It was that stronger part of me taking over completely. "Do you remember what he did to you? It's time to get him back."

"Don't help him," said Jimmy, trying to make his voice sound tough, but I heard it quivering. He was scared. "Y'all let me go and we'll call it even. I swear."

Mothball hesitated, so I prodded Jimmy out onto the tree by myself. When we reached the end—where the tree went vertical—I turned him around so his back leaned against the upright part of the trunk. There wasn't enough room for Mothball to help anyway. My legs felt a little wobbly, and I had to really pay attention in order not to fall.

"I swear to God, Walter, you're going to pay for this. And pull my fucking shorts up, you bed-wetting freak."

"Jimmy," I said, reaching for the rope that was still secured against the sycamore, "would you please just shut . . . the fuck . . . up?" I grabbed the looped piece of clothesline and dropped it over Jimmy's head, where it rested loosely around his neck. I held the rope in one hand and kept my other tucked under his armpit. "This oughta keep you from squirming."

"Shit, Walter," said Mothball. "We could just make him sit on the ground."

"This way," I said, "he definitely won't move. Get the firecrackers and lighter."

"Don't do it, you fat bastard," said Jimmy. "I swear to God, Mothball, I'll get you for this. Don't fuck with me."

Apparently that was all Mothball needed to hear. He

stood on the bank and just stared at Jimmy. I couldn't really see his face, but I imagined what it looked like.

"Hurry up," I said. "We're not going to be able to light them here in a minute, the way this rain's starting to come down."

Finally, Mothball turned around and casually walked toward Jimmy's shirt, which sat about a hundred feet away. He disappeared into the darkness. I turned to look at Jimmy. He had his arms raised, getting ready to strike me.

"What the fuck are you doing?" I yelled. I don't think I'd ever been so angry.

He brought his bound hands down toward my head, but I easily dodged the blow. His fists only glanced my shoulder, which set him completely off-balance. He tottered from side to side, trying to stay upright, but he had no chance. I pulled on the rope and reached for his arm, but his feet slipped on the wet bark. His neck jerked and the tree branch swayed violently as he went sailing out over the river and into the darkness. A second later he came propelling back toward the sycamore—hanging by his neck, spinning around like a twisted yo-yo—and smacked into it, hard. I grabbed for him, but I missed and lost my footing. He went flying outward again as I made a desperate grab at the tree, trying to hold on. There was a crash in the black water, and this time when the rope came swinging back, it was empty. Jimmy was gone. The clothesline was gone. My palms were on fire. Unable to hold on any longer, I fell to the water on my back, hitting it hard and nearly getting the wind knocked out of me.

"Walter. Holy shit, Walter." It was Mothball. He stood on the edge of the bank above me, looking down as I corked to the surface. I felt dazed and didn't quite know what was going on. I struggled in the water and managed to get to my feet. The level of the river was nearly neck high.

"What the hell?" screamed Mothball. "Jesus, his hands are tied. He can't swim."

I looked at him blankly. "What are you talking about?"

"Jimmy," he yelled. "You knocked him into the fucking river."

It took me another few seconds to realize what had happened. "Come on," I finally yelled. "We gotta find him."

I took off into the water, paddling furiously toward the spot where I thought he'd landed, though it was too dark to tell for sure. When I got there, I took a deep breath and dove to the bottom. I grasped clumps of mud and leaves, but couldn't locate him. When my breath was nearly exhausted, I pushed off the mucky bottom and surfaced.

"Mothball, get over here." He still hadn't left the bank. I started frantically splashing at the water and realized I'd been pulled quite a ways downstream. I chopped through the water, back upstream, and dove again, scouring the bottom. My hand touched something hard, and I instinctively pulled back for a second. I reached again, only to find a submerged log. And then the current forced me downstream.

Something floated by on top of the water, and I grabbed it. It was the clothesline with the noose tied at the end, but there was no sign of Jimmy. I started pulling on it so hard in my panic that my hands nearly ignited; my palms split wide open. I tossed it back into the river and yelled at Mothball once more.

"Goddammit, help me!"

"Oh, Christ," he said. "Oh, shit, oh, shit, oh, shit."

The rain had started falling hard. He clumsily made his way out to where I was.

"What do we do? Oh, shit, Walter, what the hell do we do?"

"Start diving. The current's getting stronger. We've got to hurry."

I dove again and Mothball did the same. We searched the bottom with our hands and feet but found nothing. I couldn't understand how Jimmy had disappeared so quickly. Why hadn't he come to the top? Or maybe he had, but it was so dark that I hadn't seen him. When I resurfaced once more, my body started shaking involuntarily.

"I can't see anything," said Mothball. "Holy shit, what the hell did you do?"

The rain now pounded the surface, and the trees swayed violently on the banks. The hard drops stung my eyes. The storm was directly overhead, and the current increased in strength. I tried to dig my feet into the mud, but it was useless. We fought our way toward shore and ran along the soppy bank, back toward the sycamore.

"We gotta try one more time," I said. "He landed right over there." I pointed toward the spot where I thought Jimmy had dropped. We bounded into the water once more, then dove, but again came up empty. We got ripped downstream even faster than the time before. We edged our way toward the bank, and then I saw him. He was caught between two large rocks that ordinarily created little riffles but because of the storm practically had white water passing through them.

"He's right there, Mothball," I said. "He's caught in the rocks. Jimmy, we're coming."

I let the current pull me to him and then braced myself against the largest rock, staying upstream from his body. The force of the water pinned me against the rock, and the tip of my elbow slammed against it, sending a surge of pain up my arm. I grabbed at his legs, which were closest to me, while his head and arms bobbed with the rhythm of the water flowing over him. His feet were wedged below the surface while the rest of his body floated just above the water, his face pointed toward the sky.

The current had pushed Mothball to the shore, and he looked as if he were about to come back into the water, presumably to help free Jimmy. I reached for Jimmy's legs and my fingers found the twine around his ankles. With a strength that wasn't my own, I pulled at the twine and freed his feet before Mothball made it out to us. I clenched the twine tightly in my burning hands as the river demanded that I let go. The current tugged at Jimmy's body, jerking my arms, trying to claim its prize. I probably could have held on until Mothball got there, but I didn't. I let go. I let him float helplessly down the river. For some reason, it seemed like the right thing to do. And then I heard, "No, Walter. Brothers. Why?" It hadn't been Mothball. It was Jimmy who'd said it, just after I let him go. Somehow, despite the fall he'd taken and his float downstream, he'd managed to stay alive. And after all that, I let him go. His body swiftly shot down the river, disappearing.

"What did you let him go for? Jesus, Walter, he was alive," yelled Mothball, who stood a few feet away from me in the river, crying hysterically. "Didn't you hear him pleading with you? Christ, you just killed him. He's gone, Walter. He's fucking gone."

I stood there blankly, staring downstream as the rain bubbled white spots on the surface of the river. "I heard him," I said, "but it was too late. I'd already let go."

"Bullshit! It wasn't too late. He asked for you to help

him at least three or four times. I could hear him all the way from shore. You just let him go. It was like you wanted him to die."

I looked at Mothball, not really comprehending what he said. And then anger started to well inside me once more. "I didn't want him to die," I yelled. "I was trying to save him."

I worked my way back to shore and dropped down in the mud. Mothball followed and fell down next to me. I was exhausted. The palms of my hands were bloodied from where I'd pulled on the clothesline. My forearms ached; they felt like balls of concrete.

"It was your idea to get him back," he said after a minute, whimpering. I could barely hear him above the noise of the storm and the roaring river. "You were the one who said I was a jellyfish. It was your plan. All that Houdini shit."

"I said we should tie him up and mess with him a little," I screamed. "I didn't say we should fucking kill him. Jesus Christ, Mothball, don't blame this on me. You agreed to mess with him too, remember?"

"We gotta go get help, Walter. Go tell the sheriff or something. It was an accident."

"How we gonna explain it was an accident? How we gonna explain his hands being tied up? How we gonna explain any of it? How?"

"I don't know," he said, sobbing softly now. "We can't."

We walked back along the bank in a daze, heading toward the rope swing to get my shirt and shoes. My whole body ached. My legs, my elbows, all of my muscles. My neck muscles, the muscles in my face, in my throat, the tendons in my fingers. Everything hurt. And my hands. Especially my torn-up hands.

I sat down next to Jimmy's drenched shirt, exhausted, while the rain continued to come down. I struggled to put on my shirt and shoes, and then just sat there, staring out at the river through squinted eyes. Finally, I grabbed the pack of soaked cigarettes. With a lazy toss, the box landed in the river and disappeared. Mothball pulled the lighter from his pocket and stared at it as he fingered the embossed initials.

"Can I see it?" I asked.

He handed it to me, and I ran my fingers over the initials as well.

"Don't toss that," said Mothball. "It's all we've got left of Jimmy."

"It's evidence," I said, finally breaking down.

The lighter shook in my trembling hand. I stared at it and sobbed as the rain continued to pour down on us. For some reason, I couldn't part with it. It seemed important. Mothball grabbed it from me and heaved it into the river.

"You're right," he said. "It's evidence." He picked up Jimmy's shoes and shirt and threw them in. Then he pulled out his knife and tossed that too. "We gotta get outta here," he said, his voice high and panicked.

"We've gotta get some help," I said, suddenly realizing we were in deep. "Get a search team out here to find him or something."

"We can't tell nobody," he screamed. "Just like you said." He was hysterical. He started pulling at his wet hair as if he wanted to rip it out, and he paced back and forth in the mud. It was as if we'd completely switched roles from just a few minutes before. "You hear me? Nobody. If we tell, then we're in a load of trouble. We just killed Jimmy. We stole shit. My dad'll kill me if he finds out I been sneaking out."

"It was an accident," I said. "Jesus, Mothball, nobody's gonna give a shit if we snuck out and stole a couple of things. Jimmy's fucking dead."

He dropped to his knees, pounding the mud with his fists. He started pulling at his hair again as he wailed.

"Jesus, Walter, what are we gonna do?"

"You're right—we can't say anything. We'll figure something out."

Suddenly, in unison, we both turned our heads downstream. Even over the pounding of the rain and the whip of the wind, I heard the unmistakable sound of something shuffling through the leaves. And then there was a splash. A big splash, as if someone had just jumped into the water.

"What the hell was that?" asked Mothball, his eyes now popping from his head.

"Let's get out of here," I said, scrambling to my feet. "We gotta get home."

We raced through the pea field, now muddy and sloppy, toward town. Once on the road, we started running as fast as we could, Mothball keeping up with me step for step. Under the streetlamps, the rain fell almost horizontally, smacking me hard in the face. I was numb to the pain. At the corner by the crape myrtle, we stopped and caught our breath, Mothball breathing far heavier than I.

"What was that . . . we heard . . . in the woods . . . Walter? That was definitely . . . somebody."

"I don't know. Maybe a deer or something."

"That was no deer . . . You know it wasn't . . ."

"Maybe a tree branch breaking in the wind. I'm not sure."

"When's the last time you heard a tree branch run through the leaves before it fell in the water?"

"Just forget it, okay? It was nothing. And when we wake up, we play dumb," I said. "We don't know where Jimmy is."

"But his mom, Walter. I was thinking about her while

we were running. We gotta at least tell her what happened. She needs—"

"Do you think if it had been you or me to drown in that river, Jimmy would have told *our* parents?"

He looked down at the wet pavement glistening in the lamplight. He knew I was right. He walked off toward home, and I carefully made my way to the back door of my house, praying that of all nights my mother hadn't awoken during the storm with an urge to come check on me.

CHAPTER 11

I HOPED THAT EVERYTHING from the night before had been a bad dream. As I stripped the wet comforter from my bed, my hands started to burn again. There were rope marks on both of them, red and glistening and coated with some kind of clear pus. I looked underneath the bed and found my rain-soaked clothes wadded up in a ball. It hadn't been a dream. I gingerly grabbed the clothes and dropped them on the bed, then pulled the sheets off. Every movement sent pain through my body; I was sore everywhere. As carefully as I could, I wrapped the sheets around the clothes. Mom wouldn't think twice about it. She knew my problem.

From downstairs, my mother's voice immediately set my heart jumping. I'd slept late, so I knew Dad was already at work. We hardly ever had company, so whoever Mom was talking with must have had something to do with Jimmy. Mothball and I were busted, I just knew it. And now we'd really be in a heap of trouble because we hadn't reported it. Nausea settled deep in my gut.

As I slipped into a pair of dry shorts, the bedroom door swung open. My mother—still dressed in her pink bathrobe and slippers—looked at me. Her face eased for a moment when she saw me standing there getting dressed, then transformed back into a stricken look of anxiety and fear. Her expression told me all I needed to know.

"Walter, have you seen Jimmy? Do you know where he might be?"

"What . . . What do you mean?" I casually stuffed my hands into my pockets.

"Lydia Haddsby is downstairs. She's a mess. Jimmy wasn't in his bed this morning. She said he didn't sleep there last night. Do you know where he might be?"

This was the moment of truth. I could tell everything, get it off my chest, and deal with Mothball when the time came. But I didn't. "No, ma'am," I said. "Maybe he's over at Mothball's."

"She already checked there. Hurry up and get downstairs, we have to help her."

"You wanna help her? You don't even talk to Jimmy. And you hate the Haddsbys." My voice projected louder than I'd meant it to, but I didn't care.

"*Hate* is a strong word," she said, trying to keep her voice down. "I don't hate the Haddsbys. Besides, Walter, that's her child. Her baby is missing. Someday, when you're a father, you'll understand. I don't know where you ever got such a crazy idea. Hurry on down."

"I'll never be a father," I said, but she'd already closed the door and left. I wanted to tell her I'd gotten the "crazy idea" from reading her diary, but now was definitely not the time to bring that up. Telling the lie had been easier than I'd thought, though that had been to my mother; I'd been lying to her forever. But she had just lied to me too: she did hate the Haddsbys. As easy as my lie had been, playing dumb to Mrs. Haddsby or Sheriff Walls might be a different story. And my hands. I had to watch my hands.

My mother's words, *that's her child,* kept reverberating in my ears. Paranoia enveloped me. I started sweating again, the perspiration beading on my forehead. *That's her child.* I decided right then and there that I had to tell Mrs. Haddsby. For once, I knew I had to do the right thing. She didn't deserve the pain she was going through. *That's her child.*

I put on a T-shirt and a baseball cap to hide my messy hair, pulling the bill low over my eyes. I headed downstairs—every muscle in my body throbbing as I did so—dreading her reaction, but strangely I also felt a sense of relief. Mrs. Haddsby, my mother, they'd both have to understand that Mothball and I had been scared, that we hadn't known what to do. They'd pity us and sympathize with us. That's what ladies always did with kids. As I hit the bottom step, I put my hands in my pockets and felt another flood of relief. I headed for the living room, where I heard a voice consoling Mrs. Haddsby.

Everything changed when I entered the room. Mrs. Haddsby sat on the couch, her pretty face stained with dark blue streaks of mascara. It struck me as strange that she would take time to put on makeup when her son was missing. Wrapped tightly around her fist was one of Mom's handkerchiefs, also smudged with blue. Sitting next to her on the couch was Mothball's mother. It was her voice I'd heard consoling Mrs. Haddsby.

Mrs. Cleilsky was short and fat, just like Mothball, and her feet barely touched the floor; she had her arm around Mrs. Haddsby. Sitting in the wooden rocker across from the women sat Mothball, rocking nervously, a concerned look on his face. The chair creaked every time he went forward. He saw me and gave a slight shake of his head in the negative.

"Walter," said Mrs. Haddsby, "have you seen Jimmy? He wasn't in his bed this morning. I went in to wake him for breakfast, and . . . and he wasn't there."

She looked as if she might start crying again. I glanced at Mothball, who'd temporarily stopped rocking and stared back at me. He gave another subtle turn of his head. All of my plans to reveal the truth sank away. He obviously hadn't said anything, so I couldn't either, though I think my idea of confessing was only a fleeting one anyway.

"No, ma'am," I said, shaking my head. "I haven't seen him. Not in a couple of days. We sort of got in an argument and really haven't been talking lately."

My mother came in and handed each of the women a

cup of coffee on a saucer. She had used her wedding china, which hardly ever came out of the cupboard. Mrs. Haddsby's hands shook as she placed the cup to her lips and blew over the surface of the coffee. Watching her hands made me realize that mine had started throbbing.

Mom looked at me. "I know Jimmy was often hard to get along with," she said with her sweetest smile, "but what were you two fighting about?"

"Nothing, really. You know, guy stuff. It doesn't matter anyway."

"Walter," said Mom, "it might be important. Maybe he was upset and ran away."

"I hardly think he ran away over a fight about a basketball game. It was stupid."

"Well, maybe so," said Mom, and then turned to Mrs. Haddsby. "Lydia, I'm sure you or Macon already called the sheriff, right?"

Mrs. Haddsby wiped her face with the handkerchief and shook her head. "No. I ain't even told Macon yet. He left this morning to finally go look for work at the quarry."

"Maybe Jimmy went with him," said Mrs. Cleilsky. "Yes, maybe that's it. He probably just went with him. A father-son thing."

"No, I was up with Macon this morning. Cooking him breakfast and all. I even went out to the truck because he'd forgotten his lunch. Macon was alone."

"Well, let me call the sheriff for you," said Mom. "If

Walter had ever gone missing, I know the first thing that Gene and I would have done was call the law. I mean, that's *our child*." She headed for the kitchen, her bedroom slippers skipping across the wood floor. I'd never really seen her talk with Mrs. Haddsby before, and I couldn't believe how she was acting. It seemed as if she almost enjoyed the whole situation. As for me, I couldn't stand it. My mind kept seesawing on whether to blurt out what had happened or to just remain quiet.

"And Raymond," said Mrs. Cleilsky, "you're sure you haven't seen Jimmy?"

"No, ma'am," said Mothball. "Like I said, last time I saw him was yesterday evening, just before the storm. Then I came over here to talk to Walter for a few. Jimmy wanted me to patch things up between them, and that's what I done. We were planning on getting together today and go swimming down at the river. Weren't we, Walter?"

Mothball's mentioning the river unnerved me, but other than that, I couldn't believe how smoothly he acted. He'd picked up on my lie about the basketball game and gone with it. He seemed like a completely different person than the kid I'd known my whole life.

"Yeah, we were gonna go swimming," I said.

"Maybe that's it, then," said Mrs. Cleilsky. "Maybe he's down at the river."

Again I was unnerved. Mrs. Cleilsky had no idea how right she was.

"He'd have waited for us, Mom," said Mothball. "Besides, Mrs. Haddsby already said it didn't look like he slept in his bed last night."

Mrs. Haddsby nodded with Mothball's words.

"Oh, that's right," said Mrs. Cleilsky. "I forgot about that. I guess you're right."

The room went silent with tension, and we could all hear my mother talking on the phone. After she hung up, she came back into the room, carrying a cup and saucer of her own. "I talked to Laura at the station," she said. "She sent out a call to the sheriff. He was over in Niggertown sorting out something or other. Lord only knows what. You know how their kind are always carrying on. She said he'd be over as soon as he could. I just told her to have him come over here." She seemed to glow with every word, as if she were now a key player in the mystery. "Don't you worry, Lydia. I'm sure everything's going to be just fine." She gave a broad smile, trying to convey reassurance, but all I saw was some type of strange satisfaction. She was taking pleasure in Mrs. Haddsby's pain, and I felt pretty sure I knew why.

The next twenty minutes of waiting were pure hell. Mrs. Cleilsky and Mom, with a sappy smile on her face the whole time, talked about what a fine boy Jimmy was while Mrs. Haddsby nodded and agreed.

When Sheriff Walls knocked on the door, I went to answer it. He was stout, with unkempt blond hair creeping from the sides of his brown Mountie-style hat. He nodded at me and removed his hat when I opened the door. I prayed he wouldn't try to shake my hand.

"Young'n," he said, his voice gravelly, "your mama at home?"

"Yes, sir," I said, opening the door wide to let him in. As the sheriff walked past, everything about him creaked. His polished boots, his belt, his holster, it all creaked. Despite the fact that he was smoking a cigarette, he smelled fresh and clean. His presence intimidated me.

He asked Mothball and me if we'd seen Jimmy, and as we gave the same answers we'd already given our mothers, he jotted down some notes on the inside of a black pad. Then he asked if we wouldn't mind going outside for a few while he talked to the ladies in private. I thought that was the best idea anyone had ever suggested.

We walked down the walkway in front of the house and sat on the curb next to Sheriff Walls's parked prowler. Heat from the engine wavered off the hood. The car made noises like a house settling, even though the ignition was turned off. Refrigerant dripped from underneath the car, creating a little pool that meandered toward the curb and our feet. Inside the car, a radio squawked unintelligible static-filled messages every so often.

"We gotta say something, Walter. We're gonna get caught. The cops always catch the bad guys."

"We aren't the bad guys," I said. "And if you were so

itching to tell, you had your chance. Why didn't you say something to Mrs. Haddsby or the sheriff?"

"I was scared. I didn't know what you'd say."

"Mothball, we didn't do anything. Besides, it's too late to say something now."

"What do you mean? It's not too late."

"Sure it is," I said. "We've already told everybody, including the sheriff, that we haven't seen him. How do you think it would look if we all of the sudden decided to change our story? 'Oh, yeah, Sheriff, I just remembered, we did see Jimmy last night. We snuck out and went swimming at the river. I plumb forgot. And by the way, I put a rope around his neck and hung him like a sack of onions from the rafters.' How do you think that'd sound? Next thing you know, he'd have us in jail for murder."

"That's crazy," said Mothball. "They don't put kids in jail."

"They do if they think we murdered our friend," I said. "We've got to stick to our story. You're the one always watching *The Rockford Files*."

"Yeah, so?"

"Well, then you know that changing your story is the worst thing you can do. Once you do that, it's all over. Have you thought about what it would be like if we told? Even if we were found innocent, everybody would look at us funny and gossip about us for the rest of our lives. There'd always be people talking behind our backs."

"Shit, Walter. We're in deep."

"Yeah, we're in deep. Real deep," I said. "You scared?"

"Are you kidding? I'm shitting bricks. I've never been more scared in my life. I kept tossing and turning last night, thinking about everything. Thinking about Mrs. Haddsby needing to know the truth. Freaking out over the thought of getting caught. Wondering what went through Jimmy's mind. You know?"

"Yeah, me too. Exactly the same."

We both stared off down the street toward Jimmy's house. It seemed strange that the rest of the town continued to carry on as if nothing had happened: people drove by, going about their business, waving if they saw us; the birds sang; the Simmons sulfur stunk as bad as it ever did. Nothing had really changed.

"Last night," said Mothball, "when I was in bed and playing it all over in my mind, I started wondering about something."

"Yeah? What's that?"

"When I went to get the lighter, why did Jimmy yell? What did you do?"

"It all happened so fast. He tried to hit me, just like he'd hit you earlier. I dodged him, he slipped, I tried to grab him, and then he was gone. But he didn't yell."

"Yeah, he did," said Mothball. "Just before everything happened, I thought I heard him say, 'What the hell are you doing?' Or, 'What the fuck are you doing?' Or something like that."

"He did? I think I said that."

"No, I'm almost positive it was Jimmy."

"No, it was me," I said. "I think I yelled that just before he splashed in the water. Or maybe it was when he tried to hit me. I don't remember."

Mothball looked at me strangely for a second, almost as if he didn't believe me. "That's really weird," he said. "I could have sworn it was Jimmy."

"Think about it, Mothball. That doesn't make any sense. Why would Jimmy say that? He tried to hit me, and then next thing I know, he went flying off."

"Yeah, I guess you're right. It doesn't make any sense. None of this makes any sense. Jesus, Walter, Jimmy's really gone." Tears formed in the corners of his eyes.

"I know. It doesn't seem real," I said.

"Walter," he said tentatively, "after we found him in the water, why did you let him go? I mean, you knew he was alive, right?"

"I think you were hearing all kinds of weird stuff last night," I said, turning to look him straight in the eye. "He didn't say anything until after I let him go. I'm positive."

"I might be wrong about when y'all were on the tree, but I know I heard him before you let him go. I heard him before you even got his feet loose from that rock."

"Well, maybe that's it. Maybe I was under water trying to get his legs free and didn't hear him. Shit, I don't know. But I never heard him until it was too late."

Mothball looked at me strangely again. He said, "Walter, I heard him while you were holding his feet. I know for a fact because that's when I started trying to wade back out to y'all. I was coming to help. I remember thinking that I couldn't believe he was still alive. I couldn't believe that he had actually survived."

"I was standing right there, and I didn't hear shit," I said, starting to get defensive. "I was looking right at him. It was dark, but I saw his face. His eyes were closed and he looked unconscious. Or dead, I guess. I don't know. Maybe the storm and the rush of the river made it hard for me to hear."

Mothball looked at me again. His eyes told me he still didn't buy my story.

"What?" I said. "You don't believe me? You think I knew but let him go anyway?"

He looked away and stared at the sheriff's patrol car. "I didn't say that. It's just weird. I don't see how you couldn't have heard him. He was practically screaming."

"I didn't hear him, okay?" I yelled, then lowered my voice as I turned around and looked at my house. "The only time I heard anything was just after I let him go."

"Okay, I believe you," he said, but it was unconvincing. "And one thing I know we both heard was that splash in the water. What the hell was that?"

"Like I said last night, I think it was probably a deer or something trying to get out of the storm. It probably got confused, or couldn't see, and accidentally fell into the river."

"Maybe it was Jimmy. Maybe he somehow revived and made his way out," said Mothball, the excitement rising in his voice with each new thought. "Maybe he's still alive."

"If it was Jimmy, why did we hear something in the leaves *first,* and then a splash *after?* Think about it. That makes no sense."

We both sat there in silence. The possibility of Jimmy still being alive bothered me. What if he walked up to us while we sat on the curb? What would he do? What would he say? But I knew that wasn't possible. I couldn't explain what the splash was that we'd heard, but I knew it hadn't been Jimmy. It couldn't have been.

I stared at the road, which the heat of the morning had already dried after last night's storm. Night crawlers lay curled and crisp all over the asphalt, a lot of good fishing bait wasted. Eventually Sheriff Walls came out with Mrs. Haddsby and Mrs. Cleilsky. He opened the doors of his prowler and helped them get in. Just before Mrs. Cleilsky got in the car, she said, "Raymond, come on with me. I want you to come home."

"I think I'll walk," he said. "I'll be home in a minute."

She glanced at Sheriff Walls for guidance. He nodded, giving her assurance.

"Okay, but hurry back."

Sheriff Walls closed the door behind her and creaked his way around the car to the driver's side. Before he got in, he said, "Don't y'all worry, boys. Everything'll be fine. He'll show up soon, and we'll get all these questions answered. He probably just ran off for a little while. That's usually the case." He forced a smile.

Apprehension and nausea welled up in my stomach once more. I wondered if Mothball was experiencing the same thing. The prowler pulled off and headed down the road.

"What do we do now?" asked Mothball. "I mean, what's gonna happen?"

"I don't know. When Jimmy doesn't show up, they'll start looking for him, I guess. Search parties and stuff."

"Jesus, he's in that river somewhere. They might not ever find him. I'm scared."

"I'm scared, too. But I guess we just stick to our story. We can't tell anyone, ever. You're gonna have to die with this secret, Mothball."

"Maybe we should've told somebody last night."

"Well, it's too late now. Look, I've been thinking about it. Whether we told or not, Jimmy'd still be gone, right?"

"I guess so."

"So, we chose not to tell. We might've screwed up, but now we gotta deal with it. We didn't know what we were doing. I let go of him when I should've held on a little longer. Maybe we could've saved him, maybe not. We'll never know. At this point, the only good that telling would do is maybe they'd find Jimmy's body a little faster."

"You're right, Walter. Shit, I'm sorry. I ain't accusing you of nothing. It's just all so weird. I don't know what the hell I'm thinking. Maybe I didn't even hear him yell. I don't even know no more."

"Forget it," I said. "We just gotta play it cool and act like we don't know anything. Shoot, that should be easy for you."

Mothball gave a little chuckle as he stood up. He still had tears in his eyes.

"I guess I better go feed Mike," he said. "He's probably starving."

"Come by later and we'll walk to town. You know, things are gonna be different now."

"Yeah, no kidding. Who's gonna give me hell and try to kill me from now on?"

Now I chuckled, which only hours before I didn't think I'd ever be able to do again. "It won't be me. You know that."

"I'll stop by later," he said.

He smiled and turned to go. I swear he looked relieved, almost happy. I think I felt the same way.

Chapter 12

Mothball never came by, and it wouldn't have mattered anyway because Mom said I wasn't leaving the house. She was afraid some maniac might be on the loose and I'd be next. She'd been on the phone all day, talking back and forth with Mrs. Cleilsky, trying to get any information she could.

"The sheriff set up a search party," said Mom as we sat at the table that night. Supper was almost unbearable since I had to concentrate so hard on not showing my hands. But somehow I managed to keep them hidden, even though I could hardly hold my fork and knife. "And if Jimmy doesn't show up by tonight, they're going out looking for him tomorrow. I heard they might even get bloodhounds from over in Lafayette."

"Is that right?" said Dad, who seemed more interested in his pork chops than any of my mother's babble. My heart jumped at the thought of bloodhounds showing up on my back porch, yelping and causing a commotion.

"But they don't know how much good that'll do, seeing as how we had that storm last night. They're treating his disappearance as suspicious. That's what Mildred said."

I wondered where they got their information and how

much of it was actually true. A missing boy was probably big news in any town, but in Woodley, where nothing too exciting ever happened anyway, this was an epic event. I'd even found myself getting caught up in the hoopla, and I knew the truth. And as strange as it may sound, it was kind of neat knowing the real story while listening to all of the wrong theories Mom gathered from the neighborhood women. I should have been sad about Jimmy being gone, I guess, but I was more worried about being found out. The idea that I knew the real truth sort of excited me. As if I held all of the cards.

"If you ask me," continued my mother, "I think Sheriff Walls should start the investigation right at Jimmy's home, beginning with that no-good Macon Haddsby. I wouldn't be at all surprised if he had something to do with it. Not to mention that tramp of a mother, who—"

My father slammed down his fork. Half of his snap beans still stuck to the tines, half were in his mouth. "Good Lord, Louise, would you give it a rest? Where do you come up with this nonsense?"

"Don't you try and tell me, Gene Sithol, that you haven't been thinking the same thing. You know good and well that man comes from questionable upbringing. I bet there's not a soul in all of Woodley who doesn't have at least a smidgen of suspicion about Macon Haddsby. Mildred said he didn't even act concerned when he came back from Lafayette and Lydia told him about Jimmy.

Apparently he just got himself a beer and turned on the television."

"Hell, I'd have probably done the same thing," said Dad.

"He killed his own brother," said Mom, "that much we know for sure."

My heart raced with her words. Dad gave an exasperated sigh as he went back to his pork chop. "That was an accident, in case you forgot," he said. "Walter was there. He saw the whole thing."

"It was an accident, Mom," I said. "He didn't know that snake would kill Ox."

"Seems to me that even a God-blessed imbecile would know that a rattlesnake can kill you," she said. "Anyway, I still think the sheriff should start at their house. They say most crimes are committed by someone the victim knows."

That sent my heart racing again.

"Who in the hell is 'they,' Louise? Who exactly said that?"

"I don't know. That's just what I heard."

"For Christ's sake, you're talking like the boy is dead. He's been missing for what, twelve hours? He probably has a girl or something. You know how boys do."

"I'm perfectly aware of what boys are capable of when it comes to girls," said Mom, casting a vicious look at Dad. "You don't need to remind me of that." Dad looked back down at his food as if he were a dog just scolded by its master. She turned to me. "Does Jimmy have a special girl, Walter? Someone he's sweet on?"

"No, I don't think so."

"You see?" said Mom, looking at Dad. "Something bad has happened. I just know it. I get a feeling sometimes, and ever since this morning, even before Lydia came over, I knew something had happened to that nasty boy."

"For God's sake," said Dad as he slid his chair back from the table. He dropped his fork on the plate, left the kitchen, and went out the back door.

I helped Mom clear the dishes, bringing them to her at the sink. I was intrigued with the idea that Mr. Haddsby could possibly become a suspect. In fact, I thought it might be fair justice if somehow he got arrested for Jimmy's death.

"Walter, what happened to your hands, child?" asked Mom when I brought the last of the dishes to the counter. "They look awful."

Panic filled my head, though I'd already prepared an excuse. "I was swinging on some kudzu vine and lost my grip. Slipped all the way down. It's nothing, Mom."

"My hind foot, it's nothing. Give me those hands."

She examined my wounds for a moment, then ran to the bathroom and came back with a can of Bactine spray and some bandages. She grabbed my wrists and sprayed my palms. The burns instantly began pulsing, and a white foam bubbled up over the gashes as the medicine killed the germs. Mom raised my hands to her lips and started blowing, soothing them. She wrapped both hands in gauze. I looked just like I did after I had tried to catch that turkey for Mothball.

"You need to be more careful," she said. "You've got to tell me when things like this happen so I can doctor you up. I swear."

"Yes, ma'am," I said, relieved that I no longer had to hide my hands. "I will."

❧

Two days later, Jimmy still hadn't been found. The blood-hounds had come from Lafayette, just like Mom said, but they hadn't picked up a trace of anything. I felt pretty safe that Mothball and I were in the clear. I just wanted to move on and not have to deal with that nagging worry that always seemed to be in the back of my mind: *What if? What if somehow they figure out I was with Jimmy that night?* Or worse yet, *What if Jimmy suddenly shows up alive and tells everyone what I did?* I didn't know how I'd explain that one. *What if it was him who made that splash? Or what if someone else was in the woods and rescued him? What if that was what caused the splash? Another person?*

The state police had been called in to aid in the investigation, and police cruisers were at Jimmy's house almost constantly. There was a rumor circulating that they were going to dredge the river soon, once the high water subsided. The storm had been really violent north of us, with tornadoes and torrential rainfall, and all that water was still filtering down from upstream. There was no telling how far downstream Jimmy had been pulled. I wondered if the carp and catfish had gotten a hold of him yet. A strange, hollow feeling filled my gut when I thought about that. I don't think it was guilt or remorse, but whatever it was, it was uncomfortable.

The day Jimmy's body was found, four days after Mrs. Haddsby had discovered him missing, Mothball and I had gone to town and were right there when the commotion started. Mom had finally consented to let me out, after a lot of begging and pleading, as long as I was with Mothball and home before dark. We were sitting in front of the abandoned gas station, pelting the metal Phillips 66 sign with stones, when several cruisers ripped through town. A station-wagon ambulance followed. They stopped at the bridge, right in front of the path that led to the Troll's shack. We ran down the road to see what was happening. Police officers stood on the other side of the guardrail, blocking the path, but they couldn't stop us from walking on the bridge, so that's what we did.

Looking downstream from the bridge, we saw a throng

of men on the riverbank, about fifty yards past the Troll's shack. Directly below us, oblivious to the goings-on around them, a pair of huge carp, at least fifteen pounds apiece, lazily fed in a patch of alligator weed, their backs reflecting the gold of the sunshine. A snapping turtle as big around as a tire sunned itself on the exposed part of a boulder jutting up out of the river. Once the commotion got to be too much for him, he slipped off the rock and disappeared into the water, barely causing a wake. On the bank stood police officers, firemen, and a group of local men—including my father, as I found out later—who were part of a volunteer search crew. I could see a few men wading in the water, shrouded in a vast patch of water hyacinth, the purple flowers floating like a fleet of toy boats around them.

Reporters showed up almost immediately. The officers wouldn't let them down to the actual scene, so they set up cameras on the bridge right next to us, like carrion crows. I don't know how they found out so fast, but they were there. It was really too far to see what was going on, and a half-hour passed before anything of interest happened. At first, all I saw was a group of men standing around in circles near the riverbank. But there was no mistaking the white sheet covering a body that two men eventually carried away on a wooden gurney. Mothball started crying when he saw the sheet. He'd been Mr. Cool for as long as he could manage, but seeing the sheet broke his back.

"Jesus, Walter," he whispered. "It's really happening now."

"I know it, Mothball," I replied, careful to keep my voice down because of the reporters. A crowd had formed all along the bridge, most leaning against the concrete railing to try to get a look. "But what did you expect?"

"I know," he said. "But now it's real. Before it all seemed like a dream. But not now. He's under that sheet down there."

We struggled to keep our position against the railing as more people shoved their way in to get a peek. A group of coloreds strolled across from the other side of the bridge. I saw Oreo among them. When he saw me, he broke through the crowd, sidled up on my right side, and said, "Hey, boy. Ain't that your brother that's been missing?"

"He's not my brother," I said, guilt welling inside. "But, yeah, that's my friend."

"No kidding? I always thought you was brothers. I'm sorry for you, young'n."

"Thanks, Oreo."

He watched the men carrying the gurney and said, "Don't look too good." Tears started filling my eyes, not so much because of Jimmy being found, but more because I think Oreo was genuinely sorry. "You come by and see me tomorrow and I'll give you a free bag."

"Okay," I said. I wiped my eyes with the bottom of my shirt. "Thanks, Oreo."

Everyone watched as the two men carrying the gurney walked through the canebrake, past the Troll's shack, and up toward the street. The police had cordoned off the road with tape and orange cones, so now we were all trapped on the bridge. The men placed the gurney in the back of the ambulance and shut the door. The crowd moved to the sides as the ambulance weaved around the cones, over the bridge, and off toward Lafayette. Murmurs of foul play kept coming up in different conversations. It seemed that murder was what the crowd wanted to believe; things were more exciting that way. I knew they would never admit to it, but I also knew it was true. Death was interesting and exciting, and murder even more so.

If nothing else, that's one thing I learned that day. People will usually show their good side and how they are such fine, loving folks, but in reality they are all a bunch of hypocrites. It's true, I know, because I'd been feeling the same way since everything happened. It was just like the time my mother and I passed by a bad car accident on our way back from Lafayette one day. A Duster had taken a curve too fast and flipped over on its roof, partially submerged in swamp water that lay in a channel next to the road. Garbage, newspapers, beer cans, broken glass, parts of the car, and all kinds of other stuff were strewn about. In the road, in the water, in the cattails, everywhere. I remember seeing a mangled baby stroller mashed up against a pine and instantly wondered if a child had been in the car. I had sort of hoped there was. I knew it was wrong, but I couldn't help it.

And I wasn't the only one. Even though my mother kept saying things such as "Oh, how awful" and "I hope no one is seriously hurt," she went past extra slow even though the officer on the scene waved her by. She craned her neck the whole time, not even watching the road, looking to see whatever horrible things might lie crushed beneath the caved-in roof. The look on her face told me she was hoping to see something unspeakable.

Mothball and I stuck around town for a while, watching the bedlam. More police cars than I thought were in the whole state of Alabama filled the streets. Because of Mothball's prodding, we eventually went to my house to eat some lunch. Mom, with tears in her eyes, made us baloney sandwiches. She'd heard the news about Jimmy well before we got home.

"I'm so sorry, boys," she said. "Your father was part of the search team and was right there when they pulled him from the river. He's awfully shaken up."

"Dad was there?" I asked in disbelief. "Where is he now?"

"He's upstairs in the bedroom. He wanted to be alone. Walter, I want you and Mothball to stick together at all times until they catch the monster that did this."

Mom had just called Mothball by his nickname. She'd always said it wasn't proper. I was stunned. Mothball even took a minute to stop chewing his second sandwich to give me a look. Something was definitely wrong.

"What do you mean, 'monster'?" I asked. "What's going on?"

"Boys, I might as well tell you since you're going to find out sooner or later. Your father saw Jimmy's body up close." She hesitated for a moment before she continued. "He said there was no doubt in his mind that Jimmy was murdered."

Mothball and I looked at each other in disbelief.

"What do you mean?" I asked. "Why does he think that?"

Mom got flustered and lost control of her emotions. She started bawling right there in front of us. She came over and hugged me tightly as I sat in a chair at the table.

"You'll have to ask your father," she said through sobs. "I can't bear to repeat it."

"Come on, Mothball. I wanna know what he saw."

Mothball stuffed the last of his potato chips into his mouth and scooted away from the table. We headed for the stairs. Halfway up, he pulled at my sleeve.

"What is she talking about?" he mouthed to me, barely audible.

"I have no idea," I said, whispering back.

"What do you think he saw?"

"I don't know. But if they think Jimmy got murdered, there're going to be a lot more questions for us. I guarantee it."

"Maybe we should've just said something right at the beginning."

"Jesus, don't start that again," I said.

"I can't help it," said Mothball, tears welling up, clouding his brown eyes. He looked as white as the wall behind him in the stairwell. He reached out and grabbed the banister. I thought he might faint. "Holy shit, Walter, I'm scared. We're gonna go to prison. I just know it. We're doomed. We should've told the truth."

"We don't even know what my mom is talking about. You know how she exaggerates. Let's go talk to my dad first, then we'll figure things out."

I tapped on the door, then opened it just a pinch to look in. Dad lay on top of the bedspread with pillows propped behind his head. His hands were locked behind his neck, his elbows pointing out in front of him. The window-unit air conditioner pumped out cool air. The shades were pulled, casting a blue glow around the dark room.

"Dad?" I whispered. He turned to see my head poking from around the door. "Can we come in?"

"What? Uh, yeah, come on in." He unlocked his hands and scooted himself up, repositioning his body.

We crept in slowly. Mothball shut the door behind him.

"How you fellas doing?" He spoke in the gentlest voice I'd ever heard come from his mouth. I'd seen my dad get mad, angry, exasperated, but I'd never seen his face as troubled and anguished as it was at that moment. He looked old, even fragile.

"I'm okay, I guess," I said.

"Fine, Mr. Sithol," said Mothball.

"Here," he said, pulling his feet up to sit Indian-style, "take a seat."

I sat down. Mothball sat next to me at the end of the bed. I looked at the dim room and the framed pictures of me from each year's school portrait—from kindergarten through eighth grade—all in a perfect row along the wall. Dad reached over to the nightstand for his glasses and slipped them on. In the locked drawer of the nightstand, I knew, was Mom's diary—the diary that had told me so many of her secrets. I thought about what I'd read as Dad reached for a sweating glass of water sitting on a white doily.

"Dad," I said, nervous about uttering the words. "Mom said you think Jimmy might have been murdered? Is that—"

He made a sudden movement as he grabbed his face and exhaled heavily. He rubbed his hands across his cheeks, over his eyes, and up through his hair.

"—is that true?"

"Goddammit," he said. "I told her not to say anything."

"She said we would find out soon enough anyway. Is it true?"

He exhaled again. "Yeah, it's true. At least, that's what I think. And everyone else that saw his body thought the same thing, including the law."

"Maybe he just drowned," I said. I stared ahead at the pictures—with all of my own faces staring back at me—not able to turn and look at him. "Couldn't that be it?"

"I don't think so. I mean, yeah, I think he drowned, because his body was bloated. But someone did it to him, no doubt about it. But I'm not supposed to say anything. The sheriff told us not to say a word because it might hamper the investigation."

"He was our best friend," I said. "We deserve to know."

"I can't," he said, and then hesitated for a moment. He appeared to be in deep thought, pondering something. "Well, maybe I can tell you a little, but I can't tell you everything. And y'all have to promise me you'll never let it leave this room. Understand?"

"Yes, sir. I promise."

"Yes, sir, Mr. Sithol," said Mothball. "I swear."

"Dave Green and Grumpy Barrett were the ones who first found Jimmy's body. They were part of the search team that I was on. We were split off into pairs, walking a grid. They were the team working closest to the bank. I was about twenty-five yards away with Mr. Jenkins. You know him, the old colored janitor at the elementary?"

"Yes, sir," I said.

"We were going through the canebrake when Grumpy Barrett yelled that he'd found something. We all ran over to see, and sure enough there was Jimmy, though at first it was hard to tell. He was twisted in the roots of an old sycamore along the bank. Only his left leg was above the water, the rest was tucked underneath the tree. None of us dared touch him. They'd warned us not to if we found anything."

Dad grabbed the glass of water and took a sip. Mothball and I looked at each other; he looked as uncomfortable as I felt.

"About a hundred cops, it seemed, were there in a second. It took forever before they pulled him out of the water, but I guess they knew what they were doing."

Dad paused again, taking a deep breath. He exhaled slowly.

"When they set him down, it was clear to me right away that his neck was broken. It didn't look right. I could see a big bump poking out, nearly popping through the skin. And there was a red scar from ear to ear. As far as I could tell, someone strangled that boy. There's no question about it in my mind."

My brain raced around, recreating the scene of just before Jimmy went into the water. "Did Sheriff Walls say
anything about who he thinks did it?" I asked. "Or why?"

"He didn't say anything about that, and I don't expect
he could have even if he did know. They have to be real
careful how they handle those kinds of things. You know
how all that stuff goes."

"Yeah, I guess so," I said.

"I'm so sorry about everything, boys, but that's all I
can say. I said too much already. The sheriff promised that
he'd find the animal that did it. He swore on it."

Mothball started sobbing, but I stayed strong. I refused
to cry in front of my dad. He'd always said crying was for
women and girls, not men.

"Why don't you boys go on now. I want to be alone for
a while."

I got off the bed and nudged Mothball in the ribs with
my elbow. He got up.

"Thanks for telling us," I said.

He put his hands behind his neck again and nodded.

"Come on, Mothball. Let's leave my dad alone."

"Okay," he said, crying. Snot bubbled at his nose. "See
you around, Mr. Sithol."

"All right, Raymond. And remember, boys: I told y'all
all this in confidence."

As I went to close the door, I looked back at Dad and
could have sworn I saw tears starting to stream down his

face. I turned my head away quickly, not wanting him to think I might have seen him. I couldn't help but glance at the locked drawer of the nightstand once more before I shut the door.

We walked down the stairs and out the front door, taking a seat on the porch under the shade of the awning. The heat hit us hard after being in the air conditioning.

"We're in a load of shit now, Walter."

"No, we're not," I said. "We're gonna be fine."

"We killed him. You said I should pay him back. You called me a jellyfish."

"Mothball, we didn't do anything."

"Yeah, but we didn't tell the truth about being there, and now they think Jimmy was murdered. If I'd known all this was gonna happen, I'd've told right away."

"But you didn't know," I said. "There was no way for us to know."

"What are we gonna do, Walter?"

I thought for a moment, contemplating our bleak options. "We're gonna do just what my dad said to do. We're not gonna say a word. We can't."

❦

The town of Woodley was in an uproar like no one had ever seen before. Parents demanded answers, they wouldn't let their kids outside, and a wild panic swept through the neighborhoods. Newspaper reporters came from as far away as Atlanta, and there was even a television crew that filmed some footage and did a story on the six o'clock news. They showed a picture of Jimmy on the screen with his full name below it: Jimmy Dean Haddsby. If Jimmy had seen that, he'd have had a fit. He hated his full name. As I watched the report, I got that familiar feeling of knowing more than everyone else. It pleased me.

A few days after Jimmy's body was discovered, I found myself walking between my mother and father as we headed into the church for his funeral. Right inside the door, behind a piece of glass, was a message on the marquee made with white plastic letters on black felt.

> **SATURDAY**
> **JIMMY DEAN HADDSBY FUNERAL**
> **SUNDAY**
> **CATFISH FRY AND WATERMELON CELEBRATION**

It was the same church where Ox's service had been a few months before. There was no air conditioning, and I found it hard to breathe. Mom made me wear a pair of wool slacks and a matching blazer that she'd bought at a pawn shop in Lafayette. The clothes were unbearably hot. Jimmy's funeral was held at noon on the hottest day of the summer so far. Every woman in the church held a paper fan in front of her face, and they all fluttered them like hummingbird wings.

All I wanted to do was get out of that church and into some comfortable clothes. I'd already dealt with Jimmy's death now for more than a week. It was still a shock for everyone else, but for me, well, I was pretty numb to it all by that time. I felt guilty for the way I felt, but it was kind of like when I'd seen that crushed baby stroller against the pine tree after the car accident; I just couldn't help it. And in a weird way, I was sort of glad he was gone. Now it was only me and Mothball. Neither of us had to worry anymore about what Jimmy might do next. About what he might say.

As hot as it was, the odor from all the perspiring bodies was masked to some degree by the smell of the fresh flowers that filled the church. The choir sang a lot of songs, much to my mother's delight, and there was plenty of crying from most of the women. Strangely, Mom didn't cry. Even though she didn't like Jimmy, I thought she would have at least cried to make herself look good, but she didn't. Mrs. Haddsby bawled continuously throughout, and I noticed that my father never took his gaze off her. He didn't cry, but he seemed even more distraught than when he'd been up in his room telling me and Mothball about finding Jimmy.

While the preacher talked, I found myself thinking about other things. I didn't think about the night Jimmy died at the river, or the firecrackers, or even the possibility of me and Mothball getting caught. Mainly I reflected on something that had happened to Jimmy and me when we were a whole lot younger, around six or seven. We'd been down the street at the construction site where the O'Kanes' house was being rebuilt. It was weird, because at Ox's funeral I'd thought about the time I burned the house down, and now, at Jimmy's funeral, I found myself thinking about something else that happened there.

On the day that I was now thinking about, Jimmy and I had been stomping around the grounds, searching for soda bottles. We could get a nickel per bottle if we returned them to the grocery store; the grocery was still up and running at that time. As we looked for bottles, I kept reflecting on how fascinated I'd been as I'd watched the house burn. At one point, as we rummaged around, I'd almost confided in Jimmy that I was the one who set the place on fire. But even then, at such a young age, that stronger part of me said to keep quiet.

The house wasn't finished yet, though it at least resembled the shell of one. It was framed, and there was plywood up all around, but the windows weren't installed yet. No front door either, no carpeting, nothing like that. The grass was gone too; it was all just bare red clay, with water-filled tire tracks from heavy machinery streaking through the yard. The deepest parts of the tracks were filled with brown pools of water, and, if stirred with a stick, they began to stink like a dead animal on the side of the road.

We found a handful of bottles and stacked them by a pile of scrap wood. We also found several beer bottles, which weren't any good for deposit money, so we set them up around the property for the purpose of smashing. One bottle sat on the ledge of the future kitchen window— where I'd watched the old one melt the year before— another on some two-by-fours, and I managed to get one to hang from the branch of a pine tree by forcing the mouth of it over the end of the limb, stuffing the needles inside. We grabbed stones from the driveway and got ready to blast the bottles.

"Those are the gooks in the jungle," said Jimmy, "and we're the Americans. We gotta kill 'em."

We took turns whipping rocks at the bottles. Jimmy connected with the one in the windowsill, sending it into the house, where it crashed. Since the house sat back from the road, nestled in a grove of pine, no neighbors seemed to notice as we smashed the bottles in our crusade against the Viet Cong. Jimmy had just clipped the bottle hanging from the tree limb, though he didn't break it, and I was readying myself for a shot when a voice suddenly made me halt in mid-throw.

"What the hell do y'all think you're doing?"

I froze. Jimmy stared, wide-eyed, at someone behind me. I turned to see who it was. The owner of the voice was a skinny teenager, maybe seventeen or eighteen. He had long stringy hair flowing down from under a blue baseball cap, and his eyes were haunting and weird. Like they were too close together or something. He was one of those guys who looked like trouble. I knew we were in for it.

"Y'all think it's okay to go around busting bottles?" he asked. "What if someone sliced their foot on a piece? And who do you think is gonna clean up all this mess?"

Jimmy and I dropped our heads, hangdog, not saying a word.

"I said, who the hell is gonna clean this up?" He yelled it this time. I felt tears welling, but I clenched my teeth in order not to cry.

"We will," said Jimmy, barely audible, almost a whisper.

"You're goddamn right, you will," he said. I lifted my eyes for just a second to see the guy glaring down at us. "But first y'all need to be punished. What you both need is a good whipping. Come on," he said, pointing toward the open doorway. "In the house."

Despite my attempts to squelch the whimpers, I simply couldn't. My lower lip trembled and my breath became short. Jimmy remained stonefaced, though I could tell he was equally scared. Just as I thought about trying to run, the boy grabbed each of us under an arm and shoved us toward the house. When I tried to pull away, he squeezed my arm tight. He steered us onto a pair of two-by-fours that acted as a ramp leading up to the front door; the steps hadn't been built yet. The boards bucked slightly as Jimmy and I walked up the ramp, and then bounced violently as the boy climbed on behind us. Inside, the house smelled of fresh pine and sawdust, though there was still the faint odor of burnt wood; muddy footprints stained the floors.

"Come on," he said. "Head to that back room." Jimmy led, and I followed right behind him, sniffling. The back room he referred to was apparently a bedroom. The room already had sliding closet doors installed, as well as a regular door. The boy closed it behind him as he shut us in, turning the lock in the knob.

"I'll teach you scumbags to break bottles," he said. "What y'all both need is a good punishment. You," he said, pointing at Jimmy, "get in that closet."

Jimmy grabbed my shoulders and shoved me toward the teenager.

"Okay," said the boy, glaring at Jimmy, "you'll go last. That is far worse." He grabbed my arm above the elbow and led me toward the closet door, where he slid it open and pushed me inside. He closed it, shutting me off from the two of them. I backed myself into a dark corner and shook, waiting for the unknown.

"Don't you move a muscle," said the boy to Jimmy. "You stay right there until I'm ready for you. You understand?"

"Yes, sir," said Jimmy. I barely heard him.

The closet door slid open, rumbling along its tracks. He stood at the opening for a moment before walking in and closing the door behind him. I backed up even tighter into the corner. His breathing was raspy as it bounced off the confines of the closet.

"Pull down your pants," he said, but in a different voice. This voice was soft and gentle. I was too young to understand his intention, but I knew it wasn't anything good.

Trembling, I dropped my shorts. Though I couldn't see him as he went to his knees, I felt his warm breath brush my face. He cooed, "See, I won't hurt you."

But just before he was about to touch me, the door to the room slammed.

"Shit," said the boy. "Goddammit, I told him not to move." He stood up and ripped the sliding door open. He pulled so hard that it popped out of its bottom track. The light shocked my eyes. "You stay right there. Don't even think about leaving."

I stood in the corner, crying and shaking and not knowing what to do. I waited for a moment, then finally pulled up my shorts and ran from the closet, out of the bedroom, and exited the house, bouncing along the two-by-fours. I didn't see either Jimmy or the boy anywhere. I ran down the street, heading straight for home.

I was a blubbering mess by the time I got to my mother. I told her everything that had happened, and she called the sheriff.

Only a few days after the boy tried to molest me, my mother and I were visiting over at Papa's house. Mom had already told Papa about everything the same day that it had happened, and Papa had been irate. He'd made me describe to him exactly what the boy looked like, down to the tiniest detail. He'd talked to Sheriff Walls personally and demanded that the boy be caught, but they had no leads. I'd never seen, before or since, Papa as angry as he had been during the days following the incident.

As it turned out, on the day we were at Papa's, the boy's picture showed up in the local paper, not as a suspect but as a missing person. In the article, it said that the boy's mother had reported him missing just two days after he'd taken Jimmy and me into the house. The mother stated that she remembered hearing something, a disturbance of some sort, late at night, but didn't think anything of it and fell back asleep. The next morning, when she awoke, her son was gone. His wallet was still on the nightstand, never touched. The newspaper said the incident was being treated as suspicious.

When I saw the paper on Papa's kitchen table, I told my mom and him that the boy in the picture was the same one who'd tried to hurt me. Mom immediately called the sheriff. Quickly, the boy's disappearance status changed from being suspicious to a case of a runaway. The sheriff told Mom that the boy probably got scared and fled before getting caught, though it seemed strange to me that he didn't at least take his wallet. They never found the boy, either alive or dead.

The whole incident—the attempted molestation, Papa's anger, the boy's disappearance—hadn't really affected me all that much at the time. Probably because I was so young and because nothing had actually happened to me. It wouldn't be until years later that I'd finally figure out how significant the whole thing had been.

I never blamed Jimmy for pushing me and making me go into the closet first. I believed that Jimmy, in fact, saved me by slamming the door and running away. At the time, I felt that if I hadn't escaped—if the boy hadn't given chase and had instead stayed with me—Jimmy would have told his mom and I would have been rescued anyway. But now, as I sat on the pew at his funeral, I wasn't so sure that he would have.

My mother grabbed my elbow, whispering for me to get up. I'd gotten so lost in thought that I hadn't even realized the service had ended. The next thing I knew, I was back outside in the crushing heat. I got in the car with Mom and Dad, and we drove the half mile over to the cemetery. As I got out, I still felt as if I were in a numb daze. The sun was extremely bright, and I envied my father, who had on a pair of dark sunglasses. I would have given anything to have a pair, not only to stifle the glare, but also to hide behind.

A crowd of people had formed at the back corner of the cemetery. A large open-sided tent hovered over the ditch where Jimmy's casket would soon be lowered, and there were a few metal folding chairs lined up underneath it, resting on a square of artificial turf. Mr. and Mrs. Haddsby sat while everyone else stood in small groups, talking quietly. Mothball stood next to his mom and Carver on the far side of the tent. Though he was a good ways off, I could tell he'd been doing a lot of crying.

Sweat dripped from my head, and the wool of the suit started scratching and irritating my skin. Different headstones sprang vertically from the ground, seeming to encircle me on every side. Some were so old that I couldn't even decipher the writing on them. They had turned nearly black from years of exposure and were sporadically splotched with lesions of gray lichen. There were other markers that lay flush with the ground, in similar states of ruin, which couldn't be read because of the thin fingers of Bermuda grass creeping over them. Those headstones made death seem so real to me. So permanent.

The preacher said some words, but thankfully he kept

it short. A few men then proceeded to lower Jimmy's casket into the ground. Mr. and Mrs. Haddsby each grabbed a handful of red clay from the pile next to the ditch, tossed their respective clods on top of the lid, and then it was over. Mom, I could tell, wanted to socialize, but Dad got us out of there quickly. It appeared he wanted to leave just as badly as I did.

CHAPTER 13

TWO DAYS AFTER THE FUNERAL, Mothball came over in the late afternoon and asked if I wanted to go to town, just to bum around. I let Mom know where we were going.

"You two be careful and stick together," she said. "And be home before dark."

"Yes, ma'am," I said. "We'll be careful."

We walked toward town, meandering along the streets, crisscrossing whenever there was a good stretch of shade offered by either the elms lining the sidewalk or the mimosa trees, with their fernlike leaves, arching softly over the blacktop. At the Big House, we stopped for a moment, looking at the little bare spots on the fence where Jimmy had stripped it for toothpicks. I glanced at Mothball, but he only stared down at his feet. We walked the rest of the way in silence.

We sat on the steps of the five-and-dime, our bodies shaded thanks to the awning hovering over the entranceway. I grabbed a handful of pebbles from the road and pitched them in front of us, one after the other. Across the street, on the front porch of the hardware store, two old men dressed in overalls sat in wicker chairs, a table in between them, playing dominoes. I recognized one man as Grumpy Barrett, the man who had helped find Jimmy's body. The men didn't look up, and they didn't seem to notice or care that Mothball and I stared at them; they were highly focused on their game.

I looked down the street and wondered why Oreo wasn't at his stand. It seemed like the perfect time to be set up, what with all the strangers—reporters, sightseers, policemen from neighboring counties—driving around town and all.

"What do you think will happen now?" asked Mothball.

"Shoot, I don't know."

"Mom told me the sheriff was determined to find Jimmy's killer. Said the state police would probably be around for a while, investigating. You know, hunting for clues and all."

The sun slipped behind the top of the hardware store, creating shadows all along the center of town. Soft light gently crept in, relaxing me. The town seemed peaceful.

"Well, I don't see how they could possibly get us for anything," I said. "I mean, we tossed everything in the river. The storm erased our scent and tracks. Everyone feels sorry for us because we lost our best friend. We aren't suspects. I'd say we got it made."

"You think so?"

"Yeah. Eventually, after they don't find anything,

they'll call it an unexplainable accident and that will be the end of it."

"I hope so," said Mothball, "but they think he was murdered, Walter. They're not going to call it an unexplainable accident if they think there's a killer on the loose. You and me know there ain't some psycho running around, but nobody else does."

I smiled at that. "Everything's going to be fine. Just make sure you keep your mouth shut."

Up the road, toward the bridge and the path leading down to the Troll's shack, Sheriff Walls's prowler sat parked next to the guardrail. I pointed it out to Mothball.

"I wonder what he's doing down there?" I said.

"Maybe looking for clues. Putting it all together, just like on *The Rockford Files*."

"Yeah, I guess so," I said. "It feels kinda cool knowing the real story, doesn't it, when no one else has any idea?"

"That's really weird, because I've been thinking the exact same thing lately. Like when someone says they heard this or that, and I know they are wrong but I can't say nothing."

"Exactly," I said. "One thing my mom said early on was that they should look in Niggertown for Jimmy. Then she said the sheriff was going to check the quarry for his body. And I'm thinking the whole time, *Just go check the river. That's where you'll find him.*"

"Well, I hope we ain't got nothing to worry about no

more. I need to start taking better care of Mike. I haven't even written to the *Guinness Book* yet."

"You haven't? You better hurry up and get on it."

"I know. You think I can borrow your typewriter?"

"I've already told you a million times that you can," I said. "Just come over and type the stupid letter."

"Yeah, I gotta do that soon," said Mothball, looking up the road toward the bridge. He nodded his head. "Here comes the sheriff."

Sure enough, the brown prowler was making its way slowly toward the center of town, the red globe on the roof sending out a flash that glanced off the storefront windows. The siren was off. We watched from the steps as the car passed, heading toward the station. I made to wave, but I'd only raised my hand about halfway when it got stuck, frozen in mid-address. In the back, staring directly into my eyes, sat the Troll. He turned and locked his gaze on me as the car passed. Judging by the way he moved, with his shoulders stiff, I figured the sheriff must have had him handcuffed. He twisted his head around as if he were an owl and flashed a quick grin at me as the car disappeared down the street. So quick, in fact, I'm not sure if I even saw it. Regardless, chills prickled my neck.

"What the hell's going on?" asked Mothball. "What's he doing in that car?"

"I don't know," I said, confused. "Maybe the sheriff's got himself a suspect."

"But he didn't do nothing. Why would the sheriff be taking him in?"

"I don't know, Mothball," I said, smiling. "But what better suspect could there be than the Troll?"

❧

News about the arrest of the Troll spread rapidly. Before I'd gotten home to tell Mom what I'd seen, our phone had already started ringing. For the next hour, she stayed on it, either answering it or calling someone else, tears in her eyes all the while.

On the news that evening, I finally found out more. The newsman sat at a desk with a picture of the Troll hanging over his shoulder and also a school portrait of Jimmy. The Troll's name, said the anchorman, was Earl Addam Swit, thirty-three, a veteran who'd completed several tours of duty in Vietnam. The reporter said he'd joined the military in July of 1961 and didn't return to Woodley until 1965 or so. Apparently, he stayed around town for about three years, then suddenly left, joined a Special Forces unit, and went back to Vietnam for another tour. The newsman said he'd grown up just outside of Woodley, out in the country. He'd lived with his mother, and when she died shortly after his final return from the war, he'd had nowhere to go. His mother owed back taxes on the property, so the house was seized after her death. Sometime around 1970, he established himself under the trestle and had been there ever since. That was pretty much the whole biography that the newsman gave us. As he talked, the TV showed some footage of the Troll's shack. A wide shot showed its close proximity to the area where Jimmy had been found. The newsman didn't go into any detail about why the Troll had been arrested. All I really found out was that there was "sufficient" evidence to apprehend him.

"I had a feeling about him," said Dad. "Something told me he might be the one."

"I don't think he had anything to do with it," I said, my mouth speaking before I knew what I was doing. "I think they got the wrong guy."

"Don't be ridiculous, Walter," said Dad. I noticed that Mom hadn't said a word; she just sat in her rocker in the living room, nervously working on a hook rug. "The sheriff knows what he's doing, and he's got his man. That guy's nothing but trouble. You could just look at that beast walking down the street and know that he's been guilty of plenty during his day."

"Well," said Mom, glaring at Dad as she finally spoke up, "plenty of people are guilty of things they don't ever get caught for. What if he didn't do it? What if he's innocent?" Tears formed in her eyes.

"They'll find him guilty, all right. I was there. I saw. They found Jimmy's body not more than a hundred feet from the man's shack."

"So what?" said Mom. "That doesn't make him guilty.

If they'd found his body in our backyard, would that make us guilty?"

Mom's ironic words chilled me for a second. And I found it odd that she would take up for the Troll. Usually she was the one jumping on the bandwagon and riding it across town. And then I heard *How's Louise doing?* in the back of my mind.

"Yeah, Dad," I said. "That doesn't make him guilty."

"You know what I mean, Walter. I know why your mother's acting this way, but I thought you'd be happy they arrested the man that killed your best friend." His words were sharp and were intended to cause harm—to my mother more than me, I gathered—but I didn't quite understand how. Something strange was going on. The Troll knew my mother's name. He knew mine. And I felt sure that he'd smiled at me when I'd seen him in the patrol car.

"He wasn't my best friend," I said as I got up to leave the den.

My mother continued rocking nervously; tears streamed down her face. Dad seemed to be enjoying it. I walked up to my room, not knowing if I wanted to see the Troll set free or not. Obviously, it would help me out if he was found guilty, but I struggled with the new set of problems this caused. When I'd entertained the idea of Mr. Haddsby possibly being picked up for Jimmy's death, that was one thing, but when someone who I knew was innocent got arrested, it was a whole different story. And why was my mother acting so strangely about everything?

I couldn't believe I suddenly found myself feeling sorry for the Troll. After all the worry he had caused me, all the anxiety, all the fear, I should've been relieved to know he'd been locked behind bars. But as I sat on my bed, thinking, I realized that he hadn't caused any of it. I'd created everything in my mind. The fear of him was all part of something that Jimmy, Mothball, and I had brought upon ourselves. He hadn't ever done one thing to me, or anyone else for that matter, as far as I knew. Carver had said he was like a snake, don't bother him and he won't bother you, and I think I saw what he meant.

But still, the Troll was the perfect scapegoat. I had to keep reminding myself of that. I also knew that if I felt sorry for the Troll, then Mothball definitely would be feeling the same way. I needed to talk to him, and quick. I had to see what he was thinking. We hadn't talked since we'd seen the Troll in the back of the patrol car a few hours earlier. We'd each gone home to tell our families, and then I'd watched the evening news. Now we had to talk and get things figured out. I had to make sure he didn't get all emotional and start blabbing everything. If that happened, I'd be in real trouble.

"Hell, no, we're not saying a word," I said after I had walked over to Mothball's house and found him feeding Mike. I stayed outside of the pen as we talked.

Just as I'd figured, the news report had softened Mothball. "Walter, this ain't right. It was one thing when we thought the police would say Jimmy drowned. Even when they suspected murder, I still wasn't really sweating it because we knew it had been an accident. They wouldn't be able to prove nothing." Mothball fed Mike with the eyedropper as he talked. "But now they're looking to send an innocent man to jail."

"It's the Troll, Mothball. Who cares? He can save us."

"What do you mean, 'who cares?' I care, that's who."

I walked into the cage, trying to get up close to Mothball's face. I realized I might have to get tough with him, maybe even threaten him, in order to keep him quiet. He didn't seem to pay me any attention. He set the eyedropper in the bowl, secured the hood over Mike's knob, and let him go. Mike started walking around, dropping his hooded stump toward the ground as if pecking for food. Mothball passed by me and exited. I followed him out. He flicked the switch, turning off the floodlight that shone into Mike's pen. It took my eyes a minute to readjust.

"It's very simple," I said. "It's like when we were trying to figure out if we should tell Mrs. Haddsby or not. The answer is to keep quiet. Things have gotten way too deep for us to jump in and start spilling our story now. If we thought we looked guilty before, think what it would look like at this point. Think what it would do to your parents, Mothball. It'd kill them."

"I don't care," he said. "I'm going down to the sheriff's office tomorrow and tell him everything. Tell him it was all a big mistake. An accident."

"And how are you gonna explain his broken neck?"

"I'll tell him the truth," he said. "I'll tell him we were screwing around, things got out of hand, he got his neck caught in the loop and then fell in the water."

I laughed. Not exactly a laugh caused by humor, but more of a laugh that said he was stupid. "He'll never buy it. Just listening to you right now makes me think you're full of shit. And I know the truth. What do you think Sheriff Walls will say? You'll be locked up faster than you can blink."

"Not if we both go and tell him the same story. Walter, the Troll is innocent. He might spend the rest of his life in jail for something he didn't do. For something we did."

My mind churned; I had to convince him. I felt desperate.

"What do you think Jimmy would have done if he was alive and it was one of us that was dead?" I asked. "Do you think he'd tell, knowing there was a chance, no matter how small, that he might get in trouble for it? Maybe even face charges for murder?"

"No, he wouldn't," he said. "But I don't think Jimmy

was the best role model. He wasn't exactly the most moral person in the world. We need to do what's right."

"What's right," I said, my voice rising, "is to shut the hell up and save our own skins. Mothball, it's the Troll. It's not like it's somebody that really matters. Maybe he didn't kill Jimmy, but I bet he would have if he'd ever gotten the chance. Remember that day in front of Oreo's? He looked like he wanted to kill him then. Just forget about it."

"I've got a good mind to go down to the sheriff's station tonight and tell him everything. But I won't, since maybe they're just asking him a bunch of questions. If they keep him, I'm going down there tomorrow to tell."

"No, you're not," I said.

"Yes, I am. And there's nothing you can do to stop me either."

I couldn't see Mothball's eyes because of the shadows, but I wanted him to know that mine were on him. I got right up in his face, so close I could feel his breath on my chin. "We'll see about that, Mothball," I said, anger rising in me. I felt the stronger part of me starting to take over, the part I couldn't always control. "If the sheriff calls me in for questioning, you know what I'm gonna tell him?"

"The truth, I hope. That he slipped off the tree and hung himself on accident."

"That's not the truth," I said. "But I'll tell him the truth, all right. I'll use my innocent face and my puppy-dog eyes and make it so convincing that he'll have to believe me. I'll tell him I didn't say anything before because I was so scared. So scared of you."

"Of me?" said Mothball. "What the hell are you talking about?"

"I'll tell Sheriff Walls all about the firecrackers and how you wanted to get Jimmy back. That it was you who put that noose around his neck. That it was you who tied his hands. That it was you who then strangled him. I'll take him right to the rope swing and give him the proof he needs. I'll show him how you cut the clothesline with the knife you stole and then used it to kill him. How you wrapped it around his neck and started pulling and squeezing until Jimmy couldn't breathe. I'll tell him that you intentionally murdered Jimmy because you resented him. Resented him for all the pain and trouble he'd caused you and your family."

"Jesus, what the hell is wrong with you?" he said as he slowly backed away from me. "You're freaking me out. He'd never believe that."

"Maybe, maybe not," I said. "But is it worth taking the chance?" My hands trembled, yet I felt powerful and in control.

"You've lost your mind, Walter. You're nuts."

"Then go down there tomorrow and tell him your story and then we'll find out, won't we? Just leave it alone, Mothball. What's done is done. Fuck the Troll."

"What's wrong with you?" he asked. "What the hell has happened to you?"

"I'm just trying to save our asses. You say anything and we're both dead."

"Sounds to me like you're nervous," said Mothball. "Sounds to me like you don't want me to tell because you know you killed Jimmy. And maybe it wasn't such an accident. Maybe you don't want them to find out you let him go while he was still alive. While he was begging for you to save him."

He hurriedly walked away and headed toward the house, letting the salt seep into my wound. My control from a second ago turned to an anger that grew so intense that I wanted to grab a two-by-four and clock him upside his fat fucking head. How dare he try to blow everything now, just because of the Troll. How dare he accuse me of killing Jimmy on purpose.

"I'm the one who wanted to help your lard ass," I yelled at his back. "Have you forgotten that, you fat bastard?"

Moths fluttered around his head as he walked up the back stairs and under the porch light that was loosely fastened to the facing boards of the house. The screen door squeaked and then slapped shut as he disappeared inside. He gave no response, and I walked home, suddenly scared and unsure about everything.

CHAPTER 14

THE TRIAL STARTED FOUR MONTHS after Jimmy's body was found, on a Monday in the middle of October. Mothball and I hadn't talked since I'd made threats to turn him in on murder charges, but I guess it worked because he never said a word to Sheriff Walls. I spent most of the remaining summer tucked away in my room, reading and trying to keep cool as I waited for school to start. I hoped that once the trial ended, maybe things would get back to normal between Mothball and me.

On the morning when the trial began, Mom and I awoke early because we had to travel all the way to Lafayette. Dad went to work, saying he couldn't afford to take the time off. When we got there, a throng of reporters, photographers, and other important-looking people, all dressed in suits and ties, stood on the steps of the courthouse, trying to shove their way in. A line of police officers held them back.

The courtroom was already full and most of the people turned to look at us when we entered. I saw Papa standing in the back corner with some of his friends. Directly in front of me, at the end of the aisle, was a swinging wooden gate attached to a banister rail, serving as a barrier between the spectators and the attorneys. The spindled balusters had the same color and luster as fall chestnuts, shining in places where they reflected little rectangles of sunlight. On the other side of the banister sat the prosecutor's table and the defense's table, one to the right, the other to the left, respectively. Sitting at the defense table next to his lawyer, his back turned to me, was the Troll. His bushy hair gave him away, though if it weren't for that, I probably wouldn't have recognized him; he sported a nice jacket instead of the army-issue coat I was so used to seeing him wear. My heart gave a little jolt when I saw him sitting there. On the far left side was the jury box, already filled with jurors, mostly all white men, though there was one colored man and one white woman. At the head of the room was the judge's bench, the seat empty.

Looking to my right, directly in front of the banister, I glimpsed an arm up in the air, waving at us. It was Mrs. Cleilsky, motioning for us to join her. She'd saved two spots for us in the second row, and we squeezed through the other people to sit next to her. Since Mothball was going to be a witness, he wasn't in the room. When I'd heard that he would be testifying and I wouldn't, I was jealous at first, but then relieved, knowing I wouldn't have to lie in front of everyone. But I was worried as to what he might say. If he cracked, our whole cover would fall apart.

In the first row, right in front of me, sat the Haddsbys.

Mrs. Haddsby wore a print dress covered with scarlet be-gonias, held up by spaghetti straps. Her hair was shiny and silky, falling down over bare tanned shoulders. She turned to look at me after I sat down, nodding and giving a forced smile. She still looked pretty, despite the circumstances. It appeared that Mr. Haddsby had on a nice suit, though I couldn't tell for sure since I couldn't see the front of him. He never turned around to acknowledge any of us.

The Troll, however, did turn to look when we sat down. He glanced at me, and then a little longer at my mother, then turned back around. In that brief moment, I got my first real taste of what he looked like. Of course I'd been near him before, but his hair and beard had always hidden his face. Now his hair was pulled back and he had a clean shave. He had piercing green eyes and was actually kind of handsome. I was terrified of him, but at the same time I wasn't. When he looked at me, his eyes weren't at all menacing as I'd always imagined, but almost kind, like an old dog's might be.

So that's how things got started, and the scene didn't vary much each day after that. I couldn't help but think that the whole thing—the reporters, the jury, the lawyers, all the people—was because of me. Well, technically be-cause of me and Mothball, but I mean, it was sort of thrilling knowing that I was the cause of it all. The trial took a full week (Mothball and I got to miss school) and became more interesting with every day. The beginning, however, was boring. In fact, it was tedious, and I couldn't wait to get to the good stuff. Lots of different people came up to give testimony, including the two men who'd first found Jimmy, but nothing overly exciting came from any of it.

Things started to pick up—a little, at least—when, much to my surprise, Oreo was called to the stand. The prosecuting attorney, Mr. Lavender, was a tall, balding man who seemed fully in control. He asked Oreo about what happened the day we'd all been in front of the peanut stand and Jimmy had yelled at the Troll. Oreo recalled the event just as I had remembered it, but I didn't understand why his testimony was all that significant. The only important thing about that day, as far as I was concerned, was when the Troll had asked about my mom, but of course that never came up. Then the defense attorney, Mr. Westmoreland, who was also tall, with bright orange hair, asked Oreo a few questions. It seemed as if he'd rather be out fishing and drinking beer than trying to defend the Troll. He appeared to be going through the motions as part of his job.

When Mothball was called to the stand, things finally began to pick up, but I got nervous. Since all of the testimony up to that point hadn't been all that enthralling, I'd remained rather calm. But when Mothball's name got called, my heart started pounding and my hands and feet began sweating. I hated knowing that my fate rested in his hands.

Mr. Lavender was gentle with Mothball, at first asking him basic questions about his friendship with Jimmy, but it didn't take long to get to the heart of why he was up there. It had to do with his knife. Not the knife he'd stolen, but the original one that his grandfather had given him—the one he'd lost the night we'd gone to hit the Troll's shack with rocks. It had been found next to the path when the police had been searching for evidence. As it turned out, both Mothball's and Jimmy's fingerprints were on the knife, not to mention a small splotch of blood, which was found to match Jimmy's blood type. None of that was too surprising to me, since I knew how the blood and fingerprints had gotten there. What was surprising was Mothball. He told Mr. Lavender that Jimmy had had the knife with him on the night he disappeared. He said that Jimmy had borrowed it earlier in the day, which was a flat-out lie because Mothball had lost it several days before. I couldn't believe it. All along, I'd been worried about Mothball singing, and instead he got up there and did the exact opposite. It looked as though things might turn out better than I'd expected.

The knife seemed to be the first piece of damning evidence against the Troll. Mothball's testifying that Jimmy had it that night seemed to prove that Jimmy had been on the Troll's property. I felt that Mothball, single-handedly, was setting the Troll up for murder. He must have thought hard about what I'd said, about us going to prison and all. About the threats I'd thrown at him.

After Mothball testified, he was allowed to watch the rest of the trial. During a recess, when most of the adults went out to smoke cigarettes, Mothball and I finally got a chance to talk to each other. We worked our way into a far corner of the foyer outside the courtroom. I was nervous, since the last time we had talked had ended so badly.

"How do you think I did?" asked Mothball.

"Are you kidding?" I whispered. "You lied on the stand. You know, you can go to prison for that. It's called perjury."

Mothball gave me a wicked look and whispered, "Oh, yeah? Well, *we* could go to prison if I had told the truth. It's called murder. I thought you'd be happy. I kind of feel horrible about it and you ain't making me feel no better. Besides, I didn't lie."

"Have you lost your mind? That knife vanished days before Jimmy died."

"Yeah, but Jimmy borrowed it all the time. He could have lost it that night just as easily as me. What's the difference? I mean, that's the way I thought about it, but now I'm starting to feel guilty."

"You know what, you're right," I said, chastising myself for being so stupid, realizing Mothball was a delicate situation. "He could've just as easily lost that knife. You did well, Mothball, real well." I then tried to change the topic. "Were you scared?"

"I was at first, but then I relaxed some. I kept thinking it was either us or him, and I decided I'd rather it be him."

"You did the right thing," I said. "You did what you had to do."

"I guess so. But I still feel guilty."

❦

I walked back into the courtroom with Mothball. I found my seat and waited for things to get going again. The first major witness was an officer from the military. He'd been the Troll's commanding officer in Vietnam, when he'd gone back the second time. He explained that the Troll had been in his Special Forces unit and that he had trained him. One of the Troll's main duties was to sneak into dangerous territory where the Viet Cong were holed up and "dispose" of certain enemies. Though they used many methods to kill, one of the main ways they did it—and this was what Mr. Lavender focused on—was garroting. The officer explained that garroting was most efficient because it was quick and silent. The man who did it had to be made of strong nerve and have a gift for stealth. He said that the Troll was one of their top men as far as that was concerned.

When Sheriff Walls took the stand, that's when the

evidence really started piling up. First, Mr. Lavender asked him about the state of the body when it was discovered. Sheriff Walls explained that when Jimmy's body had been found, he was naked except for his shorts, which were caught on the twine around his ankles. He said it looked like Jimmy's neck had been broken. He also said there was a dark red line running across his throat from ear to ear, and also around his neck. The sheriff said, "The line was deep. It looked like somebody wanted to take his head plumb off."

Then Mr. Lavender began to focus on the actual evidence that the sheriff had found in his investigation. Even though it was all wrong—but only Mothball and I knew that—the way Mr. Lavender tied it together almost made *me* feel as if the Troll were guilty. Sheriff Walls said after Jimmy's body was found, his men began a large sweep of the immediate area. The first thing they found, of course, was Mothball's knife. He said they then expanded the search to all of the woods along the river.

The sheriff said, "Upstream from Earl Swit's shack is where we found most of the evidence. Most of it was sitting around a tree, out in the middle of the woods." He said they found a section of clothesline, a camouflage-patterned bandanna—which Mrs. Haddsby confirmed was Jimmy's during her testimony—and disintegrated scraps of firecrackers. The very things Jimmy had used to cause such havoc were now being used to convict an innocent man of his murder. I glanced at Mothball, who looked back at me.

The sheriff said his men also found another piece of clothesline—a little downstream—that had washed up on shore. He stated that that piece had been tied in a noose, and trace amounts of blood had been collected from it. Immediately I got nervous, knowing my hands had held that piece—the piece that had been wrapped around Jimmy's neck, the piece that had ripped my hands wide open when I'd found it in the river. What if they found my blood instead of Jimmy's? If the blood didn't match Jimmy's, the case might fall apart. But a forensics expert was able to determine that the blood on the clothesline was the same as Jimmy's blood type: B positive, which, as it turned out, was the same as mine. Blood brothers until the end.

After Sheriff Walls had collected the evidence, he got a warrant to search the Troll's shack. Mr. Lavender asked him how the Troll had acted when Sheriff Walls and his men showed up at the door. The sheriff replied that he'd been cooperative and helpful. When they entered, they didn't find much at first, but then one of the sheriff's men found a packaged coil of clothesline on the floor next to some tools. It appeared to be brand new, but after further inspection they realized that a small section—about five feet or so—had been cut from the original fifty-foot section. Mr. Lavender then held up the plastic bag with the piece of clothesline they'd found washed up on shore and asked the sheriff how long that piece was. The sheriff said, "About five feet." That revelation sent gasps running through the courtroom.

The judge, Judge Trible, a rather meek man with bad acne scars marking his cheeks, had to use his gavel for the first time to quiet the audience after that. The Troll's guilt was becoming more and more convincing, and I couldn't help but enjoy it. Later, when the owner of the hardware store testified, he confirmed that the Troll had bought a coil of clothesline from him not too long after the incident in front of Oreo's stand. And forensics verified that the piece of clothesline with the blood on it had indeed been cut from the coil found in the shack.

But my elation at the mounting evidence was short lived. The sheriff went on to tell that after they'd found the package of clothesline, they'd also found an abundance of the Troll's writing. Stacks and stacks of notebooks were then brought out for everyone in the courtroom to see. Apparently the books contained fictional stories that the Troll had written. The sheriff stated that the Troll had told him that day in the shack about how he wanted to someday be a novelist and short story writer, though he'd never been published. Mr. Lavender asked the sheriff to read some of them for Judge Trible and the jury.

The first few were graphic stories about Vietnam and

the different ways that the characters would kill their enemies. Then the sheriff read one about a boy mutilating animals, and another about a father killing a pedophile who had harmed his child. But the one that almost knocked me over was the one he read about two boys torturing another boy with firecrackers. I couldn't believe it. The story was about us. I looked at Mothball in amazement, and he looked at me, stunned. We were obviously thinking the same thing. It couldn't have been a coincidence; the Troll had seen what happened. And if the Troll had been spying on us all along, then how much else had he actually seen? What exactly did he know? More important, what did he know about the night Jimmy died? What might he tell? As the sheriff left the stand—and just after I'd felt things were going so well—everything seemed to unravel right before my eyes.

The most damning evidence against the Troll came from the medical examiner, Mr. Perkins. He said the actual cause of death was drowning, but there was no question in his mind that someone had tried to strangle Jimmy before he died. He also said Jimmy's neck had been broken. I thought, of course, that since he'd fallen from the tree, it seemed to make sense that the rope around his neck could have made it look as though he was strangled, and I had no doubt it broke his neck. I mean, when he fell, his head jerked like a rag doll's, so that made sense too. With his neck broken, and his hands and feet bound, he had no way to swim. And since he was alive when I let him go, of course the cause of death was drowning.

And then Mr. Perkins let loose the biggest bomb of all, sending the whole courtroom into a wild frenzy. It took Judge Trible forever to get the place settled down. Mr. Perkins said that while examining Jimmy's body, he found that Jimmy had been sexually molested. Sodomized, to be precise. He determined that the molestation had taken place sometime shortly before Jimmy's death, but he couldn't say exactly how soon before. Mrs. Haddsby broke down crying, while Mr. Haddsby didn't do anything. He didn't even try to comfort Mrs. Haddsby; he just stared straight ahead.

Mothball and I looked at each other, probably thinking the same thing: Mr. Haddsby deserved to be on trial just as much as we did, only for a different reason. I reflected back to when we'd first met up that night, shortly before we stole the cigarettes and stuff. I remembered that I thought it looked as though Jimmy had been crying. Now things started to make horrible sense.

I didn't see how the Troll had a chance against the jury unless he went up there and told what he knew. And if he did that, we were finished. If the Troll had been there that night and saw what had happened, what would I do? It took me only a second to figure that out—I'd lie. I'd deny everything. The way I figured, with all of the evidence they already had, there was no way the jury would believe him over Jimmy's best friends.

Mr. Westmoreland questioned the medical examiner on the possibility of Jimmy's death being a suicide. The idea that it might have looked as if Jimmy had hanged himself intrigued me. A murder looking like a suicide was something I'd never thought of before. But Mr. Perkins brushed that possibility aside. He said there was no way Jimmy could have managed to hang himself while his hands and feet were tied together. Besides that, in a hanging death, the rope marks wouldn't reach the back of the neck the way they had on Jimmy's body, where they'd formed a faint "X." Mr. Perkins dismissed the idea, stating that the marks around Jimmy's throat and neck were absolutely consistent with garroting.

As it turned out, all of my worry about the Troll revealing what he knew never amounted to anything, because he didn't take the stand. After Mr. Westmoreland cross-examined Mr. Perkins, he said, "The defense rests." He stated that the Troll had refused to talk to him or anyone else since the initial day of his arrest, and there was no way to force the man to talk. Mr. Westmoreland said that after the sheriff arrested the Troll, from that point forward, he'd completely clammed up. Mr. Westmoreland suggested that either the Troll had a fear of talking in front of crowds, he was protecting someone, or maybe he was mute, but of course that wasn't true. He'd talked with Sheriff Walls when they'd searched his shack, and I'd definitely heard him speak to me on two separate occasions.

The news of the Troll's refusing to testify sent the courtroom into another uproar, but I'd never felt such relief in my life. After thinking about what had happened to Jimmy—what Mr. Haddsby had done to him, I mean—I couldn't help but feel sort of sorry for him. At least now I thought I understood why Jimmy had acted the way he did sometimes. But what could I do about it now? What was done was done.

When Mr. Lavender went through his closing arguments, he went over all the evidence again. He said the Troll snuck into Jimmy's house—using his Special Forces training—and then took him back to his shack. He said the Troll probably tried to use Mothball's knife on Jimmy, which would explain the blood, but he then realized that killing him at his shack would be too messy. So he took him into the woods, where he bound his wrists and ankles, and then tied him up with the first piece of clothesline— the piece that had been wrapped around Mothball—and raped him (the prosecution never did determine where that piece of clothesline had come from, though Mothball and I knew Jimmy had taken it from Mr. Haddsby's shed). Mr. Lavender said the Troll then used the other piece of clothesline to strangle him before dumping his body in the river. He said the Troll made a mistake by killing Jimmy upstream from his shack. If he'd done it downstream and then thrown him in the river, Jimmy would have probably never been found. Other mistakes were that instead of throwing the bandanna and the first piece of clothesline in the river, he left them there. Not to mention that he kept the packaged clothesline in his shack, as well as the stories about torturing and molesting boys. Mr. Lavender suggested that the Troll had started to unravel after he threw Jimmy in the river, so that's why he hadn't gotten rid of the other evidence. I was pretty impressed with the arguments, even though I knew that none of it was true. I couldn't see how the jury could possibly find the Troll not guilty.

Mr. Westmoreland then gave his speech, and though he made a lot of sense, it seemed inevitable that the Troll would be convicted. He said the Troll was the victim of circumstantial evidence, stating there was absolutely no proof that the Troll had broken into Jimmy's house. He said the only thing the Troll was guilty of was having the bad luck of living close to where the body was found. He posed the question—and this was the part that really got my heart beating—that if the Troll had strangled Jimmy, why weren't there any rope marks found on his hands? And if he'd used gloves, and then disposed of them, why wouldn't he have gotten rid of the other evidence too? He gave a pretty good argument, and afterward I thought the jury might find the Troll not guilty after all. But it wasn't to be.

The Troll was found guilty of murder in the first degree,

as well as a whole list of other charges. And once sentencing came, the jury suggested life in prison. However, Judge Trible said that in the state of Alabama he had the option of overriding the sentence the jury agreed upon. And he did. He said that in a decision earlier that year (he called it the Furman decision) the death penalty had been reinstated in the United States. He informed us that the death penalty could be enforced when a person was found guilty of intentional murder with one of eighteen aggravating factors. I had no idea what he was talking about, but he said the Troll had been found guilty of a lot more than one aggravating factor. He ended everything by stating that the Troll was sentenced to death by means of the electric chair at the state facility in Atmore.

After the sentence was read, the crowd erupted one last time. The Troll didn't even flinch as the bailiff took his arm and led him away through one of the doors at the back of the courtroom. I just knew that at any moment he would turn his head and stare at me, Mothball, and my mother, but he never did. My mother bawled, as did Mothball, which I guess everyone—everyone but me, that is—thought were tears of joy. I thought to myself, as I looked at Mothball and then watched the Troll walk away, that I would soon be responsible for another death.

CHAPTER 15

SINCE WE'D BEEN THE ONLY TWO KIDS at the trial, for the first few days after Mothball and I returned to our high school, we were celebrities. But that eventually faded and we went back to being regular students. We weren't talking to each other much, but I was content with just going to school and reading in my room.

Ironically enough, right after the trial, the book Miss Nehemiah assigned my English class was *To Kill a Mockingbird*. I'd never read it before, though it was practically like the Bible in the state of Alabama. I read the whole thing in two days, staying up almost all night the second night to finish it. Miss Nehemiah said she thought it might be good for us, considering everything that had taken place with Jimmy's death and all, and she was right. Of course, she had no way of knowing how right she was, especially the part about Tom Robinson being convicted of a crime he didn't commit.

I was handling everything okay, I guess, though sometimes things would start bothering me. Mothball seemed to be having a more difficult time dealing with the conviction than I was. That was a lot of the reason we weren't talking or doing anything together. Every time we were alone, he wanted to bring it up again, while I just wanted to drop it altogether. His conscience had really started to eat at him.

About two weeks after the trial ended, Mothball showed up at my house one day. Mom had gone shopping in Lafayette, so I was the only one home when he knocked.

"Hey," he said when I opened the door. He seemed sullen. "I was wondering if I could use your typewriter. I thought I'd finally write that letter to the *Guinness Book*."

"You still haven't done that?"

"No. You know, with the trial and everything, and then all the schoolwork, I just ain't never gotten around to it. Besides, I think it needs to be typed."

"Well, yeah, you can use it. Come on upstairs."

When we got to my room, I loaded a piece of paper into the typewriter and then sat on the bed. "You want me to help you? I'm pretty good on that thing."

"No, thanks. I'll do it myself," he said, sitting down at the desk. "I'll figure it out."

The mood between us felt stiff, as though neither of us knew what to say, but all the same I was glad he was there. I realized I missed hanging around with him.

"Walter," he said, "this whole thing has been so messed up. I'm still scared."

"What are you scared of? It's a done deal."

"I don't know. Don't you worry they might figure out

that the Troll didn't have nothing to do with it? Don't you think maybe they'll figure out we was there that night?"

"No, I don't. It's over now, Mothball. You have to live with it until you die. That's all there is to it. Maybe we made a huge mistake by not telling, but it's over now."

"But it's not over," he said. "The Troll's in prison over in Atmore. They're gonna kill him, and he didn't do nothing. What if we went to the sheriff and told him everything?"

"You can't be serious," I said. "You committed perjury. You could go to jail for that."

"Just for telling a little lie?"

"Don't be such a dumb-ass. It wasn't a little lie, Mothball. You told the court that Jimmy had the knife. That was definitely a huge part of getting him convicted."

Tears welled up in his eyes. He wiped them with the end of his sleeve. "Everything is my fault," he said. "It's gonna be me that kills the Troll."

"We made some huge mistakes," I said, trying to be consoling. "But we gotta live with them."

"I can't live with them, Walter. I can't."

"You have to. There's nothing we can do about it unless you want to tell the sheriff you killed Jimmy and then lied on the stand. I don't think you want to do that. What's the point?"

"But the Troll, Walter—what about him?"

"He didn't even go up on the stand. It's almost like he wanted to go to jail. Shit, he'd been spying on us. He could've told all kinds of stuff about us if he'd wanted to."

Mothball looked around the room for a moment as if he wasn't sure what to say next. "Do you think he saw us tie up Jimmy that night? You think he was watching?"

"I don't know," I said. "He could've been. Maybe he was what caused the splash we heard that night. You know, if he saw what happened, maybe he jumped in to try and save Jimmy. Or maybe he didn't see Jimmy on the rope swing at all, but he heard us searching in the water, so he jumped in to try and save him as he floated away. I don't know. I mean, it must've been him that tied that piece of clothesline to the rope swing. He must've known we went down there sometimes. So he could've been there that night."

"But if he'd been there," said Mothball, "and if he saw us messing with Jimmy, or even if he just saw us trying to find Jimmy in the river, why didn't he say something at the trial?"

"Because he knew nobody'd believe him. That's what I think, anyway. He knew he was screwed."

"So he might've saved us, Walter. He might've known we had something to do with it but didn't say nothing about it. Man, I don't think my own father would protect me that way."

"Yeah, I know what you mean," I said. "My dad wouldn't. Not even close."

"So why would he protect us if he knew we'd done wrong?"

"Maybe because of what Jimmy did to you with the firecrackers. Maybe the Troll knew we were trying to pay Jimmy back. I don't know. Or maybe, like I said, that splash we heard was him. Maybe he realized that things had gotten out of control but realized it too late and couldn't save Jimmy."

"So he might've seen everything," said Mothball. His eyes narrowed as he apparently thought about something. "That would mean only you and him really know exactly what happened to Jimmy."

"And you," I said.

"I never saw *exactly* what happened. I mean, it was dark and my back was turned when you and Jimmy fell off the tree. Kind of weird that everything happened while I went to get the firecrackers, huh? Kind of a strange coincidence."

"So what are you saying, Mothball?" I asked, that familiar anger rising once again. "You accusing me of something?"

"I keep thinking about what the Troll's lawyer said at the trial, that's all. About the fact that his hands were fine. But your hands, Walter, they were torn up pretty bad. And

I thought it was Jimmy that yelled before y'all fell, not you. And I never saw exactly what happened. And the way you let him go while he was still alive and then insisted on covering it all up."

"So once again you think I killed Jimmy on purpose? Is that what you're saying, Mothball?" My cheeks burned as I got off the bed and started pacing the room. "Some friend you are. If that's what you think, then why don't you go tell the fucking sheriff? I guess you've already forgotten that I did all that shit to help you. To get him back for blowing your ass up. And this is the thanks I get? You accuse me of murder?"

Mothball turned sheepish. "That's not what I meant. Shit, I'm so confused over everything. It was your hands— that's all. That lawyer just got me to thinking."

"My hands were fucked up because I grabbed the clothesline as it floated by. I was angry. Maybe if you'd gotten your lazy ass in the water faster, you'd have seen me do that. While I was searching, you were stuck to the bank like a fat piece of sausage on a plate."

"I know. I'm sorry," he said as tears streamed down his cheeks. "Just forget it. Please? I don't know what the hell I'm even saying no more. I swear to God I don't."

I continued to pace, opening and closing my fists, wanting to punch Mothball, or at least a wall or something. He sat in the chair and sobbed while I walked back and forth, hissing through my teeth. After a few minutes, I finally started to calm down.

"I'm sorry, Walter," he said. "I know you wouldn't do nothing like that on purpose."

I looked at Mothball's pathetic face, all swollen and wet, and instead of wanting to punch him, I suddenly felt sorry for him. "Forget it, Mothball," I said. "This whole thing has been really hard for both of us. We'll be all right. We just have to stick together."

Mothball wiped his nose with the cuff of his sleeve as his crying slowed. He gasped involuntarily, sucking gulps of air as he said, "I'm sorry. I'm really sorry."

"Forget it," I said. "It's over with."

Things went awkwardly quiet again. The only sound was Mothball's gasping every now and then. It unnerved me to know what he'd been thinking. How he'd tried to piece things together. Finally, I decided to change the subject.

"How's Mike doing?"

"He's doing good," he said, looking relieved to be talking about something else. "You should see him. I've been feeding him more, so he's fattening up."

"How long has it been now? I mean, since you cut off his head?"

"About five months. Can you believe it?"

"Mothball, I don't know if I've ever believed it. It just

doesn't seem possible. What was that chicken's record? Eighteen months?"

"Yep," he said. "Only thirteen more to go and we'll have tied the record."

"I hate to break it to you, but until the *Guinness Book* people come out and verify it, I doubt they're going to give you any credit. They'll probably have to start counting from the day they first see it." I was sorry the second I said it, because I realized Mothball had never thought about that.

But he surprised me. "Oh, yeah, I guess you're right. They probably won't take my word for it, huh? But it don't matter anyway. I don't really care no more."

"What do you mean, you don't care? That's all you've talked about for nearly a year."

He looked up at me, his eyes flat and tired. "Since everything's happened, I just don't seem to give a crap about nothing. I haven't done shit in school, and I don't care."

"Are y'all reading *To Kill a Mockingbird* in your English class?"

"You know I'm in the dipshit class, Walter. We're reading a book about a couple of rich boys at some boarding school in New Hampshire. I haven't even started it. And we're studying poetry too. We just read Edgar Allen Poe, 'The Raven.' And some other poem called 'Enema,' or something like that."

"'Enema'? Are you sure?"

"Yeah. I think so."

"Mothball," I said, chuckling slightly, "an enema is something you stick up your ass to make you crap."

"Well, whatever it was called, it was pretty cool. It was a poem, but it was also a puzzle."

"Oh, yeah," I said. "I read that once. Did it have a hidden message in it?"

"Yeah, that's the one."

"I think it's called 'Enigma.'"

"Yeah, that's it. 'Enigma.' 'Enema.' Sounds the same to me. But, I'm telling you, I just don't give a shit no more."

"Well, you should read To Kill a Mockingbird. You can borrow it if you want."

"Maybe some other time. Anyway, I need to write this letter." He looked at the typewriter, readying himself. He looked intimidated as he put his fingers on the keys, as if he were standing on the edge of a bridge, afraid to jump.

"You sure you don't want some help?" I asked.

"I can handle it. But do you think I could have a little privacy?"

"You want privacy to write a letter about chopping off your turkey's head?" I was joking, trying to lighten the mood, but he didn't laugh. I'd never seen him so down.

"Please, Walter. I gotta do this, okay?"

"Sure, okay. There's a dictionary on the desk if you need it."

He didn't reply, so I left the room and headed down-stairs. I wondered if he was so self-conscious about his typing and spelling that he wouldn't even let me in the room. But that didn't seem like Mothball. He was a horrible speller, and he'd just admitted that he was in the slow English class, so I couldn't figure out what his problem was.

About a half-hour later, he came down and went straight for the door without even saying goodbye or thanks. I caught him on the porch and asked, "Did you get it done?"

"Yeah," he said, holding the letter close to his chest. He clearly didn't want me to see it. "I'm gonna put it in an envelope and drop it in the mailbox as soon as I get home." He turned to go.

"All that shit that happened upstairs," I said, "let's just forget it. I'm not mad at you. It just took me by surprise, that's all. It's not every day you get accused of murder."

Mothball didn't reply.

"You want to meet up tonight?" I asked. "Sneak out or something? Or we could walk together to school tomorrow? I'm ready to be friends again, Mothball, if you are."

"I don't know. Maybe. I guess I could walk to school with you. Yeah, sure," he said, though he didn't seem overly eager. "I guess so."

"Are you okay?" I asked. "I mean, you really don't seem like yourself."

"I'm fine. I just need to go."

"You want me to proofread the letter or anything? You know, I'm good at that."

"You're good at everything, aren't you, Walter?" he suddenly snapped. He quickly folded the piece of paper and stuffed it into his pocket. "So smart. So clever. Mr. Know-It-All's got a plan for everything."

"What's that supposed to mean?" I asked, taken aback. I started getting mad again. I'd let him borrow my typewriter, offered to help him, brushed aside his accusations of murder, and here he was acting as though I'd done something wrong.

"I gotta go," he said. He walked toward the street and off into the twilight that had settled over the neighborhood. Immediately I became highly suspicious. I went upstairs and checked my garbage can to see if he'd thrown away any bad drafts of the letter, but I found nothing.

❦

The next morning, I walked to school alone. Mothball never showed up. Thanks to him I hadn't gotten a good night's sleep. He'd kept me up most of the night, not to mention that damn letter. That letter had kept me up all night too.

That afternoon, I again ended up walking home by myself, reflecting on the day before. My head was down and I didn't really pay any attention to what was in front of me, so when I looked up and saw the sheriff's car sitting by the sidewalk in front of my house, my knees went weak. I thought I might collapse right there in the front yard. My first thought was Mothball's letter. I knew he hadn't written a letter to the *Guinness Book* people. He'd probably written about everything we'd done and then somehow given it to the sheriff, but I didn't see how that was possible. Then I started thinking that maybe the Troll had finally started talking. He'd probably told the sheriff how he saw me and Mothball with Jimmy that night. There was no telling what he might have said; it all depended on what he'd seen. I didn't want to go inside but knew I had to.

When I opened the front door, I saw my mother sitting on our couch in the living room. She was sobbing. Sheriff Walls sat in the rocker and stood up when he saw me enter. I was scared. I didn't know what all he might have figured out and had no idea what amount of trouble I was in. But with Mom bawling the way she was, whatever was going on couldn't be good. I know I must have looked pale, and I figured the sheriff could see my knees knocking. He walked toward me as I stood frozen in the foyer.

"What's going on?" I asked, trying to sound as innocent as possible. My mother looked up when she heard my voice.

"Walter," she said through heavy sobs and tears. "Walter, it's . . . it's Raymond. Do you know . . . ?" She started crying so hard that she was unable to finish.

I had to figure out what was going on. I had to figure out what exactly the sheriff knew. The excitement, the adrenaline, the fear, it all started pumping through me once again.

"Do I know what?" I asked, giving her my sweetest voice. Until I knew for sure I was busted, I'd continue to play the game. "What's happening? What did he do?"

Mom really started crying then. "He's gone, Walter. Raymond is gone."

"What do you mean? Sheriff, what's she talking about? Where'd he go?"

Sheriff Walls came up next to me, creaking. It all reminded me of that last time he'd been to the house. He led me to the couch next to Mom. "Why don't you sit down, Walter," he said. "I need to talk to you about a few things."

Judging by the gentle sound of his voice, I didn't think I was in trouble, but I still didn't know for sure. "Mom, what are you talking about? Where's Mothball?"

She had her face buried in her hands and continued to wail.

"Walter," said the sheriff, "this is going to be difficult to hear. But, as you can see, your mom ain't in no condition to tell you. So I guess I better just say it."

"What?" I asked. "Say what? Where's Mothball? Just tell me."

The sheriff grabbed an ashtray off the end table and

then went back over to the rocking chair. He set the ash-tray in his lap and propelled himself backwards, the soles of his polished shoes pushing against the wood floor, while his hands and fingers gripped the clawed ends of the rocker's arms. When he pushed back, his shoes and belt moaned, and on his way forward the chair answered with a squeaky response.

"This morning a man from over at Niggertown went down to the river to do some fishing," he said. "Water's been down lately, and he saw something strange on the rocks, just under the bridge. Water was so shallow, he was able to wade out there without having to go in over his knees." The sheriff lit a cigarette, which drove me crazy. Not the actual lighting of the cigarette, I mean, but his de-laying of the story. It was as if he wanted to impede the news on purpose, just to make me nuts. "It was Raymond in the water," he said, tilting his head upward and exhal-ing a stream of smoke. "He was dead."

"What?" I asked, though I'd heard him. It was just that I didn't know what else to say. "What are you talking about? Did you say he's dead?" My head started swim-ming and everything in the room began to spin. The smoke hovering in the room made me nauseated.

"I'm afraid I did. That Negro run straight to me this morning to tell me."

"What the hell? How? I mean, how did he die?"

"It looks like it might be suicide. Apparently he jumped

off the bridge sometime last night. Either that or he was pushed off. Can't say for sure. We haven't found a note or anything yet. Like I said, water's been so low, there wasn't more than a foot of water where he landed. Broke his neck on the rocks from what I can tell. If nothing else, it don't look like he suffered none. I'm awfully sorry—Walter, I really am. You've been through a whole lot lately. Ain't no boy deserves what you been going through."

Mom looked up at me, her red eyes in terrific pain. "He's gone, Walter. I'm so sorry, baby," she said, trying to put her arms around me, but I pushed them away.

"I just want to ask you a few questions, son," he said. "Same as last time. I hate having to put you through this again, but I'm afraid I have to. Is that all right?"

"Yes, sir," I said, staring at the long ash growing on the end of his cigarette. When he flicked the butt with his thumb, some white flakes missed the ashtray and littered his lap like falling dandruff. "I'll tell you what I can."

I had another night of fitful sleep. All of the horror, all of the death, it kept haunting me. I replayed the information I'd given Sheriff Walls over in my head as I lay in bed the next morning, making sure I'd covered everything: how Mothball had come by while Mom had been shopping; how he seemed depressed; how he used my typewriter to write a note, supposedly to *Guinness Book*.

It was just me now. No Mothball, no Jimmy. I only had one thing on my mind as I got dressed; there was only one thing I had to do. I had to get over to Mothball's. I also noticed that, for the first time in forever, I hadn't wet the bed.

Mom was at the kitchen table, sipping on coffee, when I came downstairs. Dad had already left for work. I found it hard to believe that he hadn't taken the day off to maybe at least console me some. When Jimmy had been missing, he took off work to assist with the search party; he even went to his funeral. Then again, maybe it wasn't so hard to believe.

Mom looked horrible. Her hands shook as she tried to drink her coffee, and her haggard face was damp with tears.

"Hey, honey," she whispered, her voice rough. "You want something to eat?"

"No. I gotta go over to Mothball's."

"You ought to leave them alone right now. Let me get you something to eat."

"I don't want to eat," I said. "I gotta go over there. I gotta take care of Mike."

"Mike?" she said, trying to figure out who that was. It took her a second to understand. "There's more important things to worry about than that stupid bird right now."

"Mothball would want me to take care of him," I yelled. "I have to feed him."

"Walter, you're not—"

"Shut up," I screamed. "Just shut up. I'm going over there."

I stormed out of the kitchen and slammed the door on my way outside. In the street, I heard my mother's wails traveling all the way from the house. I'd never told my mother to shut up before, but I just couldn't help it. The only thing that made sense to me was getting over to Mothball's. I had to take care of things. Make sure everything was in order. Mike had to be fed, and I knew I was the only one to do it. None of the Cleilskys would even think about it. Mike was my responsibility now.

The sun had just barely risen, and the cold morning air stung my face as I ran down the street toward Mothball's house. White puffs of cotton shot from my mouth as I loped along. My mind raced around in circles. Sheriff Walls had said it looked like a suicide, but he planned on doing an investigation to rule out all other possibilities. Suicide made sense to me. The way Mothball had been acting since the trial, his depression, his guilt about everything—it all made sense. Suicide was believable.

Yellow light snuck from the kitchen window as I reached the driveway, but I didn't want the Cleilskys to see me. Likewise, I didn't want to see any of them; I didn't want to see their faces. I knew what they'd look like, and I wasn't ready to deal with that yet.

As I entered the backyard, a few startled peahens scurried haphazardly through the dew like water bugs over a murky pond. Mike was already out of his little house, poking around in the straw, his black hood covering his stump. I approached the pen, opened the door quietly, and entered. He must have felt my footsteps because he ran over to me, stopping at my feet.

"Hey, buddy," I said softly. "How you doing?"

I squatted and ran my hand down his satiny feathers. He stayed right next to me, arching his back and crouching like a dog getting a good scratching. "You hungry, Mike? I'll take care of you—don't you worry about that. Let me go get your feed."

Mike followed me to the door. I nudged him back with the toe of my shoe and quickly closed the gate. I walked to the chicken shack and entered the dark building. The ammoniac odor of moldy straw and chicken shit hit me as I blindly fumbled around for the light string. I found it hanging in front of my face, pulled on it, and then located the feed. I poured some into a clay bowl, added water, and stirred.

When the slurry reached the right consistency, I turned to leave. As I exited, I noticed, in the opposite corner of the shack, the *Guinness Book* sitting on the same oak log that Mothball always used to decapitate the chickens. Only it wasn't *sitting* on the log—it was propped up against a rock, as if it were on display in the front window of a bookstore or something. There was a piece of paper, larger than the book itself, placed inside, protruding from the top edge like a giant bookmark. The book had obviously been positioned that way to be found. The paper, folded in half, marked the page that described Mike the chicken's record. I unfolded the paper and began reading the typed note. My hands shook worse than my mother's had just a little while before.

I know I look lame. Even dumb. To hurt everyone
must appear selfish, for obvious reasons.

"Why?" he yelled, drowning, overwhelmed, never
talking again, since killing is absolute.
My devilment is severe. The underlying remorse
burns every day.
Internally, guilt equals torment. Suicide is clearly
knocking. I'm frightened.
I truly hope I never know other friends in turmoil.

It seems troubling, right? And not God like? Even
displeasing Jesus? It might.
Mom, you made our true happiness, because ardent
love lasts.
Christ, an unrelenting guilt has taken over now.
Sorry. Only, I panic under stress. Hell, everyone
does.

Haddsby is murdered over foolish fun. Taken
heartlessly.
Everlasting blame rests inside.
Damning guilt entered and never died.
Woodley rages over the enigma.
True happiness is suicide, life eternal . . .

The Troll's evil remains.
Take heed, everyone, the real ogre lives locally.
    Also, kids are wicked and love trouble.

Earl receives electrocution. Lies remain a secret.
I'll take Hell over Life.

Alas, Mothball exists . . . nevermore.

I read the note three times over. It definitely didn't sound like something Mothball would write, not to mention be capable of writing. And what did it mean? He must have used my dictionary, because I think he even spelled the words right. In fact, I didn't notice one misspelled word, which was very un-Mothball-like. And what about his references to the Troll, and Jimmy's death? If he had wanted to reveal the truth, why hadn't he just come right out and done that instead of writing these mysterious ramblings? Regardless, I knew I had to show Mrs. Cleilsky, and that terrified me.

I headed for the back door of the house, trying to figure out what I would say. As I walked up the back steps, Mrs. Cleilsky opened the main door and then the screened one. I trembled all over. I saw right away that she was trembling even worse.

"Hello, Walter," she said in a weak voice. A bathrobe covered her round body, and she hugged it to her chest, staving off the cool of the morning. "Come in."

"I don't . . . I was coming over to feed Mike," I said. "I went into the chicken shack to get his food, and I . . . I found this." I shoved the note into her shaky hand.

"What is it?"

"It's Mothball's . . . just read it. You'll see."

She looked at me, confused, then began to read. I stood on the bottom step, restless, fidgeting with a loose string hanging from my shirt sleeve. I turned away as she read, examining the dead azalea bush next to the steps, then the similarly dead tomato plant decaying in an old rusted milk can on the other side—anything I could find to keep my eyes averted from her. After she finished, she began crying. Not loud sobs, just anguished little whimpers.

"Where did you find this?"

"In the chicken shack. It was stuck inside the *Guinness Book*. I just thought . . . I mean . . . Mothball came over the other day and wanted to use my typewriter. He said he wanted to contact the *Guinness Book* about Mike. I guess that's when he wrote it."

"Yes. Thank you, Walter. I don't know what he's saying. I don't know why . . ." she said, pausing as the tears started coming heavier now, filling the cracks and wrinkles of her face. She looked at least ten years older than she had the last time I'd seen her.

". . . why he would do this? Do you know why? Did you see this coming?"

"No, ma'am."

"What did I do wrong, Walter? What did I do?" A few tears moistened the paper. Her hands continued to shake. She couldn't lift her eyes from the note.

"You didn't do anything, Mrs. Cleilsky. I don't know why," I said, looking down at my feet. I nervously wrapped the loose shirt string around my finger, cutting off the blood, turning the pad white. I kept my head down and repeated the process, not knowing what to do next. I thought I should probably cry, but couldn't.

"I just don't understand. He was such a good boy. Such a happy boy."

"Yes, ma'am. I don't know. I'm sorry."

She stared at the letter. "He didn't even sign it. He could have at least signed it."

There was another moment of torturous awkwardness before she said, "I've got to show this to Robert. To Carver. Maybe they'll understand it better."

"Yes, ma'am. I'll go ahead and feed Mike if you want me to. I mean, I can do it from now on if you like."

"What? Do what?"

"Feed Mike. Mothball would probably want me to do it."

She looked over my shoulder, out to the chicken shack, the soft light of the morning sunshine causing her to faintly squint. I wasn't sure if she had heard a word I'd said.

"Yes, that's right," she said, the tears subsiding slightly. "He would want that. Why don't you just . . . Why don't you just go ahead and take him, Walter. Lord knows what we'd do with him. You think your folks would let you keep him? None of us can care for him."

"Yes, ma'am, that'd probably be all right. I can ask. I don't think they'd mind, especially . . ." But I stopped before I said *especially under the circumstances*. I figured that might not be the right thing. She didn't seem to notice that I'd stopped midsentence.

"That would be fine," she said. "I need to show this to them. Thank you, Walter. Thank you for everything. You were such a good friend to Raymond."

"Yes, ma'am," I said, thinking she'd feel otherwise if she knew even half the truth.

Chapter 16

When I got home, I told Mom, more than I asked her, that Mike had to come to our house. She still looked distraught but seemed better than earlier.

"Your father isn't going to like it one bit," she said. "I don't know if he'll go for it."

"I don't care," I said. "Mike is my responsibility now."

"You know how he is about the yard. He doesn't want it looking all junked up like we're a bunch of hillbillies, even if the neighbors choose to live that way."

"He'll just have to understand," I said. "Both of my friends are dead, Mom. Don't you think he might have at least a little bit of compassion for once?"

"Don't talk that way about your father. He has compassion. He loves you."

I ignored her comment and said, "I'm gonna go make a pen."

I spent the rest of the morning building a sorry excuse for an enclosure in the backyard. It wasn't as large as what Mothball had built, but it would temporarily suffice. It was a bit of an eyesore, and I knew Mom was right: Dad wasn't going to like it at all.

After lunch, I made several trips back and forth to

Mothball's house, getting the feed, some straw, and the little house Mothball had built. On my last run, I got Mike himself. He seemed to acclimate to his new surroundings without too much of a problem. I stayed with him for the next couple of hours, feeding and petting him. It seemed pretty sad to me that the only friend I had left in the world was a headless turkey. But that's what it had come to. And then, that evening, Dad got home from work.

"That goddamned thing is going to stink up the neighborhood," he said after he pulled into the carport and Mom and I explained the situation. "For God's sake, Walter, did you ever happen to notice the way people looked at Raymond when he walked that thing down the street?"

"I don't care what they think," I said. "Mothball never cared."

"When that wind kicks up, it's going to stink to high heaven around here. And those feathers will end up all over the yard."

"It's the only thing I've got left of Mothball, Dad. What am I supposed to do?"

That was the line I knew I might have to fall back on, and it worked. Mom jumped in at that point and the argument subsided. I had won.

The next day, the day before Mothball's funeral, I was in the backyard with Mike. It was early afternoon—Mom had let me stay out of school the rest of the week—and I was about to take Mike for a walk when Dad screeched into the carport and stormed into the house. Something was wrong—as if that weren't obvious enough from his behavior—because Dad never got home before five o'clock. He was yelling and screaming, so I put Mike back in the cage and went to make sure Mom was okay.

She sat at the kitchen table, dabbing the corners of her eyes with her apron. Dad paced back and forth across the floor, creaking the boards with his boots.

"I don't know what to say, Gene," said Mom, her voice barely a whisper.

"I've been there nearly twenty years. Twenty years. And this is what that old son of a bitch does to me."

I stood in the corner, my hands stinking like Mike, wanting to get to the sink to wash up but not daring to cross Dad's path at the moment.

"I should've seen it coming. Hell, I did see it coming. But right before the holidays? He could've at least held out until the end of the year."

"I'm sure you'll be able to find other work. Maybe at the quarry or something."

"And what if I don't? What in the hell are we going to do then? There ain't no work anywhere around here. And everybody's going to be looking."

By now I knew what had happened, but I asked anyway. "What's the matter?"

"I'll tell you what's the matter, Walter," he said, still

storming back and forth across the kitchen. "Old Man Simmons decided to shut the mill down, that's what's the matter. He shut the whole goddamned thing down, just like that. I'm sure he'll be just fine, sitting on his gobs of money, but what the hell are the rest of us gonna do? Answer me that one. What in the hell are the men of Woodley supposed to do now?"

"I'm sorry," I said, barely speaking. "I don't know."

"Yeah? Well, I'm sorry, too. I'm a sorry, out-of-work, uneducated son of a bitch, that's what I am. Shit, we don't got a pot to piss in. And what do you think that new president of ours is going to do to help? Nothing, that's what. You think he's gonna help out the poor men of Alabama when he's still got plenty of problems over in Georgia? Shit."

Dad paced the floor in a fury. His glasses hung at the tip of his nose, and his face was flushed and splotchy. All of his neck tendons were stretched taut and about to pop through. The green veins in his arms pulsed. He scared me.

"Something will come up," said Mom. "We'll just have to cut back a little until you find something else. That's all."

"You're goddamned right we're going to have to cut back." He grabbed a banana from the fruit bowl and started squeezing it as he beat a path on the kitchen floor. Yellow mush started oozing from the sides of the peel, squishing between his fingers. "But I'll tell you what, by God, we're still going to have us a Thanksgiving dinner here in a couple of weeks. Starting with that no-headed turkey you got out back," he said, looking at me.

"Stop it, Gene," said Mom. "We'll do no such thing."

"The hell we won't. That goddamned turkey came from Simmons himself, and there ain't nothing that'll make me happier than to eat that bird." He threw the banana. It smacked the wall before it thumped to the ground, leaving a mushy white stain. "That's what we're gonna do."

"That was Mothball's turkey!" I screamed. "It's the last thing I got left of him."

"That bullshit excuse ain't gonna work this time, boy."

"Gene Sithol, you stop it right now. You calm down and get yourself together."

"I'm together, Louise. And we're gonna eat that turkey come hell or high water."

"Oh, no we're not," said Mom. "I won't be cooking it. And that's final."

I ran outside, bursting into tears as soon as I made it through the door. I went into Mike's cage and began petting him, thinking that I would never let my father get his hands on him. A minute later, Dad busted through the back door and stormed to the carport. He got in the car and ripped out of the driveway. I immediately felt a little better, knowing he was gone.

Mom half opened the screen door and said, "Walter, come inside for a minute. Let's talk about this."

"I don't want to talk about it," I yelled. "He's not going to eat Mike."

"I'm not going to let that happen," she said. "Just come in for a sec."

I closed the door to Mike's pen and sullenly walked into the house. We both sat down at the kitchen table.

"Your father didn't mean—"

"Don't try and defend him, Mom," I said. "I'm so tired of you explaining to me about what a good father he is. How he loves me. How he never means what he says."

"You're right, Walter. I'm sorry. But he does love you. You have to understand, he just lost his job. He's worried about—"

"Jesus, there you go again. I'm sorry he lost his job. I know he's worried about that. But I didn't lose his job for him, did I? Mike didn't shut down the mill, did he?"

"No, I guess not."

"So why does he take everything out on me?"

Mom fiddled with the folds of her dress as she sat at the table. She nervously twisted the cloth in her hands as if drying them with a dishtowel. "I don't know, Walter. He's a complicated man."

"Well, I know why," I said. "And I've known for a while now. He's an asshole, is what he is."

"Don't you dare say that about your father," said Mom. "How dare you."

"He's an asshole, and I know you think so too."

"I think no such thing."

I felt that stronger part of me starting to simmer. It told me that the time had come. "Yes, you do," I said. "What I don't understand is why you never left him. We'd have managed somehow, and I'd have sure been a lot happier."

Her face quickly became distraught and angry. "What in God's name are you talking about? I don't know what's gotten into you. I understand you've been through more in the last few months than anyone should have to go through in a lifetime, but you've got no right to talk that way to me. You should be ashamed. How dare you say such things about your father."

I hesitated for a moment, still not sure, but then it just started to come out. "He's an asshole, Mom. I know everything."

"What are you talking about, you 'know everything'? I don't know what you're talking about. I love you. Your father loves you."

"Apparently he doesn't love me as much as he loved his other son," I said.

Her eyes went wide, and panic whipped over her face like a sheet of rain across a lake.

"I don't know what—"

"Yes, you do, Mom. You know exactly what I'm talking about. I found the key to your night table. I read your diary last year. I know what you saw that night. I know you woke up and saw everything."

She was stricken now, unable to move. "Walter—"

"Jimmy was my brother, Mom," I screamed. "We were brothers, and Dad has always loved him more. That's why he's always been so mean to me."

Mom had turned into a pathetic mess at the table. I'd never seen such anguish on her face. "That's not true. He . . . he wasn't your brother."

"Okay, half brother. Whatever. Jesus, Mom—I read your diary."

Mom spoke softly, almost inaudible through her tears. "He wasn't your brother. He wasn't your half brother. He wasn't."

The anger inside me reached its peak. "How can you sit there and lie right to my face? How? I read it. Your words. They are sitting in your diary upstairs."

"You're wrong, Walter," she said, gasping for breath. She had her hands over her face now as she sobbed. "You're mistaken."

"I am not. I know what I read," I yelled. I pushed away from the table and ran upstairs to her room. I found the key to her nightstand in the back of her Bible, unlocked it, and grabbed her diary. I then bolted back downstairs.

Blood, adrenaline, and anger shot through me. My mother hadn't moved from the table. When she looked up and saw the diary in my hands, her eyes went wider still.

"Walter, what do you think you're doing?"

"I'm going to read it to you, Mom. If you want to lie to me, then I'm going to read to you exactly what you wrote."

"Don't do this, Walter. Please, you don't understand what—"

"Page one," I said, now opening the little leather-bound diary to the first entry. "I like how you have it titled, 'A New Beginning.' That's real clever. Anyway, it's dated September fifth, 1961. It's the day after you and Dad got married. You remember that?"

"Walter, please. Don't do this."

"No, I want to read some of it to you," I said, enjoying the control I now had. "It's obvious you don't remember what you wrote. Let me skip ahead to the juicy stuff, Mom. It's not far, just a couple of weeks after you got married."

I flipped through the diary until I found the entry dated September 19, 1961. "Okay, this is the one that really got me. You know what I'm going to read, don't you? You know what you saw. What you wrote down."

Mom muttered a weak "yes," and then I began to read, word for word, what she'd written.

September 19, 1961

I'm sitting in my room and it's nearly eleven in the morning. I don't know where Gene is, and I don't care. I'm still trembling and shaking something awful. When I woke up this morning, I hoped it had all been some kind of bad dream, but I know it wasn't. I'm so scared. I'm so ashamed. I don't know what I'm going to do. How am I going to even be able to look at him?

Last night, a bunch of us drove down to the old Stafford plantation and built a bonfire. We were drinking, carrying on, and just having a good time. I didn't really want to drink, because of my situation and all, but since I hadn't told anyone about being pregnant yet, other than Gene of course, I thought it might look strange if I didn't at least drink a couple. I've been getting sick a lot lately, and figured maybe a few beers would do me some good.

Mostly I talked with Lydia about what it was like to be married so far, and also we discussed her and Macon's wedding, which is only a month away. Though if Macon finds out about what happened last night, who knows if he'll even marry her now. I've never really trusted her, to be honest. I know that she broke up with Gene more than two years ago now, right at the end of sophomore year, but I've never been sure if she was really over him. I do think she truly loves Macon, but I've often wondered if she still has feelings for Gene. I've always been positive that Gene's never gotten over her, that's for sure. The way he looks at her, even when I'm standing right there. And if I still had any doubts, I guess last night really made me know for sure.

We had run out of beer, so Ox and Macon headed out to see if they could get some liquor from a bootlegger they knew over at Niggertown. Margaret and Diane left with the Lafayette boys they had been running around with, so that just left me, Gene, and Lydia sitting by the fire. We were talking and staring at the flames when I realized that I wasn't feeling well. I'd somehow managed to get myself really drunk. I didn't think I'd had all that much to drink, but my body was changing every day, and the alcohol had affected me in a way I wasn't used to. I told Gene I wasn't feeling at all well and wanted to leave. He got up and walked me toward the car, but I could hardly stand. Everything was spinning around so fast. I thought I might get sick. Gene helped me into the car and told me he wanted to stay for a while. Said that I should just try to sleep it off for an hour or so. I was in no shape to argue and immediately passed out in the front seat.

I don't know how long I was out for, but it couldn't have been too long because Macon and Ox hadn't even gotten back yet.

"Walter," interrupted Mom, "please stop. I get the point. Please."

"I'm going to finish," I said. "You said I was mistaken, and I'm going to prove to you that I'm not." I continued on.

I awoke because I'd heard a scream. I was a little confused and disoriented for a minute, but then I realized I was in the car. I sat up and could see the fire roaring away, but I didn't see anyone sitting around it. And then I heard another yell, muffled this time. My eyes followed the sound to some high weeds, and then saw Gene on top of Lydia. The glow of the firelight faintly lit up Gene's naked body. I couldn't really see Lydia, but I could see her flailing her arms at Gene. He had one hand over her mouth, it looked like, and with the other he tried to fight off her blows. And I can't even mention what the bottom part of his body was doing.

Nor can I describe what I felt. I wanted to get out and help Lydia, but I couldn't. I wanted to scream at Gene, but I couldn't. I still felt woozy and found myself unable to move. Just a few minutes later, Gene got up, pulled on his pants, and headed for the car. I didn't see Lydia get up. I slouched down in the car and pretended to be asleep as Gene opened his door and got in. My heart pounded faster than a cornered rabbit's. He whispered my name, but I didn't respond. He started the car and we left, leaving Lydia alone in that field.

When we got home, he helped me to bed. Even as scared, as nervous, as sick as I was about everything, I still immediately fell asleep.

And so here I am now, only two weeks married, pregnant, and last night I just witnessed the unthinkable. I have no idea what I'm going to do. This baby has got to be raised with a man in the house. That's one thing that I'm set on, no matter what. Oh Lord, give me strength and help me make the right choices. I know I've done some bad things. Maybe this is Your way of punishing me, but please guide me on what I'm to do next.

When I'd finished, I looked at Mom for a reaction, but she didn't give one. She was blank and stared through me. I stood in the middle of the kitchen with the diary in my hands, ready to read more if need be.

"Why are you doing this, Walter?" she asked, her voice soft and tired.

"Because you lied to me. You've been lying to me forever."

"I haven't lied to you," she said.

"God, I can't believe you. Dad raped Mrs. Haddsby. I just read it to you. Do you still need more proof? I mean, these are your own words, Mom, not mine." I began flipping ahead through the pages to another important entry I'd once read. "This one is dated July eleventh, 1962. It is the one where you talk about seeing Jimmy for the first time. A few weeks after he was born. You remember that one? You talk about how you have no doubt that it is Dad's baby. How he already looks just like Dad and nothing like Mr. Haddsby. You want me to keep going? There's plenty more in this thing about how Jimmy continues to resemble Dad as he grows up."

"No, Walter, please," she said softly. She'd hardly moved at all during the whole time she sat at the kitchen table. She looked beaten. "I've had enough."

"So you admit that Jimmy was my brother? Or my half brother? Whatever."

She looked up at me, and I waited for her confirmation. Her eyes were red and pained. She said, "No, I won't tell you that."

"Goddammit, Mom," I said, erupting. "What's wrong with you? How can you sit there and lie right to my face? I can't believe you."

I shot through the back door and went to Mike's cage. I put his leash on him and led him out. He seemed eager to go for a walk. I left my yard and started heading toward town, so upset that I could barely stand it. All Mom had to do was admit what I'd known for almost a year now. But she wouldn't do it. I headed toward Papa's, which was a few miles away, hoping that he might offer some sort of sanctuary for Mike. And for me too, as far as that was concerned.

❦

"What in the hell is that?" asked Papa when he came out on the back porch to greet me. "I ain't never seen nothing so peculiar in all my life. What's that hood for?"

"Mothball caught him on Merchants' Day," I said, removing the hood and exposing the grayish mass of tissue. I stuffed the hood in my pocket.

"Good day in the morning," he said. "Would you look at that thing?"

"He wanted to get into the *Guinness Book,* so he cut off its head."

"Tell me how cutting off a turkey's head is setting any kind of record," he said, still eyeing Mike warily. "What kind of record is that?"

"Some man cut off a chicken's head once and it lived for eighteen months. Mothball wanted to see if he could make Mike live longer."

"Well, how long's this rascal been living without?"

"About five months or so."

"I'll be damned," he said, shaking his head. "That's the ugliest bird I've ever laid eyes on. I ain't never seen nothing like it. Walking him around like a dog."

He pulled his pipe from the bib of his overalls and dug

it out with a silver pipe nail. He smacked the bowl into his palm, discarding the spent tobacco over the railing of the porch, then packed a new load. "Where's your mama? Don't she even come say hello to her daddy no more?"

"We got in a fight, so I walked over here."

"You telling me that bird just walked with you for over three miles?"

"I had to carry him part of the way," I said. "I'm hoping maybe you'll take me back later on, if that's all right."

"That's all right," he said from the side of his mouth, his teeth clamping the stem of the pipe. He held a match over the pipe and rapidly puffed, the flame disappearing into the bowl and then popping back out again in quick bursts. The sweet smell of the pipe tobacco surrounded our heads. "Only problem is, alternator's gone bad on the truck and the new one ain't arrived yet. Won't be here for a few more days."

"I can just walk home later, I guess. It's not that far."

"Why you in a scrum with your mama? Don't ever come to no good to fight with a woman. Ain't I told you that before? They'll win every time."

"I don't really wanna talk about it," I said, not wanting to go over everything that had just happened. "Besides, I guess it was really between me and Dad."

He pulled the pipe from his lips and squinted at me. "What'd he do this time?"

"He won't let me keep Mike at the house. He lost his

job today. So when he got home, he said we were gonna eat Mike for Thanksgiving dinner."

"I heard about the closing," said Papa. "It's a shame. But I kind of side with your daddy on this one. That bird would be better off going in the oven."

"But he was Mothball's. It's the only thing I got left of him." It worked once, so I figured I'd try it again.

"That don't sound like nothing more than sniveling to me. And that ain't all you got left of him. Shoot, I lost a buddy to a trap-jaw when I was a young man, but I still got him around."

"I know," I said. "You've told me about it before. How he stepped in a nest of them and died."

"I got the memories of him, is what I got. These days I can't remember where I put my hat, but old memories and such, I don't never forget them. They'll stay with you forever."

Papa looked skyward as a formation of mallards honked and flew by overhead.

"Them ducks are heading over to the river. Coming from Yankee country. Winter's on the way." He gazed at the mallards for a moment, puffing on his pipe. "Did I ever tell you why they fly the way they do?"

"I don't think so," I said, now looking up at the birds too.

"You see how they is flying together in the shape of a 'V'?"

"Yes, sir."

"And you see how one side of the 'V' is longer than the other side?"

"Yes, sir, I see it," I said, shielding my eyes from the sun as the ducks disappeared over the tops of the trees.

"You know why that is?" Papa looked down at me with a serious expression. I shook my head. "I'll tell you why, but you gotta pay close attention, 'cause I'm only gonna say it once, all right?"

"All right."

"Okay, well, one side of the 'V' is longer than the other," said Papa, "because there's more ducks on that side."

Papa fell out laughing. I laughed so hard that tears came to my eyes. I hadn't laughed, I mean really laughed, in so long that I'd almost forgotten how.

"You're about crazy," I said.

"My granddaddy told me that a long time ago while we was sitting in a blind, freezing our asses off down on the Tallapoosa. Didn't get one damned duck that day, but I'll never forget the hunt."

Papa continued smoking on his pipe and looked out at the trees behind the house. Though mostly the woods were filled with assorted types of pine, there were some oaks spread out among them, spotting the green canopy with oranges, reds, and yellows. The soft evening sunlight seemed to make the leaves even more brilliant.

"So what are you gonna do?" asked Papa.

"Sir?"

"About the bird. What're you gonna do with him? You gonna take care of him, or are you gonna eat him?"

"Well, that's one of the reasons I came over," I said. "I was wanting to know if maybe I could keep him out here for a while. Figured maybe he could stay in the old bird dog pen."

"How does he eat?" asked Papa, bending down to inspect Mike a little closer. He blew a stream of smoke at Mike's head, which sent him scampering backwards toward my feet. "I don't see how the hell he eats without a mouth."

"You gotta mash up corn and squirt it down that hole. Same with his water."

"I'll be damned. And this was the record he wanted to go after? Couldn't he have hopped around on a pogo stick for a while? Maybe a Hula-Hoop? He always had them wide hips."

I laughed and Papa smiled back at me.

"How often you say you gotta feed him?" he asked.

"Mothball fed him about four or five times a day. Birds eat a lot. And often, I guess. I'll take care of him—I just don't want to leave him at home. Dad'll kill him."

"And what makes you think I won't?"

"Because you just wouldn't. Not without asking me first, anyway."

Papa stood up, curving his back as he stretched, and looked out at the woods again. "Walter, there ain't no way you're gonna come out here five times a day and feed that bird. There just ain't no way. And I'll tell you this: I sure as hell ain't gonna do it."

I looked down, dejected.

"Your daddy won't let you keep it at his place, and there ain't no way you can care for it proper out here. You can't let him go because he'd get killed in no time, and that'd just be a waste of good meat. Not to mention it'd be plain cruel. And you already know how I feel about that."

"Yes, sir."

"You know where I'm going with this, boy?"

"Yes, sir."

"You can do it here, and we can have us a fat supper later tonight. I got some potatoes. And a pot of October beans already soaking. We can have us a midnight feast. That way your daddy still wouldn't get his way, would he?"

I looked up at Papa and smiled. "I guess not," I said, "but I gotta get home tonight. Mothball's funeral is tomorrow morning."

"Well, that's even better. It's gonna be cool enough tonight that after we cleaned him, we could hang him up and let him breathe for a day. Makes a better-tasting bird. What better way to celebrate your buddy's life than to have us a big spread in his honor?"

"I don't know if Mothball would see it that way," I said.

"Sure he would. He'd understand you don't really got no choice, and he'd appreciate us having a dinner for him. Hell, I know that boy loved to eat. He about sent Mudcat to the poorhouse that time I took y'all out there."

I smiled. I didn't quite know how I felt about it, but Papa did make a lot of sense.

"I can kill him and clean him after you leave," said Papa. "That way you won't feel guilty about it, having to do it yourself."

"If anyone is gonna do it, it's gonna be me," I said. "And you don't have to worry about me feeling guilty."

Papa looked at the tops of the trees, where the sun had already slipped down behind them. "We still got some light," he said. "You want to get it over with?"

I exhaled deeply. "I guess I might as well."

Papa and I walked down the steps, with me leading Mike by his leash, and headed toward the skinning table in the backyard.

"I got a hatchet in the shed," said Papa. "I'll be right back. Let me go hunt it up."

I looked down at Mike, who was poking around in the fallen leaves. I pulled the hood out of my pocket and placed it over him; it only seemed fitting for an execution. It amazed me how quickly life sometimes changed. Just an hour before, I couldn't fathom the thought of Mike sitting on our table for Thanksgiving dinner. The thought had sickened me. And now, here I was, getting ready to lop off his head, or his neck, or whatever it was that was left of him. Only a few days before, Mothball had been in my room, supposedly writing a letter to the *Guinness Book* to advise them about a potential record. And now here I was, getting ready to kill that record once and for all.

"Here you go, boy," said Papa, handing me the wooden handle of the hatchet. "You sure you can do it?"

"Yes, sir. It's my responsibility. I've gotta do it."

"All right, then. He won't feel a thing. He won't even know it's coming."

Papa grabbed Mike and hoisted him up on the table. Mike tried to flap his wings, but Papa held him tight. "Goddamn, he's a heavy rascal. We're gonna eat for days."

Papa turned Mike on his side, pushing down on his breast with one hand, on his legs with the other. Mike started struggling.

"You got him?" I asked.

"Yeah, he ain't going nowhere. Whenever you're ready."

I looked down at Mike, his body now obscured in tree shadows. Grasping the handle of the hatchet, feeling the wood in my hands, I couldn't help but think about that fox; about Mothball wanting me to chop that chicken for him; about that rope in my hands when Jimmy died; about Mothball.

I dropped my arm with tremendous force, right at the base of Mike's neck. The hatchet cut it clean and bit into the wood, sticking tight. The hood and leash flopped off the table, and Mike's body went limp. A small trickle of blood seeped into the gash where the hatchet had imbedded. He hadn't felt a thing, just as Papa had said. And he never saw it coming. I decided that must be my modus operandi.

"That wasn't too bad," he said. "You've gotten better at this since you killed that fox."

"Yes, sir, I guess I have." I smiled weakly.

He picked up Mike's body, holding it in his arms as if it were a baby. "I'll build a fire in the pit and get a big pot of water boiling. We'll get these feathers off and gut him, then I'll string him up for the night. This fall air will do him a world of good."

"You think you could take care of that part, Papa? I better get walking home before it gets too late. Tomorrow I'll get Mom to drop me off and we can eat him."

"Use the telephone and call her if you want."

"No, sir, I think I'll walk. It's not that far, and it'll be good for me. It's been a long day."

"Nothing like a walk to clear a man's head. You just be careful of the boogeyman," he said, smiling.

"The boogeyman's in jail, remember?"

"I reckon that's what everybody thinks," he said, shaking his head. "But I know better. Something wasn't right about that trial. I don't buy for a second that Earl Swit killed the Haddsby boy."

"What do you mean?" I asked, stunned. "It seemed pretty obvious to me."

"I've known that fella since he was younger than you are now. That boy couldn't hurt nobody unless he had to. I don't doubt he killed people in the war, but that was his job. Killing your friend? Uh-uh. I don't buy it for a minute."

"Why did . . . I mean, how did you know him? I never knew that."

"You didn't? Your mama don't tell you nothing, does she? Shoot, she and him was practically brother and sister when they were waist-high. In fact, if you want to know the truth, I always thought they'd get married one day. But he went off to the service and that was that."

"What?" I asked in disbelief. "What are you talking about?"

"That friend of mine I told you about, the one who got killed by all them trap-jaws, that was Earl's daddy. Edgar Swit. We was best friends growing up. After Edgar died, I sort of helped raise Earl up for a while. Taught him how to hunt and trap, same as I taught you, so he could take care of his mama. He sort of looked to me as his second daddy, I reckon. He used to come over here all the time as a boy, as eager to set a trap line as you were when you started. And he was good in the woods. Knew how to keep quiet. He could sneak up on anything."

"I can't believe no one ever told me any of this," I said. And now everything really started to come together. *How's Louise doing?*

"Sure, and I'll tell you one thing more. He always took a shine to you."

"To me? I've never met that man in my life."

"Sure you have. When you was a little fella, your mama would leave you here sometimes with me and your granny. He'd come over—he lived with his mama then, just through them woods—and play games with you. You don't remember that? Hide-and-seek, things like that. He adored you. Would have done anything for you. I think he thought of you as a little brother. Or maybe even the son he never had. Used to let you play with his war medals. You loved holding them."

Walter, come back here. How many secrets had my mom kept from me? I was completely stunned. I said, "I don't remember him. I can't believe this."

"You were young. And he looked a lot different back then. He was clean-cut. Still looked military in those days."

"Well, what happened?" I asked. "Why'd he stop coming around?"

"When you was about six or so, I reckon," said Papa, "he hightailed it out of town." He gazed off into the woods for a moment, thinking hard about something. Then he looked at me as seriously as I'd ever seen him look at anybody. "You remember when that little son of a bitch tried to hurt you when you was just a little boy? When you'd been playing at that house they was rebuilding?"

"Yes, sir, I remember that. But I don't ever remember seeing the Tro—I mean, Earl Swit. I don't remember him. Are you saying he was the one who tried to hurt me?"

"Hell, no, that's not what I'm saying," said Papa. "He'd've never harmed a hair on your head. He loved you. What I'm saying is, it was shortly after that no-good punk tried to hurt you that Earl took off. It was right around that time. He reenlisted in the army and went back to 'Nam, lickety-split. Here one day, gone the next. Just disappeared. After he got back from his second go-round in the war, he wasn't never the same. Soon after he returned, his mama died, and from then on he wanted to be left alone. He had a tough life from the get-go. Some people's got it rougher than others, I reckon. But I'll tell you this: he didn't kill the Haddsby boy. Him not speaking at that trial wasn't him saying he was guilty. He was protecting somebody, the same way a wild turkey will fake a broken wing in order to keep a fox from getting to her poults. Her babies."

I had no idea what to say. All kinds of things were

coming together, but I couldn't believe any of it. I had to talk to Mom again, and fast. A horrible realization was hitting me hard. I suddenly felt as though I was going to be sick. I had to get home. I stammered, "W-well, I gotta get going. Boogeyman or no boogeyman."

"You be careful all the same," said Papa. "I still ain't totally convinced this town's safe."

"Yes, sir, I will. I'll see you tomorrow."

"All right, then," he said. He walked away, carrying Mike toward the fire pit. I turned in the other direction, went around the side of the house, and started off down the drive. A fat orange moon—maybe the harvest moon, I wasn't sure, but it only seemed fitting—had popped up over the trees, lighting up the clay tracks of Papa's driveway, showing me the way.

CHAPTER 17

As I walked along the moonlit road, I did a lot of thinking about Mothball, about Jimmy, but mostly about the new information concerning the Troll. I felt sick and wanted to puke. *How's Louise doing? Walter, come back here. He's not your brother.* I hadn't really grieved for Mothball, my mind being too occupied with Mike, but things now started to sink in. It had been the same with Jimmy. Trying to cover up his death and then worrying about the trial had kept me busy. That stronger part of me had said I was doing the right thing. But now a different part of me said I'd been wrong. Horribly wrong.

As I crossed over the bridge, I stayed on the side opposite of the Troll's shack—the side where both Jimmy and Mothball had been found. It took everything I had in me not to turn and look. On the other side of the bridge, shortly before town, I saw the road that led up to the pulp mill. Also on that road, about a quarter mile before the mill, was the cemetery: the cemetery where Jimmy was, where Mothball would be tomorrow, where the Troll would probably end up after he was executed.

Anxiety started to build as I thought about the conversation I was going to have with Mom when I got home.

As I walked along, the headlights of an approaching car momentarily blinded me. Just as it was about to pass, it came to an abrupt stop. It was Mom. She rolled down the window, and I looked at her shadowed face in the moonlight.

"Walter," she said. "Thank God. I talked with Papa and he said you'd just left. I'd have come earlier, but your daddy only got home a few minutes ago with the car. You okay?"

"Yeah, I'm fine, I guess," I said. I pulled my arms to my chest, as if hugging myself, to fight off the night's chill.

"Well, jump in and I'll take you home. We need to talk."

I nodded my head. I walked around the front of the car and got in.

She drove the car back over the bridge and then turned around in a driveway before slowly heading toward home.

"Walter, I've got some things I have to tell you. This isn't going to be easy for me to say or for you to hear. But I've been sitting at home for the last few hours, and I realize I have to."

"I think I already know," I said, my mind numb. "You weren't lying to me, were you? About Jimmy not being my brother."

My mother took a deep breath and pulled the car over

in front of the hardware store. Her hands shook as she tried to hold the steering wheel.

"No, Walter, I wasn't."

"It's the Troll, isn't it? Earl Swit? He's my father."

She looked straight ahead, right through the middle of town. "Yes," she said.

Everything began to crumble. With her simple answer of yes, I felt my whole world, my whole life, my whole everything, start to collapse. "Oh, my God," I began muttering. "Oh, my God. Oh, my God. This can't be true. How is this possible?"

Other than her shaking hands, Mom acted remarkably calm. She wasn't even crying. I sat in disbelief and listened as she told the story. "Earl and I grew up together as friends and playmates, but as we got older, well, it became more than that, and we started dating. I was truly happy, Walter. As happy as I'd ever been. But toward the end of our senior year, things started to fall apart. He'd already signed up with the service and found out that after he graduated and did his training he was going to be shipped overseas, most likely to Vietnam. At that time, nobody even knew what Vietnam was. It was still very early in the war. All I knew was that it was a long way from Woodley, and I didn't want him to go. I begged him to stay, to marry me, even though I knew it was impossible. The service already had him.

"After we broke things off, it wasn't too long before I started dating your father. Or, well, Gene. You know what I mean. God, this is hard."

"It's okay, Mom," I said, feeling sympathy for her like I'd never known before. For the first time in my life, I saw her as a person, as someone other than just my mother. "I know what you mean. Keep going."

"Things were okay with me and your father, I guess, but my heart was still with Earl. The night before he was to leave for basic training, he stopped by the house and asked if I'd go out with him for a little while. He wanted to tell me goodbye. We went up to the football field and talked for a long time. It was during that conversation that I realized how much I loved him and how much I'd miss him. And then . . . well . . . I gave myself to him. I know that's the last thing you want to hear from your mother, but you have to know the truth."

"It's all right, Mom."

"I loved him, Walter. I hope you understand that. And if I hadn't done it, you would never have been born, so I don't regret it one bit. What I do regret is what I did to your father. It didn't take me too long to figure out, shortly after Earl had gone away, that I was pregnant. Even today, an unwed pregnant woman isn't tolerated around here. And that was more true back then. I was scared to death. I didn't know what to do. I knew it would be at least a year before I'd see Earl again, and that was too long."

"So what did you do?" I asked.

"Please understand that I was desperate, Walter," she said as she began to cry. Not heavy sobs, just little tears. She unlocked her hands from the steering wheel for the first time and wiped her face. "So what I did was sleep with your father. And then shortly after, I told him I was pregnant. As expected, he proposed, and, well, I guess you know the rest."

I sat in the car, looking out at the night, at the Hanging Woods lurking behind the barbershop in the moonlight, not knowing what to say. All that I found myself able to mutter was "I can't believe this."

"I know this is hard, Walter. But understand that you were conceived by two people who loved each other. It isn't something I regret. It wasn't dirty or ugly."

"You mean like the way Jimmy was conceived?" I said, a deliberate edge in my voice.

"Well . . . yes, I guess so."

I had so many questions I wanted to ask, but one pressed on my mind more than all of the others combined. It was the most important question of all as far as I was concerned. "Does Dad know? Does he know I'm not his real son?"

"I've never told him, Walter, but I think he suspects it.

Simple math says that you should have been born nearly two months later than you were. Certainly a month later. You were a healthy-size baby." She hesitated for a moment, as if she wasn't sure if she wanted to say more, but then continued. "I think it's the same with Macon Haddsby. I'm sure he suspected something wasn't right with Lydia, so I believe he's always been suspicious. And that's why I think he was so hateful to Jimmy. In fact, that's why I think he killed Jimmy."

"What? What are you talking about?"

"He always took out his jealousy and anger toward Lydia on Jimmy. He sort of blamed him for all of their problems, I think. Besides, there's no way Earl Swit killed Jimmy."

"Oh, Jesus, I can't believe this," I said again. An intense heat burned in my brain. It was difficult to breathe, but it was important for me to know for sure if my father knew, so I asked again. "So you never told Dad about the Troll . . . I mean, Earl Swit? About him being my real father? Nothing at all?"

"No. Never. The only person who has ever known is Earl himself. You were nearly four years old before he found out because he'd been overseas, and I didn't dare tell him such news in a letter. You and I were visiting at Papa's one day when he stopped by. As soon as he saw you, he knew, but I wanted to tell him anyway."

"Why didn't you ever write about that in your diary?"

I asked, now becoming frantic. "Oh, God, if you'd only mentioned that in your diary, just once, things would be so different."

"Sometimes," said Mom, "it's better if things are left unsaid."

Pain and nausea, sweat and fear, guilt and remorse, it all started to eat away at my insides. I thought I might be going crazy.

Mom pulled out and began to drive off, still incredibly calm. "I know this is a lot to absorb in one day," she said. "Let's go home, and we'll talk tomorrow after Raymond's funeral. You'll have plenty more questions, I'm sure, but I'm so glad I told you. I feel better finally getting it off my chest. You've had a tough year, Walter, but maybe this could be a new beginning for us."

I don't know if she even realized it, but "A New Beginning" was exactly what she'd put on the first page of her diary. We drove the rest of the way home in silence. I thought about everything that had happened since I'd read that stupid diary. Jimmy was dead. Mothball was dead. And I'd single-handedly sentenced my father—my real father—to death row.

I wondered if what she had just said was true, about feeling better once she got it off her chest. I wanted to tell her everything. I wanted to confess. But I was scared. She'd been so brave, yet I was nothing more than the spineless jellyfish I'd once accused Mothball of being.

She'd been through so much, had given up so much, to ensure my happiness. How could I send the only man she'd ever loved to the death chamber? But then again, if I said something, then I might send her only son instead. As we headed for home, the turmoil ripped me in two.

❦

When we neared our house, I saw something that made my heart jump. It seemed like déjà vu all over again. Sitting in front of the house, one more time, was Sheriff Walls's prowler. After all I'd been through, after all I'd just learned, the last thing I wanted was to answer more of his questions.

"What in the world?" said Mom.

After she parked, we got out and went toward the house. My legs were shaky and weak. When we walked through the front door, Dad and Sheriff Walls looked up from their seats in the den. I sensed thick tension immediately, the same way you can feel someone watching over you while you sleep.

Sheriff Walls got out of the rocker and took a step toward us.

"Louise. Walter. Why don't you both take a seat," he said.

"What's the matter?" asked Mom. "What's wrong?"

"Just take a seat and I'll explain, Louise," said the sheriff.

Mom sat down next to Dad on the couch, but I remained standing.

Sheriff Walls took another step toward me and said, "Take a seat, Walter."

I instinctively took a step backwards, feeling like an animal getting boxed into a corner. Like that trapped fox. "I don't want to take a seat. What's going on?"

"The sheriff told you to sit down, dammit," said Dad. "Do what he says."

"No. I don't want to. Just tell me what's going on."

"It's all right," said the sheriff to Dad. "He don't have to sit down if he don't want to." He turned to Mom and said, "Louise, I apologize, but this is going to be difficult."

"What's happening?" asked Mom. Her poor face started to crumble before my eyes. After the talk we'd just had, seeing her that way killed me.

"I'm going to explain everything," said the sheriff. "And I'm going to get right to the point." He then turned to me and said, "Walter, I was just telling your father that I got an interesting phone call last night from Lydia Haddsby. On the night that Mothball apparently jumped from the bridge, she'd been sitting in her room, looking out the window. Said she couldn't sleep. She told me she was almost positive she saw you meet up with Raymond that night. Right on the corner. You know anything about that?"

Sweat started pumping from my forehead, and a

stinging heat needled my skin. My breath became short, and the room started to whirl. I didn't know how much more I could take. "No, sir," I said. "That's impossible. I was at home."

"I don't think so," he said. "What I think is you're one hell of a liar. A very clever liar. But I've figured you out. Figured out a lot of things, in fact."

"I don't know what you're talking about. I didn't do anything. I wasn't with Mothball that night." For a moment, I thought about bolting out the door.

"And I suppose you weren't with Jimmy the night he disappeared? Is that right?"

I glanced at both Mom and Dad and then said, "Yes, sir, that's right."

"What in the hell is going on?" asked Dad. "Just tell us what this is about."

Sheriff Walls dug into his pocket, got out a pack of cigarettes, and lit one. The blue smoke immediately gravitated toward the lamp on the end table.

"I ain't the smartest man in the world, Gene," he said, taking a pull from his cigarette and turning away from Dad to look at me. "I'll be the first to admit that. But one thing I'm pretty good at is puzzles. I guess you didn't know that, did you, Walter?"

"Sir?"

"Puzzles, son. I like puzzles. I'm not talking about jigsaws. I mean mind puzzles. I do the crossword every day.

Word searches. Anagrams. I enjoy riddles and the like—
you understand?"

"No, sir," I said, "not really." My entire body began
quivering.

"It's part of my job, Walter. I got to figure out things.
I'm not good at much, but I am good at solving stuff.
After Lydia Haddsby called, I started wondering if things
weren't as cut-and-dried as I'd first thought. So I went
back over everything, started looking around for something I might have missed. And you know what I found?"

"No, sir," I said. I glanced at the couch, then turned
away quickly when my father's eyes bore down on me.
Mom had her face in her hands.

"I found a puzzle," he said. He walked toward the end
table and ashed his cigarette into the ashtray. His damned
shoes and belt creaked as he did so.

"Sir?" I said. "I still don't know what you mean."

He took another deep draw and then reached into his
pocket and pulled out a piece of paper. "Maybe I should
put it another way, Walter. Say it so you'll understand it."
He unfolded the piece of paper and held it up for me to
see. It was a copy of the suicide note. "What I found was
an enigma." He then began to read it aloud as he smoked.
It was the first time my parents had heard it. And I have to
say, despite the circumstances, as I listened to the sheriff
read, I couldn't help but think what an amazing letter it
was. And how stupid I'd been to write it.

I know I look lame. Even dumb. To hurt everyone
must appear selfish, for obvious reasons.

"Why?" he yelled, drowning, overwhelmed, never
talking again, since killing is absolute.
My devilment is severe. The underlying remorse
burns every day.
Internally, guilt equals torment. Suicide is clearly
knocking. I'm frightened.
I truly hope I never know other friends in turmoil.

It seems troubling, right? And not God like? Even
displeasing Jesus? It might.
Mom, you made our true happiness, because ardent
love lasts.
Christ, an unrelenting guilt has taken over now.
Sorry. Only, I panic under stress. Hell, everyone
does.

Haddsby is murdered over foolish fun. Taken
heartlessly.
Everlasting blame rests inside.
Damning guilt entered and never died.
Woodley rages over the enigma.
True happiness is suicide, life eternal . . .

The Troll's evil remains.
Take heed, everyone, the real ogre lives locally.
Also, kids are wicked and love trouble.

Earl receives electrocution. Lies remain a secret.
I'll take Hell over Life.

Alas, Mothball exists . . . nevermore.

After he had finished, he continued looking at the letter—admiring it, or so it seemed to me. He stubbed out his cigarette and said, "It took me a while to figure it out. I couldn't make heads or tails of it for the longest time. I couldn't figure out what any of it meant. But finally, after studying on it for hours and hours, I realized something. The note itself, all the words, they don't mean a damned thing. Ain't that right, Walter?"

My knees went weak. I thought I might drop to the floor. I didn't reply.

"Well," said the sheriff, looking at my parents, "since the cat's got his tongue, I'll explain a little further. You see, this note here," he said, shaking the paper for emphasis, "didn't really say nothing. What I figured out was that if you take the first letter of every word in the suicide note, the note that Walter wrote by the way, not Raymond, then another message appears. It's your son's confession."

"Confession to what?" screamed Dad. "Stop speaking in riddles, goddammit, and tell me what the hell is going on."

"I'll read the message that I discovered and then let you decide for yourself what it means, Gene. I'm afraid it'll be obvious enough." Sheriff Walls snapped the paper between his hands as if straightening a newspaper, cleared his throat, and began reading the translation he'd scratched below the note. "'I killed them. As for why, don't ask. I am disturbed. I get sick if I think of it. I strangled Jimmy.

Mothball caught on, so I pushed him off the bridge and wrote this letter. The Troll, a.k.a. Walter Elra Sithol. Amen.'"

My parents sat on the couch as stunned as if I'd hit them in the face with a frying pan. And as for me, I'd gone numb. Completely numb. I hung my head, unable to make eye contact with anyone, especially my mother.

Sheriff Walls sounded pleased with himself. "I don't know who or what 'the Troll' is, or what it means, but I'd say the rest of the note is pretty clear. So now do you understand what I was getting at, Walter?" he asked. He seemed proud, almost gloating in his discovery. I wanted to lunge at him, grab the fat folds of his throat, and start squeezing.

But instead I just stood there. I'd underestimated Sheriff Walls. I'd gotten a little too cute for my own good with that suicide note. Who knows, maybe it was a hidden cry for help. But strangely, once I realized he had me, I felt a sense of relief, just as Mom had after she'd told me her story. A calmness settled in my gut, numbing me even further.

"Yes, sir," I mumbled, nodding. "I think I understand."

"After I figured out your little puzzle," he said, shaking the letter again, "I went ahead and had it dusted for fingerprints, just to be sure. Know what I didn't find?"

I didn't bother to respond, already knowing the answer. I'd known all along that it could be the one clue that would make things seem suspicious.

"Okay, I'll tell you. I didn't find none of Raymond's prints on it. He'd been fingerprinted before the trial so they could verify them on that knife of his. Still had the prints on file, so I had an expert come out and examine the note. He thought it curious that someone could write a suicide note without getting any of his own fingerprints on it. Don't you find that curious, Walter?"

I stared through the sheriff as if he weren't there. I didn't respond.

"That's about what I figured," said the sheriff. He casually strolled over to me, put my arms behind my back, and strapped on a pair of handcuffs.

"Oh, God, no," wailed Mom, the first thing she'd managed to utter since hearing the hidden meaning of the note.

It was finally over. If the sheriff had caught me a day earlier, before I'd learned about Earl Swit being my biological father, I think I would have been pleased with myself. I think I would have been excited to get to my cell so I could have gotten a good night's sleep, wondering if dear old Dad would have been able to do the same at home. All I'd wanted to do was hurt him for everything he'd done to me. To Mom. I'd wanted to hurt him for loving Jimmy more than he loved me. If the sheriff had caught me the day before, I would have fantasized about the conversations Dad and I might have had once I got locked up, each of us holding a phone and looking through the glass at each other, just like in the movies. Heart to hearts. Father-son chats. Maybe he would have told me his skewed version of the birds and the bees.

But I didn't feel that way now. What I felt was a sickening guilt and a hollow remorse. Over the last year, since the first time I'd read Mom's diary, I'd never once felt any of that. The stronger part of me had kept saying that I was doing the right thing. It told me to pull hard on that noose around Jimmy's neck and not to let go. It said that killing Jimmy was the best way to pay Dad back; that Jimmy was a bad person and I was probably doing him a favor. It said that Mothball had figured out too much; that he suspected me and was going to blow it for the both of us; that he had betrayed me by telling Jimmy that I'd wet my sleeping bag. It said that the Troll was evil and it didn't matter what happened to him.

But as I stood in the middle of the living room, handcuffs tearing at my wrists, I realized that it was gone; that stronger part of me had disappeared—it had vanished completely. If I'd just known that Dad wasn't my real father, I would have understood why he acted the way he did. If I'd just known that I had a real father out there that actually loved me, it would have all been different. And the pain that I'd caused Mrs. Haddsby. The Cleilskys. What about Papa, once he found out?

And my mother. My poor mother. When she began speaking, I snapped from my trance. "Why, Walter?" she sobbed. "What in God's name is happening?"

I looked at her but didn't respond to her pleading, though I wanted to tell her that *ardent love lasts.* The sheriff walked me out the door and to his car, pushing my head down as he helped me into the back seat. Mom and Dad stood on the front porch and watched as the sheriff pulled away. Mom buried her head into the crook of Dad's arm, and Dad responded by squeezing her tightly to his chest. Without question, it was the most affectionate moment I'd ever seen between the two of them.

Sheriff Walls didn't speak to me as we drove off, other than to make one statement. "The cell in Woodley has already got someone in it. Can't put you in a cell with an adult, so I got to take you to Lafayette. I'll make sure to put you in the same one that Earl Swit stayed in, just so you can see what he had to look at, day in and day out, before he got shipped off to Atmore."

The irony didn't escape me, but I kept my silence. Instead of speaking, I pressed my forehead against the window and stared out at the night, now lit up by the harvest moon.

Shortly after we passed through town, and right before

the bridge, I looked into the depths of the Hanging Woods and saw something that startled me worse than anything I'd experienced before. There, dangling from a rope tied to the limb of a sycamore tree, was a body. The body's head was slumped to the side, its feet were pointed toward the ground, and it barely rotated in the light breeze. I could almost hear the whine of the rope as it twisted under the strain of the load. It wasn't the black man who'd been lynched so many years ago. It wasn't the Troll, Jimmy, or Mothball. It was me. And I looked as if I belonged there. I saw myself hanging in that tree just as surely as if I'd been looking in a mirror.

December 19, 1976

Dear Mr. Cleilsky,

Thank you so much for your recent letter concerning the record you're trying to pursue. Mike the turkey sounds like a very interesting bird indeed. We regret to inform you, however, that *The Guinness Book* no longer condones such records. We understand, as you stated in your letter, that his beheading, and subsequent survival, was an accident, but we decided several years ago that it wouldn't be prudent to continue sanctioning these types of feats. Mainly we came to that decision to prevent people from senselessly harming animals just to make it into the book. So now we only print them for posterity's sake. Again, I understand your situation was purely accidental, but please also understand our position. There is nothing we detest more than an act of violence against another living creature just to satisfy one's own egotistical needs. Therefore, as aforementioned, we will not be able to put Mike the turkey in the book, regardless of whether he lives past the eighteen months that Mike the chicken managed to attain.

Please accept this latest edition of *The Guinness Book of World Records* as a small token of our appreciation for submitting your entry. We hope this letter finds you well, and we wish Mike the turkey a long and healthy life. Have a wonderful Christmas season, and we do hope to hear from you again if you come up with a new record you'd like to try and break. Thanks for reading *The Guinness Book*.

Sincerely,

Phillip Waller
Director of Records Verification
The Guinness Book of World Records

ACKNOWLEDGMENTS

I WOULD LIKE TO THANK all of the following, who in one way or another helped make this book come to life: Pinckney Benedict, for so many different reasons, but mostly for taking a chance and giving me an opportunity. Wayne Johnston, who steered me in the right direction with his vision of the big picture. Scott Miller, my agent, who decided to represent me. Eden Edwards, who believed in this book and fought to get it published. Julia Richardson, my editor, who isn't afraid to tell it like it is. Meg Williamson and Whitney Richter, who from the onset gave such insightful critiques and suggestions, and to Susan White, who came in a little later but was also extremely helpful. Eric Trethewey, whose initial enthusiasm for the project gave me the confidence to continue pushing forward. Cathy Hankla, whose careful reading and suggestions helped shape a later version of the book. Jim Trostle at Columbus State University's Oxbow Meadows, who gave me several hours of his time to explain flora and fauna in passionate detail. Rena Averitt, my late and great aunt, who at eighty-nine years of age recounted a memory that eventually helped me create several scenes and a character. And of course to my wife, Jocelyn, for her patience and support, and to my son, Mason, who figured out the perfect title when no adult could.

A big thanks also goes to the following people: Margaret and Tom Sanders (and an even bigger thanks for everything else), Laura Sanders O'Kane, Chad O'Kane, Ellen Altizer, Carlos Altizer, Clay and Courtney Altizer, Talley English, Richard Lucyshyn, Paul Barnett, Debbie Gerberich, Denmon Westmoreland, Danny Westmoreland, Denise Giardina, Mike Reynolds, and Jess Rapisarda.